MADNESS IN MEMPHIS

Patricia Gordon Stevens

HEMBURY
BOOKS

About the Author

Patricia Gordon Stevens is a writer from Memphis Tennessee now living in Kapunda, South Australia with her British husband. She spends her time putting pen to paper in the beautiful, peaceful landscape between the Barossa and Clare Valleys. Her debut fictional novel, 'Madness in Memphis', exposes the reality of living with domestic violence and the challenges many women face when they attempt to escape.

As a mature student, Patricia studied Psychological Science and Sociology at the University of South Australia, before graduating from Edith Cowan University with a Master's in Counselling in 2024. She now runs her own business, Maxwell House Counselling, where she specialises in working with clients experiencing anxiety, loneliness, grief, bereavement and trauma. She is a certified death doula and volunteers at Kapunda aged care homes. She believes that nobody should be alone on their last journey.

In her professional life, she was a marketing and corporate events manager for Barossa based companies, writing and recording radio commercials for Chateau Tanunda and The Beer Girls. Patricia and her husband also owned The Wheatsheaf Pub in Allendale North, SA, where she worked primarily in public relations and marketing, and even sometimes donned a chef's hat!

She treasures living in their 1860s cottage with her husband and any furry, four-legged being that drops by and decides to make the house their home.

First published by Hembury Books in 2025
hemburybooks.com.au
info@hemburybooks.com

Hardback ISBN 9781923517400
Paperback ISBN 9781923517332
Ebook ISBN 9781923517325

A catalogue record for this
book is available from the
National Library of Australia

Acknowledgements

To my most fabulous husband, Marcus, for your unwavering love
and support ~ Without your encouragement this manuscript
would never have found life. Thank you, my love.

To my beloved daughter, Kelley, who has lived 'life' with me ~
my closest ally and my most beautiful first born. We made it.
Love you and Summer Daye to the moon and back until my last breath.
In memory of my most precious son, Cory, watching over us from
heaven along with my one and only monumental sister, Constance.

In memory of my dearest mother, Judy, who instilled in me the
strongest love of the English language, the importance of proper
grammar, and attention to perfection in punctuation!

To Marcus' children: Alice, Matilda, Bodie, and Tess who have shown me
the truth about blended families and how to make them authentic and
filled with love. We have the freedom to choose WHO is family.

To my fellow writers in the most dynamic writing group in Kapunda,
South Australia ~ grateful for an eternity to my industrious editor and
outstanding author, the beautifully talented Rosanne Hawke for her
unrelenting support and tireless readings of my manuscript.
To fellow authors Nancy Jackson and Wendy Noble for their
uncompromising morale-boosting persuasion tactics.

Tremendous thanks to the outstanding Jessica Mudditt of
Hembury Books and her brilliant team for believing in this
story and supporting every step of the publishing process.

And finally, an enormous thank you to my 'Memphis Mates' –
the ones who continue to fill my heart to the brim with joy,
love, and laughter and who will see themselves combined into
one loving character: Lee. Thank you for an eternity of friendship:
Sharon, Wendy, Gina, Janie, Barbara, Cindy, and Diane.
My Memphis Stars.

'Morgan's roller-coaster ride navigating her domestic abuse is
frightening, yet she still manages to provide a happy and hospitable
environment for her family. Morgan is brave and kind. She is
determined to survive. Although there is no easy fix, this is an
amazing and heartfelt story of one woman's journey of survival.'

Dr. Rosanne Hawke, 2025

Foreword

This book is for you – *anyone* who has a daughter, a sister, a niece,
an aunt, a mother, a grandmother – yes, a grandmother who
might be in a situation that you recognise in this work of fiction.
Be vigilant. Always ask questions and if you think your loved one
is avoiding you due to coercive behaviours – this is the time
to get real, discuss with your loved one, and act.

This book is dedicated to the women fleeing domestic violence,
thinking about fleeing, making plans to flee, or shutting down
because they do not know where to start. There is help.
Make a plan. Gather your circle of support together. If you don't
have a tribe, visit your closest community help centre. Start there.

CHAPTER ONE

Perched on top of the kitchen counter was the monster's black leather briefcase – his armor. It was the one thing he carried with him wherever he went. It held his ammunition or everything he could use against anyone who ever wronged him. It held everything he could use against her. *What the Hell was he doing without it?*

Lee yelled, 'Grab it, Morgan. Take it and we'll drive like Hell to the Mississippi River and drown the damned thing. NOW!'

Morgan couldn't budge. Her legs wouldn't move. Her eyes were glazed over and she couldn't break her stare. She wanted to take it. The monster was pure evil. He existed just to make others miserable. *But I chose him, didn't I? My poison, my punishment would be to allow whatever deep, dark plans he had for me to go ahead and unfold. How could it get any worse?*

It could.

She and her friend, Lee, hopped into the car and quickly drove from the former house of Morgan's marriage. In many ways she felt relieved she didn't take the briefcase but received a scathing commentary on the ride to her new home.

Lee screamed, 'You know you could have destroyed in one single decision whatever power this monster holds over you.'

'Doesn't matter,' Morgan mumbled. 'I feel freer in spirit than I have in ages simply knowing I don't live with him anymore.'

She got out. The divorce may not be final yet, but she had escaped with her life and the lives of her children. Nothing else on Earth mattered. Lee dropped off her good friend on the drive to her new pad.

Morgan smiled sweetly. 'Thanks for being there for me, Lee.'

'I'll always have your back.'

The following morning the Christmas season was in full swing. Morgan's mom, Kathleen, had her grandchildren, Ollie and Opal, overnight helping them prepare for their primary school's Christmas festivities. Morgan, along with her work colleagues, had been asked to bring in a cheery tray of nibbles to be shared. The office would celebrate an outstanding year with lunch, a bit of wine, and Christmas cocktails would be on offer. *Hmmm... Christmas drinks – did that mean red and festive in colour or filled to the brim with Christmas spirits?* Morgan was unsure, yet almost excited despite her current stressful existence.

She had worked hard the night before and prepared too many appetizers. For whatever reason, she always did that. Morgan can never make enough; over-compensating they call it. *Why? Who the Hell knows?* Working with a bunch of men, she supposed she wanted or needed to do the nurturing. Bad, she knew. Wrong. Politically incorrect thinking. *How do you stop something that's instinctive?* Morgan put tremendous effort into preparing a beautiful tray of Christmas nibbles. She carefully wrapped the tray to protect it, grabbed her keys and her purse, realizing the platter was a bit heavier than she thought it would be. She'd go back and lock-up once she loaded the car.

Grinding. Sounds of sand and dirt scraping on the concrete floor of the garage. Morgan stopped in her tracks. Listened. Nothing. She told herself that her imagination was working over-time. Whooosh! There he was over her, the monster, grabbing her shoulders, putting his hands around her neck. She had no time to react. No time to bloody think. All she heard was glass breaking below her and she was trying hard to get her breath. She couldn't breathe.

Morgan screamed or what she thought was a scream, but it was more like a growl. The garage door was down. *How did he get in? Why didn't I hear anything when I was in the kitchen?* Morgan tried to scream again. This time his hand was over her mouth, and he was wearing black leather gloves. Insane. He had that look in his eyes. The same look she'd seen a thousand times before. He was already gone. He was in his zone and caught up in the madness he had created in his head – living it – only living it with his hands around her neck.

Morgan felt something trickling down her neck. Tears? Blood? She didn't know. She was shaking uncontrollably.

He was screaming in her face, 'You bitch. You dog. Since the beginning you planned to leave me. No one leaves me. I make the decisions. You're not going anywhere unless I say so. You are not leaving me…EVER!'

She realised he had been yelling for what seemed an eternity and he was spitting on her, literally frothing at the mouth. His eyes were dilated and there was going to be no chance to calm him or talk him down. She needed to get away quickly. Her eyes darted about looking for any hard object she could grab, then…she heard them – the police sirens. Two patrol cars were right underneath her garage door windows. Magic. The angels were about. At this moment, she felt faint. The monster straightened out the jacket to his suit and ran his fingers through his hair.

He was already tall, but he puffed up his shoulders and even had the balls to tell the cops, 'You can leave – this is just a small domestic misunderstanding, and the police certainly aren't needed here.'

The cops stared. They stared at him as if he had lost every brain cell he ever had.

One of the cops raised his hand, 'Stop talking – now.'

They went to Morgan and a police officer scooped her up off the garage floor and helped her walk inside. Morgan saw a kind man before her, a bit older, but wise looking and gentle. He brought her a glass of water.

'You can call someone to be by your side right after I ask you a couple of questions. Are you hurt?'

Morgan wept now and cried hard. She felt safe with this man, and she knew that the real live monster was out of sight…probably handcuffed, in the back of a patrol car.

The other cop walked through the door stating, 'He's something else. He's out there shaking his head yelling we've made a huge mistake and that she attacked him, and we'll be hearing from his lawyer.'

The second cop was a fast talker and didn't want to waste a minute. He showed the first police officer Morgan's neck and said, 'Get some good photos because that's going to be exactly what the judge needs to see.'

By this time, Morgan's neighbor had snuck in a side door and announced, 'I'm the one who phoned the police.'

The first officer looked at Morgan, 'Would you like your neighbor to stay for a bit?'

Morgan nodded in affirmation, holding on tightly to her water.

Then the officer got on his radio, 'Requesting female officer to the scene.'

'May I contact my boss?' Morgan asked.

The police officer replied, 'Certainly, in just a little while.'

'Please, I need to do this now,' she said gently.

The other officer responded, 'We'll need the name of your employer, too.'

In a matter of minutes there were people everywhere. Upon arrival the female police officer led Morgan into a bedroom.

'I need you to check for any bruising,' the officer requested.

Morgan couldn't see her own back but that's where the monster inflicted the most damage. She didn't remember being thrown against the side of the car repeatedly. She only remembered the hands around her neck and not being able to breathe. Bruises in abundance – black marks around her neck and huge, dark markings by her collarbones and circular black marks up and down her back after the female officer pointed them out. They were going to be massive. The officer got towels and draped them around Morgan's body where one could only see the damage that had been inflicted. Snap. Snap. Snap. About fifteen minutes' worth of photos taken from various angles. Then, Morgan heard her mother's voice and burst into tears.

Morgan's mother, Kathleen, had pre-warned her this man was not suitable for her, so she wasn't planning to tell her mom about this assault. Kat had asked her time and time again to please reconsider the marriage but, no, Morgan in her usual style was insistent upon going ahead with her plans. True. There were a few things she found odd, but she hadn't really been able to put a finger on one specific thing. Whatever was wrong, she could fix. Morgan saw herself as a good person, a strong woman, able to help anyone especially if they weren't confident in themselves. Plus, she was a divorced woman with two children, and it was time she built a family again. The children needed stability. They needed an intelligent and sensitive male figure in their lives. Morgan's head dropped. She had given her children a monster and she had made the delivery herself. *How could her kids ever forgive her?*

Her mother walked into the bedroom and every bit of fear and sadness was reflected on her face. She didn't say a word. Kat knew better. After all, her child was an adult now raising her own children, but she certainly was standing prominently in the middle of a mess. Morgan realized, too, there was nothing her mom could physically do except offer love, support, and encouragement.

She insisted on going into the office against everyone's wishes. This decision really caused an uproar and the people filling her house became agitated, pleading with her not to do so. But Morgan does as she wants as her mother always says.

She tidied her face, changed her clothes, making certain that no marks would be visible anywhere, and freshened her make-up and her hair. She wanted to be around her work colleagues. She wanted to be normal. *Normal?*

One officer announced, 'We'll be back with the original report, and you'll need to review, approve, and sign.'

The lead police officer turned on his heel and said, 'Get in touch with your attorney as soon as possible and make him aware of this incident.'

Hmmm, I'll do that on my way to work.

Her neighbor was busily cleaning up the shards of broken glass in the garage. Morgan leaned in to help but her neighbor wouldn't allow it.

'I can't thank you enough. You may have well and truly saved my life.'

The neighbor exhaled exclaiming, 'I've never heard anyone make the noises that were coming from your garage, so I knew instantly something wasn't right.'

Another hug. This time, more tears. Morgan vowed she'd get it together in the car. *I am not letting that bastard destroy my entire day or for that matter any other moment that belongs to me or my children.*

CHAPTER TWO

S he stopped by the grocery store and bought the nicest Christmas nibbles she could find. The purchase really pissed her off after all the time and energy she spent making splendid goodies for the office Christmas party, but she wouldn't think about that now. She had an even better idea leaving the store. *I'll go to the new wine shop and contribute two bottles of French Champagne. After all, I am celebrating being alive.*

When Morgan arrived at the office, everyone stopped talking.

'Gheeez, somebody's been spreading the word. I'm not having this. No long faces. No discussion. It happened, but it's over and thanks to my amazingly fast thinking neighbor, we are together today to celebrate Christmas.'

The office manager ran over to her with tears streaming down her face and Morgan whispered, 'No, not now. Straighten up, girl. We have Champagne to drink.'

Everyone got into line; they took their orders well and raised a glass.

Morgan swallowed. If I make it through this day, I can make it through anything.

A small prayer followed: *God, if you help me through this I will never, ever marry a man who I have any doubts about. YOU will show him to ME. As a matter of fact, God, I don't care if I ever marry again. Please protect my children and watch them grow.*

Morgan closed her eyes and bowed her head, imagining that she had just been given another chance in life to perform better. She also felt embarrassed by the fact she'd made such a dreadful and damaging choice for her and her children. *Desperate.* She admitted to herself that she had felt desperate to begin a family again and she must have forced the monster into their lives because she thought she could fix him.

She claimed a new mantra. *No more fixing. No more forcing. Those days are in my rearview mirror.*

Her phone was buzzing frantically on her desk. She tried to ignore it. It went off again. Morgan finally grabbed it. It was Lee, crying.

How does news get around so quickly? She had no clue how any information could travel this fast.

Lee sounded frantic. Morgan moved away from her colleagues to hear better.

'I'd driven by your house earlier in the morning because I simply wanted to check in and have a cup of coffee with you but, I saw cop cars and the sight gave me a jolt.'

Lee. Industrious, talented beyond words, caring and sensitive to a fault. Lee. Morgan met Lee in her early twenties, well beyond high school. Their friendship was closer to being sisters than friends. They had travelled together, won, and lost at love, seen their children happy, and watched them struggle. There was a bond that had grown deep out of respect, admiration for one another, and a true enduring love. They could finish each other's sentences. They could bark at each other and vehemently disagree, but they would always be – the best of friends. Each wanted the other to excel and above all be content and happy...and now, safe. Safe would be a good beginning and ending. Morgan carefully tried to find the proper words to calm her dear friend.

'Lee, it's over. He assaulted me, but the cops have him.'

Lee was not having a bar of it.

'Get your things. Get only the things that you really need or can't live without and pack Ollie's and Opal's necessary items and move in with me now, tonight. Please, Morgan, do this for me. For you. For your children. Please.'

Morgan smiled. *What had she ever done in her life to deserve such a beautiful person? Inside and out.* Lee never blinked an eye or hesitated about helping someone in need and it did not particularly need to be someone to whom she was close. If you needed help, Lee was simply...there.

'I can't talk now. I'll ring you later.' She would put Lee off for the moment and delay the conversation for as long as possible because she would prefer to keep her private life 'private' in *her* home involving the least amount of people possible until the storm cleared.

In the meantime, Morgan's phone would not stop. Exasperated, she turned it off against her better judgement and flowed back into the liveliness and comfort zone of the office Christmas gathering. She didn't enjoy the sympathetic looks she was receiving. *Embarrassment. Humiliation.* Morgan felt those words were tattooed on her forehead. She'd have to get used to it for a bit. The strange thing was that she felt as if she were floating above and around everyone. She could see that her co-workers were speaking, but she couldn't hear a word they were saying. Shock. A bit of shock had enveloped her body, she knew that much.

Morgan was drawn to the large, wide glass windows that were overlooking East Memphis. Outside of the office looked intimidating and scary. The monster could be anywhere.

'No, not now,' she muttered to herself, 'He's behind bars. I'm supposed to be breathing. God, why can't he stay there?'

You can't always get what you want.

Morgan's boss pulled her back into reality telling her that the receptionist (who had been diligently stationed at her front desk while the celebrations transpired, sipping champagne) had handed him a message seconds ago marked 'Urgent'.

He said, 'This guy has been ringing and ringing. He says he's been trying your mobile, but you're not answering.'

'Too right.' She took the note. The message jolted Morgan to remember she had not even contacted her attorney. Then she thought about how long it had taken her lawyer to return her last phone call. She was not particularly impressed. Her situation needed someone's complete attention; at least, it felt that way to her.

Message slip: Date and time. Samuel Ashley Downing.
Please ring at once. Urgent nature.

Who the Hell is Samuel Ashley Downing? Morgan racked her brain. She mentally went over the list of her clients. She knew most of them very well and even a few of their extended family members. Morgan waited until the atmosphere calmed down a bit.

She toasted her dearest colleagues, made small talk, but suddenly felt a bit ill. She snuck back into her office and gently closed the door and pulled the blinds.

Someone had displayed a terribly nice and expensive bottle of French Champagne, a 2009 Moet & Chandon Dom Perignon, right in the middle of her desk, not only on her desk, but they were kind enough to find a stainless-steel ice bucket and placed it on ice. *Hmmm*...Antonio, their compliance officer. Morgan knew he had a soft spot for her and great taste when it came to wines. Antonio was such a shy, gentle guy, but fierce with securities transactions, steeped in reality and if you were going to be a stockbroker, you'd better be an honest one working in the same firm with Antonio. He was a soft-spoken and super kind human being. His note read, 'This too shall pass. You simply must enjoy this Christmas. If not, the monster wins.'

Morgan sighed and smiled. *So true.*

She took out her phone and began ringing the mystery man. She wasn't sure why; curiosity more than anything. But as she began punching the numbers in, someone pecked on the door softly. The door opened slightly, and Antonio appeared.

'Don't say a word. I only want a hug. Call it my Christmas gift.'

The sight of his sheepish and genuinely concerned face made her eyes almost tear up again, but Morgan kept the waterworks at bay. She stood, walked over to him and they hugged. They embraced for a bit longer than she had anticipated, but it felt good. She felt comforted and it made her realize that it's been a long time since she had experienced that feeling.

Antonio kissed the side of her cheek and whispered, 'Merry Christmas. I'm always here if you need me.'

'Thank you' and she slid back into her large, corpulent office chair as he slipped out the door.

She could not get her thoughts to stop spinning. Her children were in school. There was no need to worry about Ollie and Opal. What was that nagging feeling? What was the anvil she felt like she was wearing on her shoulders? Why couldn't she put a name to it? Morgan could put a face to it, but when she did, she would use whatever power she had to push that face out of her psyche repeatedly.

Another deep breath, another sigh and she began to contact one Mr. Samuel Ashley Downing.

'Downing, Carruthers, Xavier, and Griffin' said a husky, sensuous voice.

'Excuse me? What company did you say?'

The woman repeated the name and asked who she was trying to reach.

Morgan stuttered. She hesitated, then quickly stated, 'Samuel Ashley Downing.'

Ms. Husky asked, 'May I relay to Mr. Downing what your call is in reference to?

But Morgan replied tersely, 'No, no you may not. I'm returning his phone call.' She imagined she heard a slight hiss, but then... silence...and a phone was ringing.

'Ashley Downing's office,' said a perky voice, Catherine speaking.'

Lord, most people would have given up by now. Morgan took a deep breath, stood up at her desk, and said, 'Look, my name is Morgan Sage and I'm returning Samuel Downing's call. He phoned me.'

Ms. Perky interrupted, Ashley, Ashley Downing.'

Morgan was about to lose it. 'I don't care what his name is. I'll be in my office for only a few more minutes. Either he can take my call now or take his chances.'

Ms. Perky, not so perky now, stated, 'One moment, please.'

'Ms. Sage, Ms. Morgan Sage?' a deep, soothing voice asked the question.

Morgan was shaking, but she certainly couldn't tell anyone why because she had no clue.

She softly replied, 'Yes.'

'May I call you Morgan?' asked Samuel Ashley Downing.

'Yes, of course.'

'Please call me Ash. My closest friends and colleagues do.'

Morgan retorted, 'May I please ask why you left me a message? Forgive me, but have we met before? I'm a bit confused.'

'Well, a dear friend of mine I've known for quite some time as we attended law school together advised me you are in dire circumstances and may need someone to look out for your well-being and that of your children.'

Morgan listened - she was dumbfounded but curious. She stopped for a second and asked, 'Who? Who would call you on my behalf?

Ash replied, 'Antonio. You're close friends, are you not?'

She couldn't believe it. Yes, they were friends from work, and she'd certainly confided in him lately, but did she appear to be a woman needing protection? *Embarrassment. Humiliation.* Again. She was right. She would be wearing those badges for a while to come. Morgan felt ashamed now, or angry, or embarrassed – she clearly felt bad.

'Look, Ashley Downing, I don't know what the two of you have been discussing, obviously me, but I can deal with whatever life throws my way. I do not, I repeat, I do not like being discussed when I'm not present.'

This time Ash listened, and Morgan could sense he did just that. He genuinely heard her words.

Then, slowly, and assuredly, Ash asked her, 'Would you like to meet at your convenience for coffee or for lunch? I would like very much to do the right thing by Antonio and for you. A meeting, Morgan, two people sitting across from one another and having a discussion. I'm a good listener and I take exceptionally detailed notes. I apologise that we discussed you in your absence, but I wholeheartedly assure you the conversation was held in the strictest confidence, and you are authentically cared for by my good friend. He is seriously concerned for your well-being.'

Morgan didn't immediately respond. She wanted to think. That damned head of hers was still in turmoil - too much stuff banging around up there.

'Morgan?'

Morgan bit her lower lip. 'I need time to consider your proposal, thank you,' and hung up. If Mr. Samuel Ashley Downing was not pleased, so be it.

CHAPTER THREE

Morgan tried to make the evening and the weekend as normal as possible for her children. Kat had picked up Ollie and Opal after school to take them out to dinner with her and to give Morgan time alone. Her brilliant neighbor had made it look as though nothing out of the ordinary had transpired. She made herself a cup of green tea, curled up on the overstuffed sofa, and sat in the darkness. The morning's incident wasn't something she was going to share with her children. They were already frightened of him and had been for a good while. She had never seen the monster lift a hand towards her children and when she asked them about it, they had promised her he had not, but that fact alone didn't matter. It was the way the monster was when he was around them. He sneered, he glared and made them all feel that they weren't wanted or needed in his space. It was as if he found them offensive. The monster went out of his way to make sure they knew that. That alone was enough.

Morgan had a gut full of it ages ago, but it took every ounce of strength and courage to muster the will to leave – to act. She alone knew what sort of aftermath was in store for them. Cold chills trickled down her spine and she felt instantly nauseated. He wasn't even around, but the simple thought of him could bring about negative, physical changes in her psyche and her body. Wine, a nice medicinal glass of wine was exactly what she needed now. Morgan would save the French Champagne for the celebration she longed for – freedom for herself and her children away from the monster. Any place. Anywhere. Away. Far from the madness. For now, she collected puzzles, construction paper, scissors, and coloured markers for the kids, and started a warm, cozy fire for when her cherubs returned.

Separations make people think, at least, the people who are willing to be introspective and want to bring about changes in themselves to lead more productive, healthier lives. Losers never look within. Morgan thought she had managed an enormous amount of reflection. She always felt she possessed a good radar and had exceptional perception abilities. But now she was not so sure. *How did I let myself and my kids down? What blocked my way of thinking? How did I land so far off course?* These were the thoughts that tumbled through her mind repeatedly, playing on a loop. Morgan wanted answers; she wanted the internal voice, that eternal loop, to cease. She knew she could never reverse the damage to her family that her decision had caused.

She remembered the early days while she drank the crisp wine, laid her head back on the sofa, and closed her eyes. The monster would float in and out of their lives - there was nothing consistent about their dates or their meetings. That should have sent an alarm off, but it didn't. She may have found the monster more alluring because he was not always available. Morgan thought, too, because she already had two children, that perhaps he needed time to adjust to the situation – the difference in dating a woman who could project all her attention unto him versus a woman whose children needed and wanted her, too. It was a big ask for any man to share his life with another man's children. She knew now that wasn't necessarily so, many men have done it willingly and lovingly, but then again, it depends on the man, the person, doesn't it? The monster was not cut out for it, and she should have recognized or understood the early signs.

Head in the sand. *Desperate.* Morgan's mind continuously races back to 'desperate'. Such an ugly word. *Was I? Was I so desperate that I forced the monster into our lives?* Did she actually push them to become the picture-perfect family she so 'desperately' wanted and needed for her children?

Yes, apparently.

But, how, how exactly did I do that? Well, for one thing, the monster asked her if she really loved him and why she loved him. This occurred two days prior to their wedding when they were in a small, intimate open-air mall. He physically seated her on a concrete planter, told her to look at him in his eyes and asked her for an honest answer. How weird. *If I had felt any doubt or reservations, I would, more than likely, have done the same thing.*

The strange thing now is that she cannot remember her answer. She also cannot recall or picture in her mind's eye the monster's face. Clearly, she had trouble looking into his eyes at that time.

'There is another clue,' she stammered. 'A million clues and I dismissed them.' She shook her head in exasperation. *DESPERATE* was flashing in big, white, Hollywood lights in her brain. This was going to be a hard image to burn away.

Kat texted her daughter they were pulling into the driveway. Morgan ran out to the car, kissed, and thanked her mom and collected her two beautiful children.

—

Knocking. Hard knocks on the front door and Morgan's heart landed in her throat. Loud noises did that to her. She couldn't shake it. When someone dropped something, turned the radio or television up suddenly, she jumped. Her mind was on high alert. Her nerves were on end. *What did that mean exactly?* She was frazzled – fried – every fiber in her body was standing at attention and it was weighing her down. She had a habit of peeking out the side window first, and always, before answering any door. She had asked her children as gently as possible to do the same without trying to raise alarms or instill fear. Her children didn't ask any questions, but children aren't silly, are they? They see more than any adult sees. Ollie and Opal looked frozen in their places.

'Stay here; I'll be right back. Please grab a book or work your puzzle by the fireplace.' She kept her voice calm and gently smiled.

Morgan saw one of the police officers who had been present at the scene of the ordeal, the situation, the dilemma, the most unfortunate discussion, or to keep it real: the crime. *Was it assault? Yes. Was it attempted murder? How in the Hell would I know? It sure felt like it.* Morgan ran her fingers through her hair, smoothed out her top, and slightly opened the front door.

The police officer reintroduced himself and asked, 'Are you okay?'

Morgan mumbled, 'Not exactly.'

'Could I come in for a moment and have you read the report, approve it, and sign it?'

This seemed odd and Morgan was confused, frowning. 'A policeman met me at my car earlier in the day and advised it was imperative to get the paperwork taken care of immediately if I was going to press charges.' Morgan had assured the policeman earlier that day and again now, 'I am most certainly pressing charges.'

The officer appeared surprised, apologised, and asked, 'Could I please step in?'

Morgan reluctantly allowed him in. She didn't really feel like talking anymore and she kept her voice low stating, 'I haven't shared what happened this morning with my children.'

Upon hearing that news, the officer nodded understandably and exclaimed, 'You need to hire legal representation urgently and get a restraining order in place. I'll leave now, but you might like to know your husband has already 'lawyered up' and was leaving the police station when I did.'

That fact did not sit well with Morgan. She felt a bit of a panic. She also didn't like to hear the word 'husband'. She closed the front door quietly behind him.

The children were looking at their books together and, luckily, they didn't seem to hear any conversations.

'So far, so good,' Morgan muttered, 'I don't have to begin telling stories.' When and how much context Ollie and Opal could know she would decide later, much later.

'Mom, we're hungry again,' Ollie said. 'Yeah, Mommy, my tummy's growling,' Opal added.

Wonderful. She would put together a late dessert, make specific plans and decisions while she filled their little bellies, and they would have a sweet, gentle, normal night together.

Later that evening Morgan decided she would ring Mr. Samuel Ashley or Ashley Samuel or Downing or whatever his name was first thing in the morning as she closed her eyes to sleep. Then, she suddenly remembered the next day was Saturday. *No worries, if he wants to speak with me so badly, he'll get in touch with me.* 'God knows now I need him,' she announced under her breath and drifted off to sleep.

The phone was ringing. It sounded far away then it became louder and louder. She drowsily reached over in the middle of the night and answered her landline. No one calls that line except her mother. Her eyes were wide open now. 'Hello?'

Nothing.

No sound on the other side except short breaths. Then - 'We're not finished. Don't you think for one minute you can do that to me and get away with it. You're so stupid to think you can leave me.'

Morgan couldn't speak. The monster's voice was awful. He was super angry.

All she could master was 'Don't you ever call me again.'

The monster roared with laughter and disconnected.

Trembling. Shaking. Nauseated. Morgan turned on all the lights in her bedroom. Then she turned them all back off again. She didn't know what to do. If she rang anyone at this time of night, what could they do? She would only upset them, and she would make them realize how upset she truly was. She would go downstairs and make a cup of tea as quietly as she possibly could. She thought for certain Ollie and Opal would hear her heart beating because it was literally pounding out of her chest. When she got downstairs to the kitchen, she found she couldn't make herself anything, she could only sit in the dark. It felt safe and there was no phone in the sitting room. That's where she remained until she saw the faintest hint of pale, pink sun filtering through the sparkling lead glass window.

'No. No,' Morgan said to herself, 'I'm not going to live like this. He's not going to make me feel sick or scared. He is not going to control me.'

But the monster was present even if he was not living in the same house.

She went into Ollie's bedroom and stared at him, snuggled into his pillow. He looked peaceful. He looked content. At present, that's all she wished for. Morgan shuffled down the hallway to Opal's room and she had fallen asleep with a book on her chest. The view made Morgan's heart smile. She couldn't remember the last time she had peeked into their rooms in the early morning hours. She had done two beautiful things right in her life.

CHAPTER FOUR

First things first. Breakfast for her precious kids and after that everyone had their Saturday morning chore list. She would throw herself into her portion of work, check on the kids to see if they needed any help, turn the volume up on the music, vacuum, and scrub away. Then she would make the phone call. *Why am I dreading it? More to the point, why am I procrastinating? Chores before phone call?* Morgan continued to have the feeling that something just wasn't right, this was happening frequently lately, but she couldn't put a finger on her apprehension. Then she became angry.

Morgan asked Ollie and Opal, 'Please will you take Dixie for a walk?'

Dixie was their other family member who just happened to be beautiful, hairy, floppy, white with four legs, dark gorgeous eyes, a button nose, a complete and utter joy, and loved enormously by all.

'When you finish walking Dixie and complete your chores, perhaps we'll check to see what's on at the cinema.'

This announcement of seeing a movie brought two huge smiles to sweet faces. They squealed with delight!

Morgan rang the attorney's office. This time a recording played, she supposed because it was Saturday, so she left the appropriate message. It was not even ten minutes later when her mobile began buzzing and she saw it was an unknown number. Morgan had a bit of a panic but took a breath and answered in her professional voice.

'Morgan Sage.'

'Morgan, this is Ash. Your message was forwarded to me.'

'Thanks for ringing me so quickly. Look, I think I'd like to meet you, but it's been brought to my attention that, more than likely, I need a restraining order against my husband. I filed for divorce, but things have taken a nasty turn. I cannot meet you today as I have my children but, first thing on Monday?'

Morgan looked up. Opal came scrambling back into the house screaming, 'Mom, Mom, Mom!'

Morgan told Ashley, 'Hold on a second.'

'Opal, what in the world is wrong?' Now, Opal was crying.

'Mom, a car I've never seen before was following us while we were walking Dixie.'

'What car? Who was it?'

Opal looked down with tears streaming. Morgan went back to the phone and told Ashley she had to go. She heard Ashley saying something, but she disconnected.

'Opal, Opal, my darling, what is it? Where is Ollie?'

At that moment, Ollie came in looking like he'd seen a ghost.

'Ollie, what's going on?' She pulled both of her children in close to her. Dixie still had her lead on and was wagging her tail with her tongue hanging out waiting to be included in the group hug. Morgan immediately locked and bolted the front door with a slight, shy smile to keep the children calm. She looked out the windows but saw nothing.

Opal continued to speak too quickly; Morgan couldn't understand her properly.

She had to keep reminding her, 'Please slow down.'

Opal, through her tears, said, 'There were two men in a brand new, shiny bright car. The man driving, I haven't seen before, but the man in the passenger seat...was him.' Opal hiccupped.

The strange thing was that Opal did not, would not mention his name. She kept saying it was 'him'.

'My, oh my,' Morgan spluttered.

Opal continued, 'I didn't know what to do, so I gave a small wave. He shouted at me. "Don't think I won't be back. Your mother's not going to take you from me - you belong to me. You're mine." 'I can't remember everything. He screamed a lot of stuff.' Opal wiped her tears, 'Mom, it was the way he looked and his voice that scared me so much.'

Morgan held her close and hugged her tightly.

Ollie chimed in. 'I tried to calm Opal down, but she ran ahead. He called me over to the car and Dixie was barking and jumping up and down and I told him I had to go home. He screamed I could go with him instead.' Ollie looked down and frowned. 'That's when

I ran. I saw the car out of the corner of my eye do a U-turn, then I heard it race up behind me and I yelled at Opal to run. Mom, what's going on? Why is he so angry? What have we done? Why is he scaring us?'

Morgan looked into the eyes of her treasured children and held them tightly. 'I'm so very sorry; you both did the right thing.'

That was it. The monster was starting a war, and he was using her vulnerable children as bait. Enough. *How dare he? What kind of human being does such a thing? What kind of a human being scares and uses children?*

She kissed Ollie and Opal and assured them, 'You'll be fine. Run upstairs, wash your faces, and change your clothes.'

She phoned her mother.

'Mom, I need you to come and pick up the kids, please, and take them to a movie, any fun movie filled with laughter that's upbeat and positive.' She knew she could count on her mom. There had never been a day she could not.

Morgan dialed a now familiar number. This time Ashley 'what's his name' answered.

'Could you meet me…someplace soon…now?'

He told her about a small, family-owned place about ten minutes from her home and when Morgan arrived, she could barely see in the dark fashioned pub but made out a figure in a corner booth. Ash, Samuel, Ashley got up and walked over to her as she approached. He was tall, undoubtedly handsome, a rugged kind of face for an attorney, not at all what she expected. But, then again, she didn't really remember expecting anything. Morgan wanted help. She wanted protection for her children and, perhaps, her extended family. *Would the monster try to get to my mother, too?*

Ashley extended his hand to hers, slightly pointed to the booth for her to sit, and said, 'Morgan, please. Now, start at the beginning and don't leave out a thing.'

Morgan started with the desperate, humiliating, and embarrassing situation, but when she heard herself speak, she wondered how pathetic she must sound to this stranger. It was what it was. There was no reason she should hide any of the truth now. Her life and her children's world had made the crossover from dysfunctional to frightening. Neither is an acceptable situation, but does dysfunctional kill someone? Perhaps. Perhaps it does, slowly and surely. Frightening is when you're not certain if you'll be alive from one minute until the next.

Ash listened and when Morgan's eyes adjusted to the light, she saw the clearest, bluest, and saddest eyes she had ever seen before. For a moment she lost her train of thought. Morgan began to recall the time she took Ollie and Opal to the wild and wonderful waterpark in Memphis.

'The monster had told me he needed to be away the entire day. I thought this strange because it was a Saturday, but still, I didn't want to waste a beautiful day, so I announced I was taking the children out and we were heading over to the new water park. The monster stopped as he was walking out the door and asked me again, "Where did you say you were going?" I repeated my last sentence, and I remember he didn't even respond; he walked out the door and got into his car. I gathered items necessary for a sun-filled day, grabbed my favorite book, water bottles, lotion, beach towels, flip-flops, and a fresh change of clothes for everyone and headed towards fun. The kids had never seen anything like it. I heard tiny shrieks of excitement, laughter, joy, and the kids' enthusiasm got me enthused, too. We found our turf and I set about organizing our necessities. Ollie and Opal were told any time they changed their minds about where they wanted to play, they had to promise to return and tell me. They giggled with pleasure and promised they would. I stretched out my beach chair and towel and dove into my book.'

Flipping through the pages of her mind Morgan continued, 'Something wasn't right. I had the sense that danger was imminent. I kept saying to myself at the time, Stupid. Stupid woman. Stop it. My mind's voice – that damned loop again – wouldn't stop. I couldn't enjoy my book; so, I closed it. My eyes did a sweep of the park and the area directly outside of it. Nothing unusual. Everyone was having a delightful time. I tried my book again, but simply couldn't concentrate. Next, I stood up and looked over the entire perimeter and saw Ollie and Opal making new friends and thought the trip was worth it because my kids appeared happy. The sense of someone looking over my shoulder remained with me throughout the day.'

Morgan went on, 'Late afternoon was upon us, so I reined in the children. We gathered our belongings and headed to the car. I had just pulled out of my parking space, changed the gears from park to drive, when…his car pulled up directly by my side. One inch, if that, separated us. How? Where did he come from? Why? Ash, this was far before a divorce was in the works. This is when I was trying, desperately attempting, to make a go of our marriage. This was one of a hundred instances that blew my mind. What makes a person do such a thing?'

Morgan found herself shaking again, uncontrollably on the inside. She couldn't help it but recalling the day brought back the dread. And why, instantly, did she feel guilty? *What the Hell was that about?*

'My children and I were enjoying an afternoon together and then, stalked by my own husband. At first, I didn't even know what to say. There was his look. There was his smirk. He owned that smirk. He had cultivated it over a lifetime. It was his trademark. I told him I thought he'd been there the entire time. The monster said he had been and said he'd been watching me. I reminded him he said he'd be out all day and advised him he could have joined us. The monster replied he'd been out all day doing exactly what he wanted to do. I was gobsmacked.'

Morgan sighed. 'If I described this day to anyone, they wouldn't believe me and then, they'd probably ask me what the monster did wrong.'

As Morgan heard herself speak, she asked Ash, 'What was so bad about it? He didn't hurt us. He didn't fight in public with us, he didn't harm us in any physical way, but who in their right mind does this? Then, he tailed us all the way home. The monster, for unknown reasons, kept one car between us. We arrived home simultaneously. When we were inside the house, he asked what was for dinner as he went upstairs smiling, stating he was famished. I suppose stalking works up an appetite.'

Morgan noticed Ash taking copious notes.

He then asked, 'Do you have a specific date for this peculiar day or dates for any other incidents?

'Well, I do keep a journal. Probably.'

Morgan continued with some of her reflections, 'When situations like this happened...if they were seriously bad, you know, arguments filled with screaming and name calling, the monster would much later, early in the morning, beg for forgiveness, cover my face in kisses, and tell me I tended to blow things up, to overinflate reality. He told me I was excellent at catastrophising. Or the monster would go an entirely different direction telling me I had better change my ways and it was my fault. According to the monster, most times it was my fault. I was the offender. If only I could keep my mouth shut and not upset him. On a few occasions he would blame his anger on the huge, growing responsibility, he had of raising Ollie and Opal. The monster would say his responsibility was overwhelming to mine because they weren't his children...do you see? Now, truly, to any sensible woman this was another warning sign of the horror that was to unfold in our home.'

Ash sat there with his big, sad eyes and simply replied, 'Not necessarily. Most people don't want to believe anything bad is happening and many believe if *they* change in some distinct way, their situation will change, too. I've always found, Morgan, if one is dealing with a paranoid individual – no amount of changing is going to fix the situation.'

Unpredictability was the only thing Morgan could predict.

The water park story had layers and continued to unfold, but Ash stared, and nodded, and yes, his initial words were true - he was committed to taking copious notes. Amazing and admirable, but throughout the telling of this story he showed compassion and empathy through those deep set, sorrowful eyes of his.

What was Ash's story? She wondered. She couldn't know now. She didn't want to know now. First priority: safety for her family.

Ash, such the gentleman, politely stood up and advised her, 'I have a good friend at the police station in close proximity to you.' *That's probably why Ash chose this little establishment to begin with.*

He continued, 'I want to get an emergency injunction, a restraining order against this man, preventing him from entering your space and stopping him from making any kind of contact whatsoever. I'd like to also include the children's names on the injunction, and I strongly advise, you should consider making the children's father aware of the current situation.'

Morgan's eyes grew wide. She hadn't even thought of that. Their father had moved on and was involved with his own, new family and Morgan and the kids rarely heard from him. But once Morgan did consider the situation, it gave her chills because it would not be the kind of news any dad would like to receive. No one wins. Everyone gets hurt. Why? *Desperation.* A mother making a serious, life-changing decision without considering proper possibilities or any consequences.

Humiliation. Embarrassment. Wear the badges. Morgan began to feel the weight of her dreadful, irresponsible past choices. She felt the badges burning against her soul.

Ash acted in an urgent manner now. He politely excused himself, went to the bar and paid the tab. Did they drink? Did they eat? Morgan couldn't remember, then she thought about how the cold New Zealand Sauvignon Blanc felt in her hands. Her own body heat had warmed the glass, and she was still clenching it as Ash dashed away.

His last words were, 'I know it may be difficult for you to believe, but you're going to be fine, and I may need to see you again tomorrow.'

Morgan remembered, too, she had forgotten to mention that she kind of, sort of, had already hired legal representation – no confidence in the firm so far, but she knew Ash would need to be advised.

CHAPTER FIVE

Lee had been standing at Morgan's front door. She was such a smart cookie. She's sincere and thoughtful, too. Lee possesses a key to Morgan's house, her car, and she even knows Morgan's Social Security number. Lee is Ollie's and Opal's godmother. There was not much she didn't know about Morgan.

'Hey, Morgan, I didn't want to let myself in because I thought if you came home and heard a noise or if you weren't expecting me, I might frighten you. That's the last thing I wanted to do.' And, she strongly stressed, 'Since you haven't moved your things in, I take it that's a 'No' to my offer?'

Morgan thought at that moment Lee was such an angel and she adored that she was a part of her life. They embraced one another and it was a good, long hug.

'Wine?' Morgan asked.

'That's what we both need.'

Morgan curled up on the fat, comfy sofa, Lee tossed her purse and keys on the marble kitchen countertop, went to the refrigerator, and poured a fine white wine. She couldn't help but notice the French Champagne.

'Oh-la-la, Morgan, are you holding out on us?' in a terribly bad French accent!

Morgan giggled. 'Antonio gave it to me for Christmas. You know we have a company policy against giving gifts. I think he must have felt sorry for me.'

'Take it for what it is, Morgan, don't read into it, but he's always been smitten with you. You can see it in his face and the way he watches you.'

'I don't want anyone watching me ever, ever again.'

Lee realised she hit a nerve and the atmosphere in the room shifted. She raised her glass, 'To my dear and most fabulous friend. I love you, girl.'

Morgan nodded and raised hers. 'Cheers, love you, too.'

The weekend went by quickly, too fast for Morgan's liking. For one thing she was happy – the routine – Ollie and Opal rising at the same time every morning, enjoying a good breakfast, arguing a bit, and catching the school bus. *Routines may sound boring, but they are extremely good for kids.* This morning, however, the routine factor flew out the door because they were running a bit late.

'Mom, we've missed the school bus,' Ollie called out.

Don't worry, hurry up, finish getting ready, and I'll drop you off at school on my way to work,' she shouted.

Morgan couldn't completely recall what happened next. She heard Ollie. It wasn't Opal, but Ollie and he was wailing. Morgan dropped everything and ran downstairs. Ollie's books had spilled out of his backpack, and he was on the floor of the garage sitting by a crumpled bag and moaning. She reached for him, but he pulled back, shaking as if in fear. *Of me?*

Morgan was holding his shoulders softly pleading with Ollie, 'Look at me.'

He only looked down and with a shocked daze, pointed to the paper bag. Morgan tugged on the bag; it felt weighted down and she pulled back the top. It was a puppy. It was a dead puppy. It was a miniature version of Dixie, and its throat had been slit. Morgan screamed. Of course, she didn't mean to, but it just came out. Opal had stayed back, a bit in the distance, looking as if she was questioning what was happening and appeared frightened to bits. Morgan rolled up the edges of the bag, covered the bag with an old blanket, and gently slid the poor little being to a corner of the garage. She scooped Ollie into her arms. Tears were streaming. She reached for Opal's hand and took them both back inside to the comfort of their kitchen. She kissed them both on their foreheads.

'I love you both so very much and everything is going to be all right. Opal, I'm contacting the school now. You and Ollie are out for the day. Both of you go upstairs and put away your book bags. I need to make several important phone calls.'

Morgan rang the school and without going into too much personal detail she told the school one of their pets had died.

Not good. I will not have my children tell lies. I must think this through. I need air. And for the first time in a long time Morgan felt very much alone. How far was she supposed to get Lee involved? Morgan didn't want to burden her best and closest friend. *And again, what could anyone really do?* She thought back to the briefcase left behind on their kitchen countertop and how she might have handled the situation differently now. *Too late. Forget it. Get over it.*

Morgan fumbled around in her purse for the officer's card. *The police? Really? Is she supposed to call the police or her attorney or both or the vet or all? What about her vet?* She couldn't leave the poor, little being that way. She certainly couldn't keep it around because of Ollie and Opal. *Will Ollie be traumatised for life?* If she chose to go up to the monster today and end his life could anyone blame her? That was not the point.

Morgan closed her eyes, took several deep breaths and after locating the policeman's card, rang his direct line. Within mere minutes, not one, but two cars appeared in Morgan's driveway. She went through the garage and opened the door and met the men inside. She showed them what was deposited for them, she supposed, sometime during the night. It takes an electric garage door opener, of which both clickers Morgan is in possession to raise the door, and the side garage door was locked. *How did anyone get in to do this hideous thing? How did 'HE'?* The police officers were irate and distraught - sickened by what they saw. It was the same two officers who assisted her the first time.

They scratched their heads, shuffled their feet, and advised Morgan, 'Get some of the best security cameras on the market installed as soon as possible.'

Morgan laughed, 'The monster does what he wants to do when he wants to do it.'

'Ma'am, listen to us, please, we're trying to help you. We're going to do everything in our power to catch him.'

By this time, they could hear the patter of feet coming down the stairs.

'Hello, I'm Ollie,' and he asked the police officers, 'Can you please get the man who did this?'

One of the officers bent over and asked, 'How do you know it's a man?'

'I'm not sure how I know, but I do. I know who did this, but I don't want to say his name because I'm scared of him. He's not nice.'

There. There it was. Completely out in the open. The thing Morgan feared the most was sheer reality. She had brought the man into her children's lives now known as The Monster and they were afraid. If Ollie expressed it, you better believe that Opal was doubly frightened. Morgan gasped. She had that same ill feeling again but pulled it together in front of the cops and her children.

The police officers motioned Morgan over to the side and told her, 'We'll need to take some crucial photographs for evidence, and we'd like to be alone when we do that.'

Morgan understood and complied. She gently pushed the children back inside, poured them both a glass of juice.

'I need to make a couple of phone calls.'

Ollie asked, 'Can I get the big National Geographic puzzle down from the bookshelves?' and Opal pleaded, too.

'Indeed.'

A quick phone call to her most understanding boss, after showing his disgust, and sorrow, and empathy, he told Morgan that someone was tugging his arm and wanted to have a word. Antonio.

'Hey, I only got bits and pieces, tell me, Morgan, tell me what happened now. I'm worried about you.'

Morgan kept her cool, described Ollie's horrific discovery, and Antonio was seething on the other end of the line.

'I'm on my way.'

Morgan squawked back, 'No, no, Antonio, please; I want to try to keep my children as calm as possible. I don't, well, we don't need any extra company today. We've already had two police officers here.'

Antonio listened and mumbled. Morgan couldn't see the disappointment in his face, but she could certainly hear it.

Antonio may have listened, but he did not obey, well, in a sense. He himself did not make a visit to Morgan's home, but low and behold in under twenty minutes, Ash was knocking on her door. Morgan was in disbelief. Not only did she not want company, but how was she to explain that Ash was not a stranger? He was most definitely a stranger to Ollie and Opal. Her phone continued ringing. Morgan ignored it and that drove the children nuts.

She did notice, however, a couple of strange numbers, but knew she could have a good look much later that evening.

Ash introduced himself to Ollie and Opal. 'Hello, I'm a friend of your mother's and I met your mom through her work.' In a roundabout way that was absolutely true. He motioned Morgan into the sitting room.

'These latest actions are serious, Morgan. You cannot sweep this under the rug and pretend it didn't happen. I want you to take the kids and go away for a few days. Do you have a friend you can stay with for a while?'

Morgan instantly thought of Lee, but she didn't want Lee this close to the insanity.

Ash pushed. 'Anyone. Can you go to your mother's?'

'Most certainly not,' Morgan said, 'And I don't want you or anyone telling her what went on in this house today. I don't enjoy seeing her upset. I'll ring my friend, Lee, but we'll only stay for a couple of nights.'

Ash looked completely relieved. He offered, 'Look, I've got a house at Pickwick Lake, and it has a great deal of space, surrounded by beautiful trees, fresh air, nature, you and your children would be in a safe cocoon, and no one would find you. I need a couple of days to have the home cleaned and freshened. You're more than welcome to stay there. I asked Antonio to speak with your boss and advise him you should disappear for a bit. I apologise. I know you don't care for people to speak on your behalf, but Antonio was quite upset when he reached me, and I had to think quickly. Go to Lee's and I'll contact you.'

Morgan was shocked and numb. She hesitated, was about to speak but Ash stood up and said, 'Go. This man is dangerous, Morgan, and I'm afraid he's not going to stop...yet. Contact your mother and tell her whatever you wish once you settle in with your friend.'

Well, Hell, I haven't even called Lee yet. Am I even in control of my life?

Calmly she walked over to Ollie and Opal, and she got grumbles. 'Mom, we've just started the puzzle.'

How could Morgan get them to agree to leave so quickly? She promised them another even larger puzzle. *Not such a bad bargain,* she smiled to herself.

Lee had the two guest bedrooms already prepared. One had a queen size bed ensuite, and the other room had twin beds pushed against opposing walls. It had been a long time since Ollie and Opal had shared a bedroom, but they appeared excited about the set-up. It was as if the family was on a bit of a holiday. They were away from the scene of the early morning terror and that, quite frankly, lightened everyone's mood. At least Opal was spared the wretched and horrific sight. That was the only good aspect of the last 24 hours, well, except for the kindness of two special human beings, Morgan's lifelong friend, Lee, and her new, very mysterious, most capable of managing out of control situations, Ashley. Her respect was growing immensely for this attorney and those thoughts took her back to Antonio. Out of darkness, the brightest stars appear. Morgan was beginning to feel and understand that some sort of protective shield was forming around her. Exactly what the hours, days, and weeks ahead required, sadly, she felt.

The house slept. Not a peep was heard from anyone. Morgan knew she had to rise early to get her kids to school since they were far away from the path of the school bus. She had been lying in her bed since early morning, but she wasn't awake from fear or stress, she needed the time to try and sort out her feelings and her next plan of action. Morgan wanted to take control of the reins; she didn't want her next move to be motivated by an outside enforcer even though the person meant well. It was her life and her children's future that depended on her making strong, deliberate, and healthy choices. This thought suddenly gave her real strength and power. They were going to be fine. The three of them would survive this horrible situation and learn to thrive again. Morgan sprang out of bed with Dixie, entered Ollie and Opal's bedroom, and woke them with butterfly kisses.

'Time to rise and shine, my sweeties. Come downstairs when you've finished getting ready and I'll make breakfast for you. I'm taking you to school today.'

The kids looked at each other. There would be no bus at Lee's. Lee's children were much older, and both were already driving and out of the house. Morgan would oversee chauffeuring. She made breakfast for everyone and there was charming chit-chat at the morning table.

Lee advised Morgan, 'I've got a full day and need to check in with my realty firm, see if any clients need me, run some errands, but, remember, I'm only a phone call away and I'll be back early afternoon.'

This shocked Morgan a bit. Surely Lee wasn't changing her schedule for her. Morgan thought she had said this to herself, but she had announced it!

'You better believe it, girl. Hard times call for harsh tactics. I am here. We'll get through this together.'

Secretly, Morgan rolled her eyes. She could only wish for normalcy which was an elusive and privileged concept at present.

CHAPTER SIX

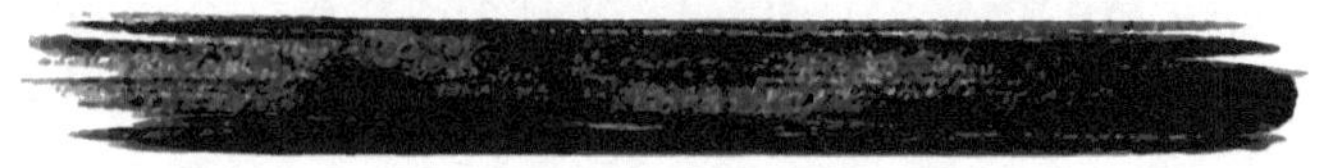

Morgan drove the kids to school, winding through the magnificent magnolia trees interwoven in the Memphis fabric. For a moment she was smiling, thinking how fortunate they were to be in a safe haven. The sun was shining. The children had a very pleasant morning, and this was going to be their new beginning. Ollie and Opal scrambled out of the car, Morgan's favorite car, an older white Volvo with red leather interior. Everybody gave her grief about her car. Everyone told her it simply didn't suit her personality. She smiled to herself thinking that this particular vehicle had sailed along with her through the brightest days and the darkest storms, and they belonged to one another. Air kisses and waves and Morgan watched her children dash to the front door of school.

Of course, she didn't need to, but Morgan wanted to go see her boss face to face. Once she saw his expression, she would know exactly how he felt about her taking time off. It probably made no difference to him at all because the Christmas season and even January were slow periods at work. Morgan ordered two special coffees at Starbuck's drive-thru, then changed her order to three because she didn't want to ignore Antonio. What to do. If she put a lot of energy into him, he might read her the wrong way. He was really stepping into her life, and even though his actions surprised her, lately he had made fairly spectacular decisions concerning her situation. Antonio was a sensitive, kind man and Morgan had wondered, more than once, why there was no special woman in his life. She pulled into the office parking lot. The building she worked in had all the bells and whistles, very contemporary, sexy in fact if a building could have sex appeal, and it had a good vibe and smelled of money. She put her trusty Volvo in park, grabbed the take-away tray, and headed towards the elevator.

Upstairs things were far quieter than usual. The receptionist was on the phone but smiled and winked at her with an 'OK' sign.

Morgan noticed the majority of cubicles were empty. Her boss, Mike, Mr. Mike the Tan Man, gave Morgan a hearty 'Hello' and ushered her into his office.

'For Goodness' sake, what are you doing here? I thought the plan was for you and the children to simply disappear for a bit?' Mike questioned with some concern.

'The kids have only a few days left at school before they're released for Christmas, but, yes, that's the plan and it is to be shared with no one. Are you sure it's okay if I bail for a bit?'

'It's not only okay. It's an order.' And, as you probably already know Antonio is aware of the scheme.'

Scheme, Morgan thought. Scheme. That sounds naughty. That sounds devious or spiteful or manipulative. Most of these words she didn't like the sound or meaning of, but it was reality. A scheme had formulated, and she and her children are the major players.

'Mike, tell me truthfully. Does anyone else at all know what's going on? Anyone? Please tell me.'

'I don't believe so. C'mon, the entire office knows you're going through an extremely rough time, but no one truly has the details, to my knowledge.'

That made Morgan feel a bit better. *How do you keep your life and your dignity private when it seems as though there is a giant magnifying glass on your every move?*

Antonio was, uncharacteristically, running late. He popped his head in with his wavy hair and posh, horn-rimmed glasses. Morgan pointed to the coffee and a huge grin appeared. He bent over, kissed the top of her head and said, 'Thanks for the coffee.'

'Are you okay?'

She nodded and the three toasted their coffee cups.

'Good,' Antonio said, 'Stay away until you heal and find your strength again. I miss the essence of Morgan.'

Morgan shook her head. *What in the heck was Antonio on about?* They pleaded with her to get in touch if she needed anything and they put an emphasis on the word 'anything' like she's never heard before. She assured them that she would.

Antonio happened to mention as he walked her to the elevator, 'I have virtually no plans for Christmas, and it's been a while since I've visited Pickwick Lake.'

Morgan looked up at him and saw sincerity in his eyes. She also sensed a complication. Now was not the time to invite Antonio to Pickwick or, for that matter, anywhere else. It was time for her to get back home and begin organising their mini vacation.

She began digging through her purse on the ground floor and was barely paying attention when she was whisked into the re-volving front, glass door. Not a soul in sight. She heard her phone ringing in her purse and walked through a line of cars, keys in hand, ready to unlock her car door. She looked up and she looked down at the parking aisle.

Morgan was muttering to herself. 'Now, I really know I'm losing it, but it's just stress. I know I parked my car here. I know I did.' She began circling the parking lot. The lot was not even that large. She retraced her steps. Her phone was continuing to go off. This time she stopped next to a brightly coloured BMW, found her phone and answered it.

'Are you looking for something?'

'I told you to never contact me. I'm calling the police.'

'Fine. They can't prove it. This isn't my phone. The car is in my name, too, and I needed it.'

Morgan screamed. Laughter. Hideous laughter followed. She was even more upset that she had screamed.

The last thing she wanted to do was return to the office. *EMBAR-RASSMENT. HUMILIATION. DESPERATION. SAD. PATHETIC.*

'You piss-poor pathetic woman,' she hissed to herself. The mind-loop was in full force and Morgan was telling it to 'Shut-up.'

She hesitated on the ground floor and went into the ladies' room before going back upstairs. Morgan's only goal at this point was to remain calm and try to find a little dignity. Just a little is all she needed. When she re-entered the office, Antonio and Mike were lingering outside of Mike's office and a look of puzzlement was on both of their faces. Morgan shared. Antonio looked as though he was going to punch the wall and he's the nice, sensitive fellow. Mike cursed. He actually dropped a couple of gems that Morgan hadn't heard him say prior to this moment. They pulled her into the office, closed the door, lowered the blinds, and told her to call the police.

'Funny,' Morgan said, 'I just happen to have a card right here. It appears to be the most popular card in my possession during this time in my life.' She could hear Antonio on his cell phone, and he was speaking urgently and quietly.

Morgan reached 'her cop'. She felt as if she had earned the right to call him that now. The cop fell silent when she explained the situation.

'This guy thinks he's playing a game, but this is one he's not going to win.'

Morgan retorted, 'Well, if you look at the score right now: The Monster – Three. Morgan – Zero.'

'Ma'am, you can't look at it that way. This man has conducted criminal behavior. We'll get him. I need to make a report and I'm on my way. Don't move.'

Delightful. Simply splendid – another meeting with the nice policeman.

She felt her energy draining from her body. Morgan drank enormous amounts of hot, steaming, black office coffee while she gave her description of events to the cop. Notes were scribbled. Times were specific. Make and model and year of the car. Her baby. She knew she would never see her most favored friend again. It was as if a buddy had been kidnapped. Stupid. Material things. Not real. Not a problem, but a necessity, especially when you have kids depending upon you. Her boss, Mike, could not keep out of the conversation. They were gathered in the private, executive, mahogany paneled conference room, but Mike was pacing, and he wanted to let the cop know exactly how vile the monster was.

'Do something, Damnit. This guy is not only hurting Morgan, but he's terrorizing her kids, too. Get him. Get him or I will.'

The cops' ears perked up. He stood up, feet wide, chest straightened out, and stated in a very demanding voice, 'Sir, I understand your frustration, but we're doing our job, and we don't need any interference, and I don't want to hear any further talk like that.'

Mike backed down a little bit. He looked puffed up, too, but he finally glanced over at Morgan and walked away.

They were putting the finishing touches on the necessary paper-work, the cop was looking at Morgan with deep concern, trying to be reassuring, and patting her on her shoulder like he would his beloved dog. The next thing she knew Ash and Antonio entered the room and Ash was beaming. I mean this guy had a smile like a Cheshire cat. Unbelievable – at a time like this. Morgan wanted to pop it right off his face.

Ash made an apology for interrupting, extended his hand, and introduced himself, 'Hello, I'm Samuel Ashley Downing, repre-senting Ms. Morgan Sage.'

Gheeez-Louise, I still haven't told him about the other firm I left a retainer with. Now, she hung her head and felt overwhelmed. Three steps forward. Five steps back. Morgan vowed to start writing things down at night before bed.

The police officer and Ash chatted in low voices with Antonio interjecting.

Then she said, 'Excuse me. My name is Morgan and I'm sitting right here.'

Apologies all around. Mr. Nice Cop came over to her, shook her hand, and said that he would be back in touch. Morgan figured when they talked again, she would share with the officer she and her children were leaving Memphis for Pickwick Lake for a small vacation. Antonio was full of himself, too. You could not wipe the smile from his face if you tried either. *What the Hell was happening?* Antonio stepped away and closed the conference door on his way out.

Ash said, 'Dreadful business. This guy is a beast and, most certainly, a big bully, and undoubtedly, Morgan, he will get the book thrown at him, but it may take a while. In the meantime, I have a very pleasant surprise for you and I do hope you'll be pleased.'

Morgan suddenly felt very tired and much older, so she continued to sip her coffee and listened.

Ash continued, 'I have another very dear friend who I've known since we were boys.'

'And?'

'Well, I want you to listen, really listen because it's my turn to talk and you need to have your life in order so you can continue to take care of your children.'

'Yes, Ash, of course I do, but what are you trying to tell me? Spit it out.'

Ash handed over shiny keys. There were two keys and there was an 'L' on the heavy keyring.

'What are these?'

'These are keys to your mode of transportation, your way to safety, your road to freedom, and your path to continue a normal life with Ollie and Opal.'

'Whaaat?' spewed Morgan. 'What are you talking about? You arrive at my place of work, no announcement, and you march in here handing me keys? No, Ashley, No. This won't do. You've helped me so far, tremendously, and I'm most grateful. But I do not, I repeat, I do not take cars from men, especially from a man I hardly know. How do you show up at my place of work handing over keys like they're a bag of sugar? No. Nope. NO. Not happening.' She knew her words weren't making sense, but she felt awkward; she felt shame and embarrassment.

Ash raised his arms gently. He placed his hands on her shoulders, 'Stop. Remember I asked you to listen? My friend owns a dealership right here in town. This is not a gift. I promise you, Morgan. This is only a temporary loaner car. It is a demo car. It's a small Lexus ES350. It has low mileage, and I've put a temporary lease for six months in my name. If this individual is going to continue to take things from you, your name doesn't need to go on anything at this point. Morgan, please. This is not a gift from me. Think of it as a community gesture. The car would not be downstairs if it weren't for Antonio. The car would not be here so quickly if I didn't have a real friend who enjoys helping others whenever possible. And, by the way, I gave no name. My guy has no clue who this is for. He has prepared the paperwork and I am on the lease. My para-legal is handling the insurance and it should be sorted by now. Temporary, did you hear me? If you're that unhappy with me, tell me what your plan is, please.'

Morgan was dumbfounded. She felt over-emotional. She began to shake and felt genuinely cold. *What is my plan?* True, she didn't know - didn't even have a baby clue. But she knew her children would be expecting her at school in under an hour. *Why are gifts so difficult to receive?* She considered because she was in such a bad place in her life, she didn't really deserve the kindness of others when she, she, was the one who got herself and her kids into this unacceptable, unimaginable situation. *EMBARRASS-MENT. HUMILIATION. DESPERATION.* She pictured these words as little creatures. *How long would these three characters be hanging around?* She envisioned them as her new ball and chain, dragging them along from her ankle. The Hollywood 'LOSER' lights were flashing again upstairs, too. *Would this be a feeling that lingered for a month, six months, or a year? Am I damaged? Are these thoughts permanently imprinted on my brain?*

Morgan tried shaking off the negative crap. Ash had been staring at her for a good while with his gentle, blue eyes. He patted her hand. Morgan, for some reason, didn't like people to do that. At this point in her life, on this day, she especially didn't care for it, but she knew Ash meant well and had her best interests at heart. So, Morgan swallowed, stood up, made the mature gesture, and extended her hand.

'Thank you. Thank you, Ash. If you would please pass on my enormous appreciation to your man, too, I would be most grateful. I promise I'll try my best to make other arrangements as soon as I physically can.'

Ash reassured her that she needed to do nothing, nothing but concentrate on living safely. Tears. Big, ole, fat tears spilling out from the corners of her eyes and Ash gave her a short, sweet hug.

'So much for me taking control of the reins again,' she uttered.

'C'mon, let me show you a couple of things about the car. She is such a splendid ride and you're going to fall in love with her.'

Morgan looked sheepishly at Mike and Antonio and walked with Ash to the new, white, shining, and most luxurious Lexus. She was searching for her dignity *again* as they stepped through the door.

CHAPTER SEVEN

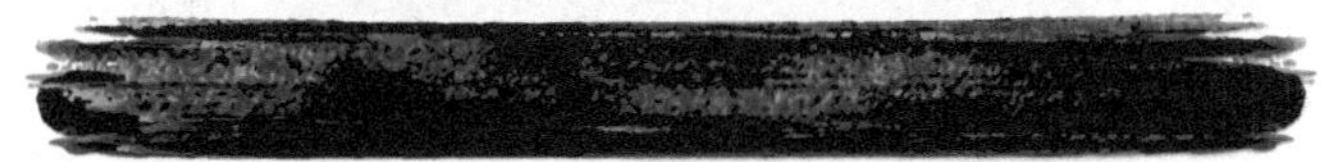

*W*ow, *this morning I left Lee's home in my most trusted car...a familiar friend, and this afternoon I'm pulling up to school in a Lexus demo that still had that new car smell. How do they do that? There must have been hundreds of people test driving this car. It must be a spray.* What was she going to tell Ollie and Opal? How would she explain away the new wheels without getting bogged down in the details or becoming a pathological liar? She'd better think fast because she saw her precious ones looking for the Volvo. Morgan stepped out of the car.

'Ollie, Opal, here. Here I am!'

The kids both looked puzzled and walked curiously towards their mom. Opal was grinning a very cheeky grin and Ollie squealed with delight.

'Mom, Mom, where did you get this? Where's our car? What happened to the Volvo? Is this ours?' Opal and Ollie were shooting rapid fire questions as she laughed.

'Calm down. The Volvo was tired and needed to take a little holiday, so this car is simply a temporary replacement. Don't get too excited. Don't get attached to it, please. I'm hopeful our Volvo will be fine after she has a check-up. We'll see. Now, buckle your seat belts.'

The kids squirmed around, making themselves acquainted with the new shiny buckles, and looking at the strange and alluring gadgets and gizmos throughout the car and on the dashboard. Morgan was still becoming familiar with it, too. *Temporary. I need to get myself settled, somewhere where I can think, and work on getting this car back to Ash.* Then she realized, what on Earth would she have done, truly, if the day had not unfolded this way? The angels had gathered and were gaining momentum, and she wondered how exactly to thank them properly.

Morgan's phone was buzzing in her purse on the front passenger seat while she was driving. She'd heard it several times. Nope. This time she was not answering. Morgan knew she could change her number, but she didn't want to alarm her mother or confuse her children, and she knew the monster would find a way to get a new number anyway. However, she wasn't going to answer numbers she didn't recognize - not any longer.

They drove up to Lee's house. Lee came out of the garage with her hands on her hip, then her hands up in the air as if, 'What's this?'

'Morgan, I've been here all afternoon trying not to worry about you, then you show up in this beauty?' She was beaming, gave them all hugs, with Dixie barking at her heels, and said, 'I've already started prepping for dinner.'

Ollie and Opal wanted to show her the car. Lee looked at Morgan who mouthed 'Later.' New car presentation finished, everyone bustled inside. Lee had made lovely fresh fruit and veggie snacks for Morgan's kids. Morgan thought Lee most certainly missed her own kids being this age. Lee eyed Morgan and went to the fridge and pulled out a fine, crisp, cold white bottle of Australian Eden Valley Reisling. Morgan gathered the wine glasses, and they sat in Lee's large family room. After Morgan finished the story, Lee looked so angry Morgan thought she might have a heart attack. Keeping screams and anger bottled up can be tough on a body. Morgan leaned over and hugged her.

'It's going to be fine. The monster keeps digging himself into a bigger hole. He may be the meanest human being I've ever known or he gets supreme satisfaction at making others suffer – the same people he proclaimed one time to love.'

Lee looked white and as if it had happened to her and the wind had been knocked out of her sails.

'This is exactly what I didn't want to bring into your household. You are wearing my pain. I love you for caring, but I hate that this upsets you so.'

'Of course, it does. You would feel the same way if the roles were reversed.'

'True.'

Then, Lee looked up and quite energetically said, 'We must stay ahead of him, Morgan. We need to be steps ahead, strategize, figure out what means the most to you and look at your daily routine because that is where he'll hit next.'

Morgan stopped. 'Lee, this is what gives me chills. You do understand that you announced into the ethos the monster's going to include my kids in his next plan.'

'No, never.'

'Yes, you did. You said we had to understand what means the most to me and that's clearly Ollie and Opal. Lee, I can't think that way. I don't want to have the mind of the monster. I don't want to live in the darkness.'

'Understood, but somehow, someway, we need to be more prepared.'

'How do you perpetually prepare for a disaster, Lee? You can't. I won't.'

Lee and Morgan both sensed real trauma and felt the tension in the room. Lee got up, took the chilled wine from the fridge, and refilled their glasses.

'Ollie, Opal would you like to help me make yummy spag-bog? My homemade recipe is the best and it's a secret, too.'

Ollie looked unsure, but Opal was keen. Lee sounded cheerful and pulled out hamburger meat, Italian sausage, yellow onions, green, and red bell peppers, fresh tomatoes, sea salt, ground black pepper, a new bottle of olive oil, garlic cloves, and a fresh bunch of basil leaves.

Ollie asked, 'Can I just sit at the kitchen bar and watch the action?'

Lee laughed and Opal joined her, and they went to work. Lee even placed a tall, white, paper chef's hat on Opal's head and an apron which was far too large to add to the fun.

Ollie warned them, 'I'm gonna write down some notes so I'll know the secret recipe, too.'

Lee teased him with a wink, 'You'd better not share it with anyone, ever!'

Morgan felt particularly guilty. Her mother was the person who had been ringing her throughout the day. It's not that she didn't want to speak to her - she didn't want to alarm her or concern her, but not communicating was going to bring about the same effect. She stammered and hesitated and then realized that she could share tiny bits and pieces, no lying, avoid telling all and most certainly nothing about the car. They would be at Pickwick Lake anyway and her mother didn't need to know anything about the car ordeal at this point. Morgan was not thinking clearly but picked up her phone.

'Hi, Mom. How are you?'

'Oh, Morgan, please do keep in touch more often. You know I automatically worry and when I don't hear from you the anxiety makes me miserable. I love you so and you're in an impossible situation.'

'Now, Mom, please don't say impossible. We both know that's not true. It's not a nice place presently, but you know I'm doing everything possible to change it.'

'He was here!' Kathleen exclaimed.

Morgan stopped still. Her mouth flew open, and she couldn't breathe properly. She wasn't sure at all that she heard her mother correctly.

'Mom?'

'Yes, Morgan, he was here. Don't worry. I didn't believe a word he said. He is such a bastard of a man, and he honestly thinks I can't see through him. He believes every word that comes out of his mouth. Oh, Morgan, he is a nasty piece of work, and I think he's most unstable. Seriously. You must watch yourself. You need to be where you can protect Ollie and Opal.'

Morgan wanted to rush to her mother to make certain she was all right. She wanted to hold her. Morgan knew that her mother must have put up a very brave front because she knew that Kathleen had never been comfortable around him.

She remained calm and soft spoken, 'You know how very much I love you. I'm so sorry you had to endure the monster. I'm terribly sorry. Mom, please forgive me, but my day's been loaded, and I feel the need to take a long hot bath to try and sleep. I promise I'll do a better job and stay connected more regularly. I promise.'

She ended the conversation, and her body began to shake uncontrollably, once again, and then…the chills set in. This must cease. Someone must stop the monster. She must stop him.

But, how? Morgan hastened downstairs to check on everyone. There was no way she was going to drop this bomb on Lee.

But she did ask Lee, 'Do you mind if I slip away for a steamy bath?'

'Go ahead and I'll put Ollie and Opal to bed after homework.' Morgan kissed the tops of their heads and she felt them watching her as she vanished.

She locked the door to the bathroom, clicked on Spotify and turned the music up as loud as she could while she ran the bath and – let it out. Her hands covered her face and she just wailed. *How, how did my life get so out of control? Please protect my mother. Please watch over my kids. Oh, God, please keep them safe.* All Morgan could do was pray and she didn't think she was doing a particularly decent job at that. She slid down into the hot steamy water, and it didn't matter anymore how much she cried.

CHAPTER EIGHT

The next morning was not as good as the previous day. Morgan felt deflated, completely flat. Her energy, her will, her, what did Antonio call it? Her essence was gone. She felt empty. She felt scared. She felt vulnerable and to be precise, alone. *Shake it off, Morgan. You are a mother. You're a good mother and you're going to go downstairs and take the day by its horns and get things happening. Concentrate. Get Ollie and Opal up. Cook breakfast. Smile. Manage. Smile. Encourage. Breathe. Smile. This situation is character building. That is all that it is. This is temporary. Antonio keeps telling me, 'This too shall pass.'* Morgan tried to gain strength and remembered a friend from another lifetime telling her to 'Fake it until you make it'. Today that would be her motto. She would need every mental aid she had available in her toolbox to get through the hours ahead.

Kids are such genuine little beings. They are smart - too smart for their own good sometimes. Ollie and Opal could sense something was off with their mom, but she looked happy. They could see she was smiling. They could see she was making breakfast, singing as she cooked, but she wasn't saying much to them. Ollie and Opal looked at each other.

'Mommy, are you okay?' Opal asked.

'I am positively smashing.'

That was their mom's favorite phrase when things were going well, and it made the two giggle. All was okay in the world for the moment.

FAKE. FAKER. FAKE. FAKER. Oh, how nice. More new negative words to add to the winding loop repertoire. This is exactly how she felt after dropping Ollie and Opal off at school. She could not alter her mind-set. She felt as if she were slipping off the edge of a cliff. There are no cliffs in Memphis. There are definitely bluffs. The grand views of the Mississippi River remain enhanced by beautiful bluffs, but that's not where Morgan is picturing herself. She is hanging on by a thread and that thread is about to snap.

After dropping her cherubs off to school, Morgan pulled over into a parking lot of an office building. One more day of school before the kids would be released for Christmas, then, they could pack up the car and head towards the lake house. Panic. More anxiety thinking about leaving her mother in Memphis. She desperately wanted to speak with someone. *DESPERATE.* Well, at least she wasn't feeling like a fake anymore. Morgan was wearing that desperate tag and dragging those other characters around her ankles, too. She rang Ash. Ash had given her his private mobile number and his direct office line, so Morgan didn't have to go through Ms. Husky or Ms. Perky anymore. A welcomed relief. It went to voice mail. *Damn. Damn. Damn.*

She took long deep breaths and imagined herself back at work, managing her clients, purchasing stocks, dabbling in a bit of commodities if she believed in the trader, and setting up individual retirement accounts for a variety of people. She missed it. She knew it was slow right now, but the rhythm of the work and the routine and the phone calls and the excitement when she concluded a money-making transaction for a client was quite intriguing to her. When she lost money for clients, she took it exceptionally hard. It was a highly stressful job, but nothing, nothing compared to the debilitating stress she was experiencing these days. She yearned for yesterday. No, she didn't. Morgan half-way smiled. *Any part of yesterday would include the monster.* A monster-free existence for herself and her family was the only aim.

Pulling into the parking lot must have done Morgan a world of good. She started to put things into perspective and was feeling slightly more positive. But the monster visited her mother. *How dare he? Anything...to get to me.* It was just as Lee said the night before, "We need to be a step ahead. He'll go for anything that means the most to you." *Bastard. Terrible. Horrible. Non-human. No one can do what he has done and be called human. Right?*

She dialed Ash again. This time he answered.

'Morgan, what's up? Where are you? The Pickwick Lake house is ready and able to receive you whenever you wish.'

'Ash, can we meet?'

'Of course. Would you like to come to the office?'

'Oh, no, I am a mess. I dropped the kids off at school, but something has happened.'

Morgan could feel Ash's uneasiness on the other end. She quickly replied, 'We're unharmed, but I feel as if I'm in a bit of shock. He must be stopped, Ash.'

'Where are you? Can you meet me at Another Broken Egg off Poplar Avenue?'

They were seated at a corner table only ten minutes later.

'You look beat. I mean you look absolutely drained.'

'Thanks, but tears will do that to you. Tears and the monster on your tail.'

'I'm listening.'

Morgan went through the entire scenario and told Ash what a brave voice her mother put on over the phone. Ash appeared disgusted. He looked agitated and seriously angry.

'Look, the first thing I'm going to do when I leave you is attempt to get before a judge as soon as possible and get him for contempt.'

'How? The monster hasn't been advised to stay away from my mother. Plus, he was right about the car. He never drove it. He had his own. He has two, as a matter of fact, but his name was on my car, also.'

'He is not supposed to contact you in any shape, form, or manner.'

'You can look through my phone and see the numbers. They are all different. How can you or I prove that it was the monster making the calls to me? It'll be my word against his. How, Ash?'

'You leave that to me. In the meantime, why don't you invite your mother to join you at the lake house?'

Morgan's mind was completely jumbled. She was not thinking clearly, but she did have the clarity to finally remember to tell Ash that she had hired an attorney and presented a five-thousand-dollar retainer about a month ago. Ash looked only a little surprised. 'What firm?'

Morgan told him.

'I know that group. I'll speak with them this afternoon. They'll keep half of your deposit or if they've performed genuine work for you, they'll keep it all.'

'Nothing. They have done zero for me and I have yet to receive a return phone call from over a week ago.'

Ash showed no facial expression and kept his mouth shut.

'I'll handle it. That's the least of your worries. Morgan, let me see how much I can accomplish this morning, and I'll get back to you. Are you going to be okay?' His eyes. His deep, blue gentle eyes again, looking inquisitively into hers.

She said with a big, fat smile. 'I'm fine, truly.'

BIG. FAT. LIAR.

Morgan watched Ash as he walked through the door. She felt glued to her seat. The dilemma was she didn't know what to do next. She didn't want to leave the comfort and safety of the booth. She didn't want to make any decisions. She wanted to sit. Think. *What happened to my brave thoughts regarding grabbing the reins and taking hold? Who am I?* She felt like a shell of her former self. When was the last time she had eaten properly, too? The server came over and poured her a fresh, steaming, hot cup of black coffee and asked if she wanted anything to eat.

'Yes, please.' But then...nothing else came.

The server looked at her kindly and said, 'Ma'am, we serve wonderful breakfasts here and I'll be happy to get you anything you like.' She had the sweetest smile.

Morgan finally looked up, 'Scrambled.'

'You'll be surprised!'

'Thanks. That would be perfect.'

Hot, moist, scrambled eggs stuffed with mushrooms, cheddar cheese, bell pepper, spring onions appeared before her eyes, with golden crispy hash-browns, thick sourdough toast with big, fat, butter pats glistening on top, a side of grits, and two crispy, bacon strips. Morgan stared. She didn't remember seeing anything like this on the menu. She didn't even remember looking at the menu. It was beautifully presented, but the plate was huge. It overwhelmed her senses. She struggled. Morgan ate a bite of the eggs as they looked as if they would taste great, but she'd lost her sense of taste. She could smell the bacon. Morgan sipped her coffee and drank a bit of tomato juice but couldn't make herself eat. She was indeed hungry, still, she couldn't swallow. Stress. The monster was doing this. *No, I am allowing him to do this.* She picked up her fork again and tried extremely hard to make the breakfast disappear. Not happening today.

The server came over and gave her a look as if she understood. 'I promise it'll get better.'

Morgan slipped a nice, larger than normal tip on the table, grabbed her keys, and headed over to her mother's house.

CHAPTER NINE

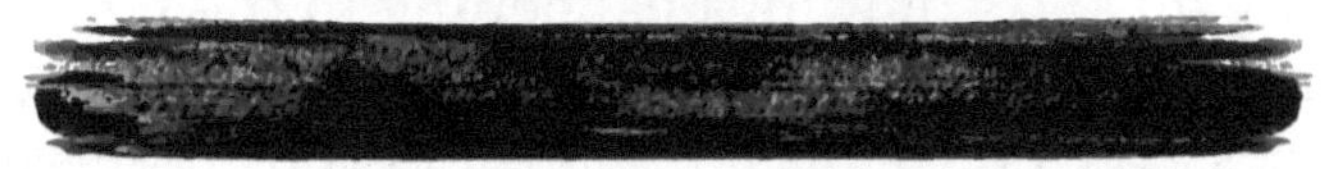

Kat unlocked the door. *Good. She is taking the proper precautions, using her head, and locking the doors.* Morgan felt truly relieved.

'Hello, my love. I'm so happy to see you. You look terribly tired.'

'Yes, Mom, that I do. I'm not sleeping very well.'

Kat poured from a new pot of steaming hot, black coffee. 'Please talk to me. I can't change a thing that has happened, but I'm always here to listen and I want to help any way possible.'

'Mom, how would you like to go to Pickwick Lake with us?'

Kat looked a bit startled, but she said the proposition sounded nice. Morgan elaborated about how she felt Ollie and Opal really needed a change of scenery. 'It'll be fun to have Christmas together in a new spot, the four of us.'

'Well, it has been difficult to even think about Christmas this season, but we must keep life as normal as we can for the children and since I have no ties or commitments here, let's do it. We can keep it simple, yet special.'

Morgan sighed with enormous relief and was grateful. They would celebrate and treat this get-away as a Christmas vacation. Morgan kissed her mom on the cheek.

'Have your bags ready and I'll be back to pick you up around 10:00 in the morning.' As Morgan pushed the front door open, she felt embarrassed, suddenly hesitating and remembering she had a different, new car in her mom's driveway. She looked down as she struggled to find her keys.

'Morgan, he was in your car yesterday. I found that quite odd, but I did not dare give him the satisfaction of saying anything.'

Morgan looked up at her mom and her eyes began to swell.

'It's quite alright, dear. You'll survive this. See you in the morning.'

Will she? Will she survive this? Will he? Morgan found herself imagining all sorts of things happening to the monster. Not particularly dreadful things, nothing tortuous, a quick death, but nonetheless, the end of his life. Monsters don't deserve to live. Monsters should not be amongst us. They especially don't need to be around children. Morgan pictured the monster getting hit by a car, she saw a huge concrete block fall from the top of a high-rise building and land smack-dab in the middle of his head, she thought because of his arrogance and cockiness that he might get into a fight with another man...and lose that fight - lose his life (that wasn't particularly creative thinking – this was a real possibility). Her last image was the monster getting hit by a bus. She had to laugh at that one. When was the monster ever by a bus stop or walking on a main street? Never. *Did he walk anywhere ever?* The stalking monster only drove...slowly...everywhere.

Ollie and Opal were in great spirits when Morgan picked them up. There were Christmas festivities and plays performed at school, but the children weren't allowed to refer to the events as 'Christmas' - only as holiday festivities. Morgan thought this was hard for kids at least, it was difficult for the younger ones who only knew about Christmas celebrations. The world was evolving, becoming more inclusive and comprehensive. This was a good thing, but Morgan liked to hear and to say 'Merry Christmas' and she would continue to do so. She was happy to hear other believers of other religions say whatever they wished to say, but she would continue to say 'Merry Christmas' throughout the season. She would defer conversations concerning this subject until the children were a bit older. And, especially this Christmas, Morgan vowed to keep conversations light and to keep those she loved remarkably close to her as much as possible.

In the car Morgan announced, 'We'll be heading off in the morning to a surprise destination for Christmas!' She thought Ollie and Opal would be overjoyed, but, clearly, they were not. *How odd.* 'Why the long faces?'

Opal immediately jumped in and said, 'Because we love Lee. We love living with her and we thought we were celebrating Christmas with her.'

Ollie chimed in. 'Yeah, Mom.'

Morgan's mind raced, she thought quickly, 'Well, kids, you know Lee's ex-husband and his new partner, her children, plus other guests will be swarming around the house by tomorrow afternoon and where would they sleep? Lee has been so fabulous to us and she adores you to pieces, but she needs some family time, too, right? Wouldn't you agree?'

In the rearview mirror, Ollie and Opal looked at each other and then looked at Morgan. 'I guess so,' Opal reluctantly agreed. Ollie agreed. 'I'll miss her and her big breakfasts!'

Morgan couldn't help but chuckle. 'And, I have another surprise for you. We're going to pick up an incredibly special person in the morning and we're taking her with us.'

Now Ollie and Opal acted overjoyed! 'Who, Mom, who are we picking up?'

'Nanna-Kat,' Morgan said with glee in her voice.

Huge 'Yippeees' coming from the back seat meant everything was settled.

Morgan had fond memories of Pickwick Lake. She didn't learn to water ski until her mid-thirties and that alone was a remarkable sight, she had been told. Morgan stated previously to others that she had never seen so many people stand up in a boat to watch her try to ski! She thought the boat might flip over due to the weight shifting to the rear with the number of onlookers, but Morgan would do anything to stay on top of the water even if it included tap dancing from side to side because she was not going under with the lake critters. And, Lord, her skinny legs – they must have looked like noodles flying above the lake. People on the boat forever swore that her feet never even touched the water. Damn. She could hold on to a rope if otherwise meant going under. Several of these individuals were her life-long friends and she reminisced over the good times, finding herself smiling.

Morgan also suddenly remembered there was only one small grocery store at Pickwick Lake and it was so long ago she wasn't sure if it still existed. She thought it would be best to stock up on plenty of groceries and supplies while she was still in Memphis. She and Kathleen would keep the Christmas dinner simple, but she couldn't forget about buying a few nice wines, too. Over the past few months Morgan had picked up various Christmas gifts here and there and most recently ordered the new and improved 300-piece Map of the World National Geographic puzzle for her kids. That present would come in handy at the lake.

Driving to Lee's, she reminded herself to make a thorough list. She hadn't even thought of asking Ash if Dixie could come along. Lee had a huge, lush, gorgeous yard with a super tall wooden custom-made privacy fence and Dixie could stay with her, but Morgan wanted it to feel like 'real family' for Ollie and Opal. If Dixie could not be a part of their holiday, it wouldn't be right. She must ring Ash. Well, hmmm, Ash had told her he would contact her. She would wait until she was grocery shopping before she tried to reach him. And, Lord, decorations. She must remember to swing by her house to pick up a box of Christmas ornaments, bits, and bobs. Tree. A Christmas tree. Now, the mental list was growing, and she was beginning to feel anxious. *No. Keep it simple. The kids will be happy in a new, wonderful space. I will not panic about Christmas.* There were other real things worth stressing over.

Morgan and the kids greeted Lee when they hopped out of the car. Lee smiled and hugged them, but her eyes were not meeting Morgan's. Lee cheerily announced to the kids that she brought the Christmas boxes filled with delights down from the attic.

'Would you like to help me decorate?'

The kids jumped up and down. Still, Lee was not looking at Morgan. Morgan smiled, walked down the hallway to her bedroom and saw on her phone a good amount of missed phone calls from Lee. She put away her things and texted Lee from the bedroom: Please. Sorry I missed your calls, Lee. Can you spare a moment to talk with me?

Morgan was changing into her soft jeans and flat, comfy shoes to go grocery shopping when Lee walked in looking down.

'Lee? Lee? What's wrong? I know you. Talk to me.'

'He was here only a short while ago.'

An urge to scream, to hit, to jump out of her skin was welling up inside of her. 'No, for God's sake, No, Lee.' Morgan began to tremble.

'He was right there.' She pointed out the window. 'In the back-yard, throwing a ball to Dixie like he lived here.'

Morgan had to sit down. She felt nauseous. She couldn't speak for a moment.

Lee suggested, 'The monster must have been following me at some point or he knew the only other places you would go would be your mom's house or mine.' She paused. 'And, he has already visited your mother, Morgan.'

Lee was right. 'That's exactly why he went to my mom's.'

'You know the way he was treating Dixie, following her around the yard, it was as if he was teasing and taunting her, and he knew I was watching him. He was sending a message, Morgan. He's going for Dixie for real the next time.'

Morgan only said, 'What did you do, Lee? I hope you called the police for your protection.'

Lee laughed. 'Well, no, I got a baseball bat from the garage, and I stormed out there like a creature from Hell. He had no clue how frightened I was. You should have seen his face. Morgan I was screaming like a wild woman and his eyebrows went over his head. I swear I scared him or at least shocked him to pieces. He told me to calm down and that Dixie was his dog and he had a right to see her. I hurled abuse at him and told him that may be true, but not on my property. He put his hands up in the air, tilted his head back, laughed, and said, "I've seen her now. Dixie remembers me. I'm going. Tell Morgan I said Hello and I'll see her real soon." I shouted in return – Never. I'm reporting you now.' Lee was pacing and rubbing her forehead. 'He laughed even louder and had the audacity to squeal his tires down the street. Morgan, his laugh is truly awful. He's not normal. He's not right in the head. I wanted to say horrible things to him. He brings out the absolute worst in me.'

And here it is – Christmas.

ANGRY. FURIOUS. ENRAGED. INCENSED. BOILING. SEETHING.

All Morgan could see was red. 'Lee, did you contact the police?'

'No, Morgan, I did not. They've done nothing so far. He does as he pleases.'

That couldn't be good.

Morgan bit her lip – a common habit these days. Her head was swimming. She knew she needed to stay on track.

Store. She needed to finish what she needed to do for the night and get the 'Hell out of Dodge' with her kids and her mom by morning.

Morgan hesitated to ask, 'Are you okay for a while? I want to get the items necessary for Pickwick and I need to call my attorney without the kids around.'

'Yes, I'm fine and I think it's best the kids remain behind with me, too.'

Morgan didn't wait to settle into shopping but rang Ash immediately from the car. No answer. *Shit.* She rang again. This time the phone rang out. *Where is he?* Morgan convinced herself to calm down and reminded her mature self that the world was not at her disposal, the Earth did not revolve around her, and that there could quite possibly be a hundred people in her shoes at the moment needing Ash's help. Perhaps not a hundred. She certainly hoped not but there could be a few. Ash would see her missed call and he would get back to her.

'I can't believe the audacity of the monster!' She snarled aloud in the car. It was becoming quite clear the monster was tipping over the edge and taking far more chances. *Why shouldn't he? He's never been stopped. He does what he wants to do. He gets what he wants or needs out of life any conceivable way he can. Rules don't matter for the monster. Rules were not written for him.* Morgan pulled into a parking spot and saw the imprints on her hand from holding on to the steering wheel so tightly. She was incredibly wound up.

She reread her shopping list and it was too large. She would scale back several items. She rang her mom before going into the store. 'Mom, is there anything special you need for the trip?'

Kathleen sounded absolutely delighted. 'Go easy on the groceries because I've accomplished a lot of baking throughout the day.'

Unbelievable. Kat the Baker. Morgan did not, unfortunately, take after her mother in the kitchen. Morgan slid her sunglasses down her nose, popped out of the car, hit the key lock, and as she turned, a police officer appeared before her.

'Ms. Sage? Ms. Morgan Sage?' he asked.

'Why? Yes.' Morgan exclaimed.

'Consider yourself served.'

Wait. What? Morgan knew this man. He was one of the first of two police officers who completed the report against her husband. Then, right behind him stood the monster. *What the Hell was happening?*

'I'll get you; you bitch! I know you fucked your way into that car and now you're going to be fucked all over again by me! DO YOU HEAR ME?'

The cop is looking at the monster. The cop is not doing anything. They're in cahoots. Something is not right.

Morgan screams. 'Officer, do something.'

The cop puts his hand up and says, 'Now, now,' to the monster. 'Sir, you need to back away. You need to leave the scene immediately.'

'Arrest him, officer. He has a restraining order against him and he's not supposed to come near me.'

The cop tersely responds, 'This is a public area. This isn't your home and I'm sure he had no idea you'd be here. Must be some sort of coincidence.'

Morgan heard herself literally growl at the officer and he advised her to watch it. Instead, she returned to the safety of her car. She could see the two of them with their heads together – talking – nothing was right about this situation.

'Oh, Ash, please ring me,' she said under her breath. Morgan saw the cop's car drive away, but only after the monster drove out in Morgan's Volvo first. Yes. The monster thought he had made her life especially tricky, so the sight of her driving a set of new wheels did not sit well with him. *Why didn't Ash or I, for that matter, see what this gesture of a Lexus would create?* She laid her head against the steering wheel and closed her eyes. The only consolation prize would be Pickwick Lake – tomorrow. Morgan wondered how this cop knew where she was. Normally, people were served in the early hours of the morning. She was definitely not telling anyone but Lee about her temporary Pickwick address.

Phone buzzing. Morgan was still sitting in her car, but calmer now.

'Morgan speaking.'

It was Antonio. 'Hey fabulous person, just checkin' in and hoping my sweet friend is working on that essence of hers.'

Morgan's heart skipped a beat. *Where was Ash?*

FAKE. FAKER. FAKE. FAKER. Morgan revved up the mental speak.

'Hi, Antonio. Life will be much better once we're on the road tomorrow, but for now we are excited and fine. Thanks so much for everything you've done. I could not have a kinder friend or colleague.' *I mean, really, how much drama can one person endure in a day? She most certainly could not relive it again by retelling the dreaded incidents. Repeating the stories kept the monster's nasty, evil energy alive. No way.*

'Antonio, apologies, but I'm in a big hurry. I must hang up now because Lee is watching Ollie and Opal and I need to make a fast run through Kroger.'

Antonio understood. 'I'll contact you soon and please stay safe.'

'Yeah, right, thank you.' *But, how to stay safe...how?*

CHAPTER TEN

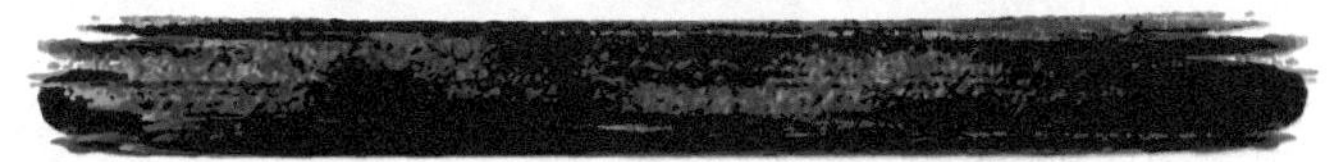

Morgan folded the stapled paper and placed it in her purse without reading it. She could deal with that later or not. She remembered Antonio was hopeful he would receive an invitation to the holiday house and Morgan was happy and relieved he didn't bring up the subject over the phone.

She felt as if she were racing through Kroger's grocery aisles. *Why? Calm down. The monster is gone. He put on his scary show and got what he wanted. Why was the cop not rattled? What were they discussing? This was wrong on many levels, but am I being paranoid? Possibly.* She gathered only the absolute necessities and decided on a medium sized turkey and one small ham. After all, she had no clue how many days they would be staying at Pickwick. If she purchased extra bread and milk, she could freeze those. She had no idea if the kitchen was fully stocked with utensils or what extra items she needed. *Damn, Ash. Please ring. Please call me soon.*

Jello. Opal loves Jello and it's been months since Morgan made any. Marshmallows. If there were a fireplace in the house they could roast marshmallows. Ollie especially loves them. Opal says they burn the roof of her mouth and are too sticky. *That's my girl.* Oh, and she must remember a couple of wire hangers in case there is a fireplace. If Ash would only ring her many of these decisions could be sorted instantly.

'My kids don't deserve this chaos,' Morgan wanted to cry. *EMBARRASSMENT. HUMILIATION. DESPERATION. SAD. PATHETIC. LOSER.* The loop began playing in her head with the word 'loser' added. Morgan told her mind to 'Stop.' Repeatedly she saw the words imprinted in her mind's eye and thought they suited the monster quite well. *Nope. I must wear them. Do not shift the blame. You got yourself into this. Those badges are yours until you get out of the cesspool. Deal with it.* Morgan had arrived at the stand to check out and she didn't even remember pushing the trolley to the check-out chick.

The cute girl said, 'Merry Christmas.' That snapped her right back into reality.

'Well, Merry Christmas to you, too.'

Morgan paid for her groceries, filled her trolley with bags, and walked briskly to the car surveying the premises using her peripheral vision.

Ash rang while she was driving. *Damn. Damn. Damn.* Again. Morgan hadn't had the chance to get her Bluetooth connected and she wasn't going to talk and drive. The phone stopped. The phone started. It was buzzing all over the passenger seat. She wasn't far from home and would have to speak to Ash when she pulled into Lee's driveway. Finally.

'Ash?' The phone disconnected.

'I did it again. I answered my phone without looking at the number – Aaaagggghhh!' Morgan was frustrated and angry with herself.

She took one sack of groceries in with her but there were plenty more. Everyone had already eaten. Lee had rounded up multiple small to medium cardboard boxes for her. Always thinking ahead. *Lee is a gem of a human being.* The phone started going off again. Ash. It was Ash. Morgan glanced quickly at Lee.

'I must take this.'

Ollie piped up. 'Mom, I can get the groceries.'

Morgan screamed, 'No, No. Ollie, you can't!' She knew instantly what she had done the moment she shouted so loudly. By the look on Ollie's face, Morgan knew his feelings were clearly hurt. She answered the phone. 'Ash, please let me call you back in about 15 minutes.'

'Certainly.'

Morgan immediately apologised to Ollie. He didn't understand at all. He thought he was being helpful. He looked so hurt and defeated. Morgan explained she had seen a dog, a fairly large one, without its owner (*LIE. LIAR. LIE. LIAR.*) and she wanted to make certain the dog was back home somewhere safely before he or Opal went out at night. *Please, God, help me to do the right thing.*

She hugged Ollie and went to retrieve the rest of the groceries. Lee had the boxes lined up. Morgan hid the surprise treats away from the eyes of her precious children and put the frozen goods away.

Morgan went over to Ollie and Opal, 'One phone call and not a very long one at that. I'll go home and get your luggage and a couple of other items. You can pack the clothes you think you'll need. I'll look over your choices and we might need to make compromises, and I promise a bedtime story. How about that?' The timing was turning into reality. The kids knew they were going on an adventure tomorrow and spending their first Christmas away from home with their Nanna-Kat. Jumps for joy. The three of them scaled the stairs. Morgan could feel Lee watching her. Lee did not miss a thing. She should have been a private detective because she would have made a ton of money.

Morgan rang Ash. Out of breath with urgency, 'Ash, I need to speak with you in detail, but I want to put my kids to bed first. So, again, I'll need to call you back only after 8:30pm if that's okay with you.'

'Morgan, slooow down, that's fine, but tell me something quickly, would you please?'

'Yes, certainly.'

'Were you served papers today?'

Morgan became curious. 'Yes, but how did you know? That's something I wanted to discuss later. Now, please, Ash. Does the kitchen have the utensils I need to cook a proper Christmas dinner? Can we please take Dixie? She's house broken and she's such a dear. She won't be any problem, I assure you. Does your home have a fireplace? Do you think we could roast marshmallows? And, you haven't even sent me a map or the address or anything. Oh, and this is important - what about Christmas decorations? I want the kids to be happy. May I please decorate? I won't do too much. I won't hurt anything of yours. Promise.'

'Whew, woah, take a breath, Morgan, Yes, to absolutely everything, except the decorations.'

Morgan felt crushed. *How could she explain to the children that they wouldn't be allowed to hang any decorations?*

'Trust me, Morgan. It is a designer, gourmet kitchen. There will be more gadgets there than you could possibly use and, well, let me finish by simply saying again, will you please trust me? I have a small dog, too, and the tiny, wooden cupboard under the large pantry is stocked fully with dog food.'

Damn. Well, that's perfect because I forgot to include more dog food and treats on my list. She also thought that she could find a tiny, little, wild branch, and make it pretty like a 'Charlie Brown Christmas tree'. Surely Ash would not object to that. She would take ribbon and their favorite family ornaments – only one each. Questions answered. 'Thanks, Ash. I'll ring you back when the kids are asleep.'

She ran downstairs. 'Lee, I need to run home quickly, grab some suitcases, and secure the house before the trip.'

'I understand. Be careful.'

When Morgan arrived at her home, it was much too dark. She decided to keep the front door exterior light on, a few interior lights, too, and keep a small backyard light shining. She remembered to turn the thermostat's heat setting to low. Pulling a heavy chair from her desk, she stood on her tiptoes to find the kids' suitcases on the top shelf of her closet. There. In the top rear and dark corner, she gave herself a jolt. She remembered the revolver she purchased from the hands of a most desperate and kind high-school friend from her past. A .38 caliber pistol she agreed to take for her friend because her friend had small children and a baby in her home. Her friend, Stevie, at the time they met, was distraught and adamant she could not keep the gun in her home and didn't have anyone else to turn to. Now, however, the fact remained Morgan had a gun in her home with small children, too. *Well, for the time being, at least it's up and out of anyone's reach and that's a good thing.* Morgan retrieved Ollie's and Opal's suitcases which were wrapped in heavy black plastic and decided on an additional smaller piece of luggage for herself. She grabbed two wire hangers for marshmallows and a small box of Christmas ornaments from another cupboard in case there was a chance she could use them. After double-checking the locks on doors and windows, she returned to Lee's as quickly as she could. *So much more to do tonight before I can catch any sleep.*

When she arrived back at Lee's, the kids had their clothes and items out and ready for packing. The children did quite well with their choices. Morgan didn't have to remove many items. She knew it might be much chillier by the lake, especially at night, so she grabbed their heavier coats and hats and gloves. Socks. Plenty of thick socks and their warmest pajamas needed to go with them. The children would be surprised when they received their brand-new dressing robes from their Nanna-Kat, too. Her kids had always loved wearing their robes. At times it was hard for Morgan to get them to change into their proper clothes.

'Don't forget to take a favorite book or two.' They each had a very worn, floppy stuffed animal they slept with, but the sleeping buddies would not be packed until the morning.

'Ollie, Opal, teeth brushed, faces washed?'

'Yes, Mom, we're ready for bed because the sooner we go to sleep the faster morning will come and we'll see Nanna-Kat.'

'You're so right, my smarty pants, hop in bed and I'll read for a while.' It was funny. Ollie complained when Morgan sat on Opal's bed to read and when Morgan switched, Opal started whining.

'Stop, you two, listen. Morning will be here soon enough.' Morgan tried to sound serious. She read aloud, but in less than ten minutes, she could have sworn she heard sweet snoring.

Even though it had been a full day, and the night was closing in, Morgan felt a bit of energy racing through her bones. She trotted downstairs and Lee was sitting, waiting.

'Wine, my dear?'

'Oh, that would be lovely, yes, please.'

This time Morgan pulled down a nice Australian Barossa Valley Shiraz and poured the lovely dark, ruby liquid into two fat wine glasses. She sat across from Lee and they toasted to one another.

Lee said, 'I'm going to miss you. This will be the first Christmas in ages that we won't be spending together.'

Morgan acknowledged her sweet words, 'I'll be thinking of you, and we'll have our own special Christmas dinner together once I return.'

'I know something happened. Tell me.'

How, how does Lee always know? 'I was served papers, and the monster was lurking behind the cop and the entire situation felt wrong. Something was up. And as soon as I finish this glass of wine I need to go report to Ash because we need to have a decent discussion.

Then Lee said something odd. 'Morgan, it makes sense the monster may have a cop on his side. You've been telling the cops your actions, your whereabouts, your plans. Now things are beginning to make sense. He's paying someone for information or he's giving something valuable in return for what he wants.'

Perhaps Morgan had not been paranoid after all, but she really didn't know. She knew nothing except her children and her mother needed to feel safe and be protected.

The besties finished their wine and said good night to one another. Morgan popped up the stairs, changed into her pajamas and rang Ash.

He answered immediately, 'Settled?'

'Yes, and thanks enormously for your patience.'

Ash proceeded to tell her he had a particularly peculiar day. 'Morgan, I've never heard so many excuses in my life. The restraining order wasn't even served properly or immediately. The East Precinct gave me ridiculous reasons why this had not been done but none seemed valid to me. I haven't seen anything like this in a long while. The police officers have a lot on their plates, this much is true. Accidents happen, papers get misplaced, I understand that but not repeatedly against the same defendant. I have an excellent para-legal assigned to your case and rest assured, there are two of us on it now, and we are on top of them. I'm sorry, Morgan, this is not how the firm operates but we don't conduct the serving of the documents. It feels a bit out of control. There are situations that just don't make sense currently. I'll get to the bottom of this.'

'Bottom, Damned straight, Bottom feeders.'

Ash asked, 'What did you say?'

'Oh, nothing really.' Then Morgan went into detail describing the events of the night that occurred in Kroger's parking lot. She said the evening was uncanny. 'The monster and the cop looked as though they staged an act.'

'Well, no, I don't think it was staged, but I do think the cop most certainly allowed the monster to be present.'

Wow, Ash even refers to her husband as the monster. How appropriate.

Ash reassured Morgan. 'Your case has top priority. I've also spoken with the initial firm you hired. You'll be receiving half your retainer back.'

That was a welcome relief. It most certainly lifted a small burden. 'Thank you.'

'Now, Morgan, I'm texting the lake house address. There is a landline in the house, too. Use that number for all your calls when you're at home. I can't explain it now, but I think this would be wise. I've attached a small map, but Google it. Finding the spot will be a bit touch and go because the smaller, winding, dirt roads will not appear on Google. Call me when you arrive and I'll navigate you towards the long driveway entrance. And remember, please, think of it as your holiday home and stay as long as you like. I'm pleased to know your mother will be accompanying you. Try to enjoy this Christmas and know that this is the last one you will spend in fear. It will be over soon. There's a unique, terracotta pot filled with succulents surrounded by other outdoor plants on the back deck, and you'll find the house key there. Look for the succulents – that's your key.' Ash chuckled.

'I can't thank you enough. I do believe, Ash, the Lexus was like pouring salt into a wound. The monster has a gaping, festering, open wound and he's running around like a diseased animal. That Lexus tipped him over.'

'Well, what were you going to do? Morgan, I did think about this. I do think about actions before I take them, but you had to have a mode of transportation. It's done. The monster needs to grow up, put those children first, and get on with his life.'

'We both know that's not going to happen,' she quipped and felt like thanking Ash a thousand times over.

'I'll call you if I have any trouble finding our Christmas holiday house. We'll talk soon.'

Morgan did not remember falling asleep.

CHAPTER ELEVEN

It was the first night she'd ever slept so deeply - the best night's sleep she'd had in over two weeks. *Delightful. Refreshing.* And now, there was a mission. This day was a day to be rejoiced. She and her children were picking up her beloved mother, no responsibilities, no homework, no real chores, no commitments, they would simply be driving towards fun and travelling towards the spirit of Christmas – together. Morgan felt like a young child filled with joy.

Ollie and Opal were already up and they were even attempting, clumsily, to make their beds. *How impressive.* Morgan got down on her knees and hugged them tightly and kissed their precious faces. Everyone was smiling. There was a big rush downstairs for a fast breakfast. Lee was already there sipping hot, steaming coffee with Dixie at her feet, and was making waffles and warming maple syrup. Orange juice was in a big, crystal glass pitcher and she had already fried plenty of crispy bacon.

A huge grin filled Morgan's face. 'Do you have any idea how much I love you?'

Lee leaned in for a hug. 'Merry Christmas, Dahlin', I love you, too.'

The kids were laughing and playing with Dixie. They began munching on breakfast while Morgan packed the car. She felt herself using her peripheral vision again as she made trips back and forth to the Lexus, but she didn't let that fact get her down. She felt uplifted, strong, powerful, and in charge.

Goodbyes were said and hugs were in abundance. Morgan held on to Lee, 'Thank you for being my safe haven.'

'Anytime, I mean it. You know my house is yours.'

Off they went to pick up Nanna-Kat. Her mother's front glass door was open. Morgan didn't particularly like that, but they would only be at Kat's home for a few minutes. Ollie and Opal ran as fast as they could to their Nanna-Kat and were showered with warm hugs and kisses on their heads.

Nanna-Kat announced, 'This is going to be my favorite Christmas ever!'

The kids squealed and held on tightly to her waist.

Morgan began lugging far too many boxes and containers to the back of the Lexus. She huffed, 'Not certain if everything will fit.'

'Nonsense. We'll make it work!'

The kids' feet barely touched the floor mats of the car, so a myriad of Tupperware dishes filled to the brim with goodness, had to be stored under Ollie's and Opal's toes. Kat went back to secure the house. The car smelled outrageously good.

From East Memphis or the edge of Germantown to Pickwick Lake was approximately two and a half hours, depending on traffic, of course. This was winter. They would be staying in the off-season, so Morgan didn't anticipate any great rush unless many others had made the same decision to choose to have their Christmas away from the hustle and bustle of suburbia. She turned on the music, checked to see if everyone was buckled in, and began the much-needed journey.

Kat commented, 'Oh, this car is luxurious.'

'Temporary, Mom.'

Kat glanced over with a twinkle in her eye, 'Well, too bad.'

Soft, easy-listening music on the radio. Lee had taken it upon herself to get Bluetooth connected and working properly. Morgan loved her friend as she was always thinking about others first. They would go somewhere incredibly nice and enjoy a terrific meal once Morgan returned.

Pickwick Lake – Memphians who craved water, skiing, boating, and fishing all flocked to this place. Some people had houses they built long ago, overlooking an edge of the lake that had been handed down to the next generation. It was the place to be seen if you enjoyed peaceful lakeside living with aquatic adventures thrown in. People would buy gorgeous, top-of-the-line boats that would be absolute stunners, and invite their good friends over to simply have a cocktail and a laugh. A few boats were not used much, and Morgan could not imagine the annual expense of mooring or storing a boat. She never owned one and didn't really know a great deal about them.

Her biggest accomplishment was staying above water on skis. That was enough for her.

Kat was busy chatting with Ollie and Opal. The kids told her about their school, their teachers, and their lunchroom and how much they liked it.

Ollie said, 'Our lunchroom has tall ceilings, big, sparkly lights that look like jewels hanging down from up above, and one whole side of the room was glass from top to bottom so we can look out on the soccer field!'

Opal added, 'Music plays during lunch and servers come by and pick up our trays wearing gloves and offer to pick up any trash. We sit at round tables instead of long, square ones and we've never done that before!'

There was nothing about the conversation that Kat didn't like as she was grinning from ear to ear. She had a sweet chuckle and exclaimed, 'How descriptive you are regarding the lunchroom!' She leaned over to Morgan and said, 'I hope the lunches you prepare for them are suitable to be consumed in this spectacular dining room.'

Now Morgan laughed. The ride was smooth and relaxing, and Morgan was falling in love with her wheels every mile they covered. She felt safe in this car, but she did miss the Volvo. The Volvo was like an old pair of tennis shoes that you've worn in and can't possibly live without. *Oh well, no time for those thoughts.*

They stopped for fuel and everyone got a refresher drink and stretched their legs. Ollie and Opal took Dixie for a stroll, too. Morgan wanted to arrive well and truly before the sun began to set and for cocktail hour. Kat didn't mind an adult beverage, but she did not drink much alcohol, only around the holidays or special occasions. This would be an incredibly special time for the family.

Her phone rang just as they returned to the car. It was Ash. He said with a heartiness in his voice, 'Hello, I couldn't help myself. I simply wanted to see if you were on the road and everything was going as planned.'

Morgan could feel his smile over the phone. 'Yes, thanks, everything is perfect and we are right on schedule.'

'Please call me when you are closer to the house.'

'Promise.'

In a short while it would be Christmas Eve. Morgan had purchased new wrapping paper, colourful ribbons, and bows. She wouldn't need much as there would be fewer gifts this year. That didn't matter. *My kids are lovely. They never ask for a great deal and are hugely appreciative of any gifts they receive throughout the year for any occasion.* She was smiling to herself now. Her mother caught it, reached over, and patted her thigh. They both glanced at one another. Sometimes you don't need words.

Morgan had an idea. She would write a heartfelt one-page letter to her mom, Ollie, and Opal and put it on their pillows for Christmas Eve. That would be a wonderful way to start off the next day. She could not believe it, but she was becoming tremendously excited about getting to their 'new' temporary Christmas pad.

Ollie perked up, 'Mom what's Pickwick?'

'Well, Ollie, and Opal, you listen, too, because you both might be interested in a little history. I'll tell you what I know. Pickwick Landing Dam is a hydroelectric facility built in the mid-1930s. The dam is over a hundred feet high and is almost a mile and a half across the Tennessee River.' Morgan remembered the marina as a tremendously busy place, a beehive of activity, stretching across the sun-lit waters. She continued, 'Pickwick Lake is the actual reservoir created by the dam and the north end of the lake provides a mode of transportation to the Gulf of Mexico. According to Pickwick Lake history, hundreds and thousands of Cherokee Indians travelled through Waterloo in the 1830s when they were brutally forced by the United States government to move west on the Trail of Tears. Many Indigenous Americans came by boat from Tuscumbia and camped there while waiting for the larger steamboats. During this time, several births, deaths, and escapes took place.'

Morgan's father had always told her his antecedents were of American Indigenous heritage. She would like to know if that tidbit of family history were true and one day would devote a portion of her time to researching it. She peered in the rearview mirror and saw Ollie taking in all the sights.

'So, Mom, we're going to be living in history when we get to Pickwick, right?'

'That's an excellent way to look at it, Ollie and, yes, history is all around us.'

It was a stunning day. The sun was shining, there was barely a breeze about, and the air was fresh and cool. The sun made all the difference in the world. Ollie and Opal had nodded off with their heads touching and Dixie snuggled in the middle. That was fine because Morgan figured they would be up a little later that evening due to the excitement of the new surroundings.

Morgan's phone was buzzing.

Kat asked, 'Should I answer?'

'Let's not even think about it – ignore it. We're the only people we need to communicate with now.'

'Perfectly stated!'

Kat and Morgan began to see Savannah, Tennessee and Hardin County signs, then Pickwick Landing Dam Road signs. They were getting close. Morgan's phone had been quite noisy for the last portion of the ride.

'Wow, beautiful,' Kat exclaimed!

Morgan agreed wholeheartedly with her mother. Ollie and Opal were stretching their arms in the back seat and Dixie's tail was wagging. The sun was glistening through the trees and beckoning to them to 'come on in.' That's exactly how the entrance felt to her. Morgan certainly didn't remember seeing the number of houses in the past she saw sprinkled around the lake now. *My goodness, it has grown enormously; Pickwick looks much larger than a village.* She continued driving slowly around the area as Siri was doing her best to guide her to their new, secret abode. Morgan knew she had just driven down the very same road. They stopped close to the marina astounded by the number of boats in their view. Crowds of people were mingling around the vessels, chatting, drinking beverages, looking as if they wanted to enjoy the sun rays for as long as possible. Mind-boggling that Pickwick could have grown to this level and in a relatively abbreviated period of time. The houses had become bigger, perhaps not better in her view, but definitely grander in appearance. She pulled over to take in the sights and sounds while she tried to get her bearings.

Siri continued to function as though she knew what she was doing – always in charge.

'No,' Morgan spats back. 'That's not right. I'm shutting you down.'

Before she had a chance, Siri shot back in her sultry voice, 'If you just said something, I did not understand what it was.'

Kat was howling and Morgan couldn't help but laugh, too. After enjoying the view, Morgan decided the most prudent decision was to call Ash. They had to be only minutes away, but each winding road looked the same to her and she didn't see any road signs that particularly stood out to her.

Ash answered with a warm, 'Hi there, tell me where you are.'

Morgan complied and Ash recognized a familiar position after her detailed description. She reversed the car and with Ash giving very precise instructions, as if he were in the car with them. She glimpsed a most significant home above them, high on an area that jutted out precariously over the lake. Well, it looked that way from her position. Ash stayed on the phone with her while she made her way up the winding, steep, graveled dirt driveway. The trees were covering the sky like a magical burnt-orange and dark caramel canopy.

'What a stunning entryway,' Morgan declared.

Kathleen and the kids were gasping at how pretty the sight was before them.

Rightio. Morgan made it to the top of the very steep driveway. 'Ash, you didn't tell me we would be climbing to the mountain top.'

Ash laughed. 'Once you're out on the deck at sunset you'll be thankful for that hilltop. Now, remember, if you need anything, ring me.'

Morgan extended her sincere appreciation and assured him she would.

One of the garage doors was already open. Morgan should have said something to Ash. She thought it only a tiny bit odd, but then, with automatic door openers crazy things can happen.

'Mom, why don't you and the kids stretch your legs and let Dixie out while I retrieve the keys?'

The back view was even more spectacular than the drive in. Morgan felt like a child, bursting with excitement. She was feeling genuinely happy and could not believe this was where they would be spending Christmas. It looked and felt like a little bit of heaven.

Ash was spot on. There were tons of pots arranged perfectly on the back deck, but only one big, fat pot filled with succulents showing off just how handsome they were. Morgan kneeled and ran her fingers along the edges. There. Her hands touched a plastic zip-locked bag, and it was full of items, and it was sealed. Ha! Every key had its own individual tag and there were two small, compact electric garage door openers.

She called out to Kat, Ollie, and Opal. 'C'mon, let's go in first, then we'll come back out and gather our belongings.' They came towards her, Dixie bouncing at their heels, but the incline was a bit steeper than it looked. Kat seemed to struggle, but she was still smiling. They gathered at the front door together.

'Let's see if I can manage to get this heavy front door opened properly.' The door clicked and when she opened it, they heard Christmas music.

Morgan flipped the inside light switch on and when she did this, a life-like, velvet wrapped Santa moved and laughed, there were mechanical reindeer that began to nod their antlers up and down, and the Christmas lights flicked on and began to twinkle in white, gold, green, and red.

'Oh, my goodness, Mom, look! This is the most beautiful Christmas house I've ever seen,' exclaimed Opal through her tears of joy.

Ollie was beside himself. Kathleen had her hands over her mouth and then reached for Morgan and hugged her – held on to her for dear life. Wow! Now everyone was in tears. They were unable to take it all in because it was wonderfully overwhelming. Everywhere you turned was something magical, whimsical, and breathtakingly beautiful. Christmas had landed at Pickwick Lake! Someone with absolute exquisite taste had decorated this house. It was their first winter wonderland of their own to behold. No one said a word for a few minutes. They walked around in awe taking in the scenery. Dixie was scampering around and slipping and sliding on the rich wooden floors. The house was lovely and welcoming. The sofas were exquisite. The rugs below their feet were antique and luxurious. Morgan could only imagine what the kitchen would be like. *This was Ash's holiday house?* It was fit for a king. He must have worked enormously long hours to accomplish such a feat. *How could he not want to live here permanently?* It was such a serene, inviting, and secluded setting.

Morgan tried to rein in the gang. 'C'mon, back to reality. Ollie, Opal, if it looks like you shouldn't touch something, use your good judgement, and don't touch it. Got it?'

They excitedly sang out together, 'Got it, Mom.'

Most items were above on shelves or big and bulky on the floor, out of the way, in a corner and her children weren't babies, so Morgan wasn't too terribly worried.

She must ring Ash.

They collected the boxes, the Tupperware containers, still smelling like Kat's kitchen, and the remaining luggage from the car. The sun was beginning to set. Morgan was hopeful she and Kat could enjoy the deck and make a toast to each other, but that may have to wait until tomorrow. First things first. She took Ollie and Opal upstairs, and they wandered through the bedrooms with their eyes and mouths wide open. The rooms were magnificent!

Morgan found a Jack-and-Jill set up with the full bath positioned between two bedrooms. Each bedroom had its own door to the bathroom, so Morgan reminded them, 'If you don't want each other to barge in, you'll need to be certain to lock the bath door when you use it.'

The children had never seen such an arrangement and loved the fact they had their own big, fluffy beds to flop in. Kathleen seemed impressed, too.

Further down the hall was a regal and sophisticated room, filled with bronze and aqua tones and a decadent chaise lounge with double French doors leading to a bathroom built for a queen. Kat couldn't say anything. The cat got her tongue!

'Mom, this is yours.'

'Oh, my, no, never. This is too nice. This is quite unbelievable.'

Morgan lovingly looked at her mother and said, 'Mom, if ever a person suited a room that person would be you and this room would be yours. It's Christmas, you're my mom, and I want to see you enjoy this luxurious space. Okay? Without argument?'

Kat sat on the huge chair in the corner with the matching ottoman and said, 'Fine, I'll take it as long as I don't have to pay for it, sir!'

Morgan couldn't help but notice a Constance Gordon-Johnson painting of abstract figures in strong and dark colours. Brilliant. Morgan had viewed pieces previously, not long ago, at Palladio's Antiques in midtown Memphis which reminded her of Constance's work. Constance's art sent her imagination into overtime. They both lingered over the painting.

Morgan helped Kat with her luggage. 'I'm going to go down the hallway and see what's on the other end. Everyone, let's meet downstairs after we've put our belongings away.'

She headed down the long corridor to a room that appeared very dark and a bit mysterious, too. She flicked on a light and this bedroom was a sight to behold. Masculine, fine, strong lines, intricately designed bedding and pillows in a soft, powder blue and chocolate brown. The custom designed valances to match hanging over the plantation shutters were the perfect touch. She didn't remember ever seeing these particular colours joined in this pleasing combination. The room was quite splendid, yet familiar, and peaceful. It felt as if this bedroom could be a study and there was an elegant, antique French Empire writing desk bureau with marble gilt ormolu secretaire – had to be c1800s. Morgan knew this because she and Antonio used to go antique shopping together. This is where Morgan would pen her Christmas letters to her family. She would lay claim to this room. She didn't care if there were other bedrooms, and she didn't wish to see them. This was to be her temporary cocoon.

'Just breathe,' she muttered. Morgan stood alone in the quiet, closed her eyes, looked down, and gave thanks just like that.

There were other rooms that she would check out later. She knew, of course, she needed to make herself familiar with the entire house.

Presently, she and Kat had priorities to get the perishable items stored quickly and she wanted to phone Ash.

Kat said, 'Help me first, Morgan, it won't take us but a few minutes if we do it together and I would personally like to thank this Ash person, too.'

The kids heard Nanna-Kat and squealed, 'Me, too, Mom. We want to thank Santa, too.'

'Santa?' Morgan asked. That title sounded most appropriate to her.

Food containers were stored appropriately. Morgan saw Kat had made a huge tub of her fabulous chicken noodle soup. Ollie and Opal could never get enough. There were chocolate pecan brownies, a red velvet cake, two pies, pumpkin and apple, M&M cookies, and even a three-layered lasagna.

'Mom, how did you have time to do this?'

'The idea of this trip got me energized and I went to work.'

Amazing. I will never be half the woman my mother is.

As Morgan opened the gigantic refrigerator built to match the kitchen cabinets, with far too many gadgets on its door, she gasped in awe. A bottle of French champagne chilling in a bucket with tiny red, squiggly ribbons tied around its neck and a little white envelope was staring back at her. She could have sworn the envelope was smiling.

'Mom, Look,' she stammered, 'Is Ash not the nicest human being on the planet? Oh, how utterly thoughtful. What a gentleman.'

Kat glanced at her with a look of concern. 'Morgan, how long have you known this man?'

Morgan hadn't really thought about it – not exceptionally long. 'Not long, Mom. He's my attorney, but the important thing is that he's an incredibly good and long-term friend of Antonio's.'

Kat looked pleasantly relieved. 'Well, if he is a friend of Antonio's he's a fine man indeed, but, honestly, Morgan, in my lifetime I have never heard of an attorney going out of their way to assist a client in this fashion.'

Morgan felt a shock swirl through her body. Those were words and thoughts that Morgan had before, too, but she had never voiced them aloud. Internally, quietly, she agreed. *Ash has gone over and above the call of duty, but, then again, her situation - the divorce was dire and unlike any divorce she had heard of before either. Special circumstances called for special tactics. Didn't they?* Morgan would ponder this later.

She excitedly slipped the little card from its envelope and quickly read it. It was sweet and simple enough: Merry Christmas, Morgan and Kathleen. I wish you both a happy, healthy, and prosperous New Year and my greatest hope is that next year, Morgan, will be a spectacular year for you in every conceivable way. Please wish Ollie and Opal a 'Merry Christmas' for me, too. Kind regards, Samuel Ashley Downing.

She handed the card to her mother. 'See, Mom? I am his client and he is my most kind and thoughtful attorney.'

Kat placed the card by the gigantic vase of flowers stuffed to the brim with red carnations, white lilies, bright, deep red roses tucked in every now and then, and heaps of lush, green foliage. It was an extraordinary floral arrangement.

'This is gorgeous and extravagant, Morgan!' Kat flicked her eyes toward the vase. The entire arrangement had to be at least four feet high or more.

Morgan gasped, 'My, oh my, Mother, I hadn't noticed. Truly. I think I simply assumed they were a part of the décor. Astonishing, aren't they?'

'Quite.'

Morgan sensed the energy in the room changing and it felt somewhat judgmental but Kat didn't know Ash. Hmmm, Morgan didn't really know Ash either, but she did know him better than her mother and he'd only shown himself to be an extremely capable, and proficient attorney, and a perceptive, kind human being. For now, that was enough. She hoped, most definitely, she would get to know such a kind man better. Morgan began pushing the mental jumble out of her head. *This is to be a light, refreshing holiday. I refuse to delve into anything too deeply now.'*

CHAPTER TWELVE

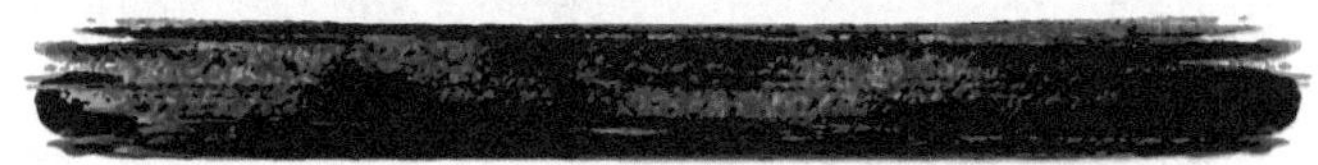

Morgan announced to her family, 'Okay, I'm ringing Ash and putting the phone on speaker. Let's all say together 'Merry Christmas, Ash, and thank you!'

The kids were keen.

Kat was, too, but she did ask, 'Please may I have my own, private 'thank you' conversation with him?'

'Most certainly.'

The phone was ringing. Ash didn't take long to answer. Four very loud voices filled with glee sang out and Ash sounded tickled. On speaker, he replied, 'No, thank *you* and I am so happy that you're happy.'

'Ash, my mother, Kathleen, would like to have a word.'

'Of course.'

Kat took the phone and walked into the lovely dining room. 'Ash, I don't believe in my years I have ever been so surprised or captivated by such a beautiful home, and I want to personally thank you for what you have done for us – for my daughter. Ash, Morgan means the world to me and I remain deeply concerned. I don't want to go into detail now, but I do want to thank you.'

'I'm touched and I assure you, Kathleen, this situation is temporary and the team and I are looking out for Morgan's best interests.'

'Very much appreciated; this means a great deal to me.' Kat handed the phone back to Morgan and she was beaming.

'Ash, we don't need to open any gifts because this house is one giant Christmas gift! I mean, admittedly, I was hurt when you told me I couldn't bring decorations. How in the Hell did you pull this off? I don't think I've seen Ollie and Opal this happy in a long time.'

'Don't you worry. I have my ways. I have friends, too.'

Morgan was walking around the spectacular, plush, yet comfy sitting lounge as she spoke with Ash and gasped, 'Is that a James King painting above the fireplace?

'Yes, how did you know?'

The artwork was a massive canvas and it looked like the opening to the universe, surreal, inviting, imaginative, hugely intense, with powerful, dazzling, bold colours that beckoned. Morgan was fascinated.

'How do you know James?'

Ash laughed, 'How do *you* know James?'

'Well, the kids and I use a doctor in Collierville and pieces of James' work hang on the walls of the practice. I've always wanted a piece for my home one day.'

'James and I go way back. He and I used to have lengthy yarns at The Tobacco Corner years ago before they shut their doors permanently. Honestly, there were more than a few of the most serious conversations I'd ever participated in occurring within those walls. On reflection, we were part of a 'Tabacco Corner Gang!' He was a talented man, and I miss our chats. Miss the damned Tobacco Corner, too. I commissioned that piece from James. I wanted something dramatic plus the work needed to be large.'

'It's divine,' Morgan sighed. 'Ash, it's been lovely chatting, but I should get back to family now. I hope we speak again soon and thanks again for everything you've done. Truly.'

'Understood. You're more than welcome. Enjoy.'

Dinner was easy-peasey because they had Nanna-Kat's homemade chicken noodle soup, fresh, crusty bread, and vanilla ice cream for dessert. Kat sliced plump strawberries to top off the ice cream and the kids loved it. It was getting late. They had an enjoyable conversation around the kitchen table and Dixie jumped after any crumb that tumbled to the floor. It felt much more intimate to eat in the kitchen instead of using the exquisite, delicate, and highly decorated dining room table. Morgan would use as few of the rooms as possible and only the ones which they felt most comfortable in. Ollie and Opal looked worn out from the sheer excitement of the day.

Kat told the kids, 'Run upstairs and I'll help with your baths. It will soon be Christmas Eve,' she reminded them and that got their attention.

Bubbles in their baths, curly hair to be dried, pajamas laid out on their massive, sprawling beds so they could quickly hop into sweet comfort. Kat was going to have to help each one up because the beds were so high.

Opal didn't look quite sure about the set-up and remarked, 'An entire family could sleep in my bed.'

Kat had to laugh as it appeared to be true. Morgan read Ollie a story and Kat read Opal one. Opal wanted Morgan and Ollie wanted Kat, so they switched bedrooms and children. Then, the children started up again stating they wanted the 'readers' reversed.

'Nope, not happening, close your eyes and listen to the story and be very happy we're together.' Those words sealed the deal. Once they closed their eyes, they were off to dreamland.

Kat and Morgan left the bedroom doors open, and they were most pleased to find nightlights in the Jack and Jill bathroom and along the hallway, too. Soft light was emitting from various sections along the floors, so the children should be fine if they woke during the night.

'We may need those nightlights, too, Mom. We don't really know our way around the place yet!'

Kat nodded. Morgan hoped there were nightlights all around and felt a genuine sense of relief once she began spotting them.

The women slowly descended the winding and seriously masculine staircase taking in the view as they headed into the vast sitting lounge.

Kat remarked in awe, 'What a day filled with sublime surprises!'

'Mom, please share a glass of wine with me. We won't open the Champagne until later, but let's have a glass and I'll get the fire started.'

'I don't mind if I do.'

Fire softly glistening, a blast from the past with nostalgic Joni Mitchell crooning in the background. Doors locked. Garage doors down. They would explore the exterior grounds in the morning. Morgan had already done a bit of research regarding their surrounds, and she had a plan for tomorrow. They slid down into the plush, enormous sofa and rested their feet on the ottomans before them. Instantly as if to bark, What about *me*?' Dixie hopped on Morgan's lap and covered her in kisses.

Morgan squealed. 'Dixie, do you like your new pad?'

Dixie barked in excitement and wagged her precious little tail which, in turn, wagged Dixie's entire body. Her furry family member – Dixie was the glue of her family, truly.

'Oh, Mom, I suddenly feel quite tired, but it's a good tired!'

'This is going to be a monumental Christmas because we'll be making new and lasting memories together. I love you, Morgan.'

Morgan's eyes welled with tears. 'I love you more, Mom and, yes, this is going to be a splendid and sweet Christmas.'

They sat quietly together. Morgan was seriously relieved that Kat was not asking her specifics concerning the divorce. Kat had this uncanny way of knowing when not to broach a subject. Kat was a much more restrained human being than Morgan, but Morgan valued and admired that unique characteristic of her mother's, and this is what she needed most from her mom at present. Quiet support inside of a lovely, fantasy-filled cocoon. Glasses of wine here and there certainly didn't hurt the situation either. Kat put her head back on the gigantic, overstuffed sofa and her empty wine glass looked as if it were about to tumble. Morgan got up, took both of their glasses to the kitchen sink, then went back to whisper in her mother's ear.

'We probably need to head to bed.'

Kat jumped, looked a bit startled, but got up. Both women said good-night and they each looked forward to pulling down the duvet covers and sinking into their luxurious beds.

Morgan suddenly remembered she hadn't even considered checking her phone. *Ha! This is a first and I love it.* This thought made her smile and feel peaceful. She closed her eyes and allowed another day to slip behind her.

The next morning not a peep; no sound at all from anywhere in the house.

'How amazing.' Morgan stretched and yawned. 'Sheer comfort. A great night's sleep and how on Earth could Ollie and Opal still be sleeping?' She didn't see a clock. She needed to find her purse to retrieve her phone and see what time it was. Quite a few missed calls, but she didn't recognize the phone numbers.

'It's 9:50am? No, how can that be?' She was flabbergasted. *Surely everyone else is up and downstairs and I can't hear them.*

Morgan tip-toed down the wooden floors and peeked into her mother's room. Kat was snug as a bug in a rug. Further down, only a short distance, in either room, curly heads were so far down in their beds that Morgan hardly saw them. Absolutely unbelievable. Morgan felt thrilled, invigorated, and happy. Happy was a feeling that did not linger too long these days, so she drank it in whenever it came around.

'Rightio, you two, rise and shine,' Morgan announced with a perky morning voice!

She thought she heard Kat wrestling with the covers in her room, too. Ollie and Opal turned their heads and smiled back at Morgan. Kids. They hopped right out of bed and argued over the bathroom.

Morgan told Opal, 'You can use my bathroom,' and Opal was off in a heartbeat.

Kat stuck her head out of her room and told everyone 'Good Morning.'

That it was. The gang headed downstairs.

'Please don't run, Morgan reminded Ollie and Opal. 'Look how easy it would be for either of you to slip in your sock feet. Be careful.'

Little things. It was hard for them to hold on to the handrail as they navigated their way down. Dixie was even struggling, missing a stair or two, looking back sheepishly as if she were embarrassed.

Kat didn't look totally awake. Everyone must have had a very deep sleep.

Morgan announces, 'I've already done my homework and since it's so late because you're such sleepy heads we are going to go to a little hole in the wall for breakfast, for brunch really. I've heard pleasant comments about this place and don't know why my friends refer to it this way.'

Opal quipped, 'Mommy, I don't want to go in a hole.'

Ollie laughed so hard he got everyone following suit. Morgan tried to explain, but she obviously wasn't doing decent job.

Kat intervened. 'Opal, that's simply an expression. Your mother is going to take us to a small, quaint cafe.'

Ollie tried to say 'quaint' because he quite liked the sound of it but couldn't quite get the hang of it. They all ended up chuckling again. Morgan broke open a banana, split it in two.

'Here. Munch on this at the counter. This will hold you over and then, when you finish, slowly walk, don't run when you go upstairs and get ready. We'll be leaving soon.'

The kids walked as fast as their little feet could carry them without running.

Kathleen and Morgan traipsed back up the winding staircase and Morgan thought to herself that the stairway kept extending, felt like it was growing longer and longer. Kat looked as if she was having the same trouble. They made it to the top and gave each other a high five. *What was happening?* They both must be worn out from the high adrenalin surge of the last few days. They absolutely needed this vacation. Morgan took a super quick shower. It was lovely. The shower was powerful, and mystifying, and a delightful aroma began wafting through the air when she turned on the shower room lights. *Probably automatic but no time to investigate now.* She was in pure heaven.

Kat was ready looking gorgeous with her sleek, white-grey bob and rose-coloured lipstick. Her Mom always looked handsome. Morgan grew up with the belief if someone looks especially nice, male or female, you should let them know it. Her mom taught her that. So, Morgan told her mother how beautiful she looked. Kat wouldn't have a bar of it.

'Now, Mom, be kind, say thank you!'

Kat shook her head with a shy thanks and they all descended the staircase. Dixie tried, unsuccessfully, to navigate the steps again. They had almost forgotten her for a moment. Dixie was yap, yap, yapping at the top of the stairs and without hesitation, Ollie went to retrieve her.

Ollie piped up. 'I hope Dixie gets used to these stairs soon because she's heavier than she looks.'

Morgan went out to the car to get their furry friend's lead.

'Please take Dixie for a walk, but only around the back yard.' Picturing their fluffy family member hopping from bed-to-bed last night, she retrieved the dog bed from the car and her chew toy, too. Goodness, she truly didn't remember to look after Dixie's needs in all the excitement last night. *Shame on me.* Ollie put food in their furry friend's bowl and let her nibble while they were outside. They waited for Dixie to do her business then they tucked her away inside, closing her into the kitchen area until she became familiar with her new home. Morgan locked the house and made sure she had the right keys and the garage door opener, and they piled into the Lexus. *Would she manage to get back down the driveway?*

Morgan's phone was buzzing again frantically, and Opal pleaded, 'Answer it!'

'No, Opal, this is our time and if someone really needs me all they have to do is leave a voicemail.'

Ollie liked his mom's response because he quipped, 'Yeah, Opal.'

The day was another stunner. Queen Kat was the one who said first, 'Merry Christmas Eve everyone,' which brought cheers from the cheerleading squad in the back.

Heading down the driveway the proper way, not in reverse, was quite novel. Morgan didn't know why she thought she would have to reverse out. This was good because they got to enjoy the views on the way back to the main road.

Morgan drove to the Dae Break Café on Pickwick Street right there in Savannah. *Lord, they open at 6:00am.* She felt as if half the day were gone, but *why did she even care?*

'Is this the hole we're going in?' Opal asked as she stared through the car window. Morgan tried hard not to laugh, 'My darling, please don't refer to it in that manner.'

'But you did. You said you were taking us to the hole,' Ollie reminded his mother!

Kat rounded up the chatty ones. 'Hush now, you need to be on your best behavior because 'you know who' is watching.

Ollie and Opal both shouted: 'SANTA!'

The Dae Break Café was unbelievably packed for Christmas Eve. The smell of maple syrup, bacon, tons of bacon, waffles, fried... the distinct smell of everything fried was in the air, and warm, friendly chatter and laughs overwhelmed the room. Coffee. Oh, the coffee smelled freshly brewed, and Morgan and Kat were past ready for it. The kids both wanted waffles and bacon. Kat decided on scrambled eggs and dry toast. The server just stared at her with a startled look as if to declare: Really, you're comin' to the Dae Break Café and you're gonna order *that*? The server never uttered a word, but it was there in her eyes. Morgan was trying hard not to laugh. She ordered French toast with extra bacon and that seemed to put their server in a mighty good mood.

'That's more like it,' she snipped with a huge grin, flashing shiny, white teeth, a few trimmed in gold.

Morgan felt as if they had stepped back in time and she loved every minute of it.

Kat leaned in. 'When you mentioned brunch, I was thinking more like eggs Benedict, but then, I should have known better with your description.'

'Stop, Mom, I bet everything tastes great.'

The place was really buzzing. Their coffee cups were never empty. *Lord, how many fresh coffee pots were brewed a day in the Dae Break Café?* Black boards were hung about the place with their plate lunch descriptions and Morgan could see Ollie and Opal trying eagerly to read the chalk written words. They had captured Kat's attention, too. *Let's see...meatloaf, home-made chicken and dumplings, mashed taters, fried okra, speckled butter beans, turnip greens, fried green tomatoes, coleslaw, devilled eggs (no one makes devilled eggs like mom), fried chicken livers, white beans, cream corn, kraut and wieners, mac and cheese, purple hull peas, hamburger steak, chicken spaghetti, lima beans, the menu went on forever!*

'How can spaghetti still be spaghetti with chicken?' Ollie asked.

'Why have we never had purple peas before because purple is one of my favorite colours and even if I don't like peas very much, I would eat them if they were purple - maybe,' Opal remarked.

Kat had a laugh. Morgan was shaking her head. 'They'll probably be closing for Christmas, but if they're open one day when we're still here, perhaps we'll come back for lunch, too.' The kids' faces perked up at the sound of that suggestion.

Then, suddenly, four plates came from above, two sets of hands sending them down to the table and no one said a word for about the next fifteen minutes. It was good. It was absolutely delicious and just what their tummies wanted.

Kat suggested, 'When we finish why don't we drive around to get a better feel for the area?'

The kids were up for it and Morgan agreed, reminding everyone, 'Dixie will need to go out soon, too.'

Instead of driving, Morgan parked around another area close to the marina so the gang could get out, enjoy the fresh air, and go for a nice walk. There were more people out than she imagined there would be. Everyone was smiling, nodding their heads, and greeting one another. She looked over at Kat, 'Well, much of Memphis must have had the same idea – Pickwick for Christmas.'

'Looks like it!' Kat seemed equally as astounded.

You could rent cabins, boats, pontoon boats, buy fishing bait, and fishing tackle. Pickwick had grown by leaps and bounds. Morgan hoped that when her two precious children grew up Pickwick adventures would become a part of their memory bank, too. She would have to work on that and put more effort into it. They didn't need to buy a boat. Many of Morgan's friends had boats and she used to receive invitations, but she must have dismissed them a few too many times because she couldn't remember the last time she was asked. When Ollie and Opal were older, they could all learn to kayak, too. Pickwick was the kind of spot that you knew was there, but out of sight – out of mind.

Her family climbed back into the Lexus, the wind had become a bit chillier, and they began the drive back home. She knew she and Kat would have to work on getting the children to bed as early as possible, never really a challenging task on Christmas Eve, as the few gifts they were giving were still not wrapped. Morgan smiled. *I want to put extra effort into my Christmas letters, too.*

CHAPTER FOURTEEN

Dixie was super excited to see them. Her tail was banging against the furniture and she was bouncing about. Ollie and Opal were fighting for the right to take Dixie outside, so Morgan attached the lead.

'Stay very close in the backyard since we didn't know the area well.'

Those words appeared to make sense to them both. 'We will, we promise.'

Leaves were floating up and above the cold, hard ground. Morgan could have sworn for one minute because the sky had changed so drastically that it might even snow.

She called out to Kat, 'Mom, come have a look.'

'The moment we wish for snow and hope for it, predict it, well, it won't happen. Best not to think about it.' Her mother lives right in the middle of reality.

Ollie and Opal brought Dixie to the back door. 'My boots are muddy!' Ollie called out. 'Will you please leave your footwear by the door? Morgan picked Dixie up, took her to the sink and wiped her little paws clean, too, with warm water. There was no way any mess was going to occur in this home on her watch. No way.

Moments later Morgan saw a text from Lee. It read: You have no clue how much I'm missing all of you. It's hectic here with the bunch I have staying with me now. Kidnap me, please? Ha! Only kidding. Love ya lots. xox

If only Lee could see this place and be here with us. It would be such a perfect Christmas. Lee had better taste than Morgan in just about anything, well, *no*, everything, and she would be overjoyed staying in this house. Perhaps sometime down the road she could ask Ash if Lee could drive out and see his home.

The front doorbell rang. At least, Morgan thought it was a front door ringing. She had not heard this distinct sound before. It was a soft and sophisticated bell, more like music than a ring, but the television wasn't on, and no music was playing, so it must be the doorbell.

Kat put a magazine down. 'Morgan, was that the doorbell? I heard something.'

'I know, Mom, I heard it, too. I'll be right back.'

She peeked out the beveled glass panels on either side of the expansive front door and to her amazement, saw no one. She pulled the heavy door open and stepped outside. Nothing. No person. No automobile. But there was a lovely, light pale pink gift bag sitting on the front step with delicately tied soft pink satin ribbons and something wrapped neatly in white tissue paper inside of the bag.

'How wonderful!' Immediately Morgan thought of Ash. Then she hesitated. *It had better not be because Ash has already done far too much. I bet he shared with his neighbors that he would have guests staying in his home so they wouldn't become concerned when they saw activity. This must be a 'welcome gift' from his neighbors.* Morgan carefully picked up the precious pink bag and took it inside.

Dixie sprang up to her excitedly!

'Who was at the door?' Kat asked.

'No one at all.'

'Well, isn't that a bit strange?'

Morgan agreed and went through all the scenarios with Kat she just plunged through in her head. Ollie and Opal acted curious, too, and everyone followed her into the kitchen.

Morgan eagerly placed the bag on the marble countertop looking for a card. No card. Hmmm. She reached inside and gently unwrapped the tissue. Morgan always took her time with presents. She drove everybody nuts.

'Any gift needs to be treated with respect.'

'C'mon, Mom, open it, please?' Ollie and Opal were both squirming.

Morgan held up what looked like an extra-large older kosher dill pickle jar. It was heavy. She held it up to the light but couldn't quite make out what was in the jar. Her mother was digging in the bag for a card. Kat pulled out a white card that had been turned upside down. When she flipped it over, they saw the card had big, black, fat, bold, block letters that read: I SEE YOU. Morgan stopped, looked closer, screamed, and dropped the jar. She didn't mean to scream. She really didn't. The glass shattered, shards and splinters went flying, and white, pinkish, gooey balls were bouncing all over the kitchen counter and onto the floor and Dixie was in dog hysterics – overly excited. Eyeballs. A jar full of pigs' eyes. Pigs' eyes flying around the kitchen – everywhere. Morgan was about to get sick.

Ollie and Opal were screaming their heads off. The scene wasn't properly registering with the ladies, but Kat managed to bring about calm, someway, somehow. 'This is the most revolting situation I've ever witnessed,' Kat hissed through her teeth.

Morgan was leaning over the kitchen sink vomiting.

Kat composed herself. 'Ollie, get Dixie. Opal, come with me.'

No one moved. They were crying and wailing, and Dixie was chewing on something.

That was definite.

Kat commanded their attention, gathered the two children, and somehow managed to get Dixie's attention. Kat was shaking and she was doing her best to remain calm. 'Everyone, breathe… just breathe.'

Once the children were upstairs, Kat ran a bath for them. She wasn't sure why, but it seemed like a clever idea.

'Well done, old girl,' she patted Dixie. Dixie made it up the intimidating, winding staircase following her favorite people. Complimenting Dixie got Ollie's and Opal's attention, and they were beginning to calm down. Their little bodies were trembling, too, through their tears.

Ollie looked at his grandmother and said, 'Hold me Nanna Kat.'

Kat's tears flowed and Opal hopped into her Nanna's arms, too.

'Watch, hundreds of bubbles mean lots of fun. I'm going to fill this bath full of magic bubbles.'

Kat was smiling and trying to hum but thinking only of her daughter downstairs. She made certain the water wasn't too hot and picked them up and plopped them in.

'Will you please stay with us Nanna Kat?' Opal asked with a gulp.

Kathleen assured them, 'I'll be back in a flash, and you can wear your favorite pajamas and get them on early. I promise a nice, sweet treat for you, too. How about your favourite strawberry Jello?'

They were flat. Her little precious bubs had lost the light in their eyes. It made Kat terribly angry – madder than a hornet, but she did not let Ollie nor Opal see it.

'Back in a jiffy – wash those feet and toes,' she said with a smile and blew them a kiss, too.

Her daughter. Kat's dynamic daughter was downstairs on her knees on the floor, snotty, shaking, picking up shards of glass, and whimpering. Morgan was making a sort of noise that Kat hadn't heard before.

'Get up, my love. Please. I'll take care of everything.' Then suddenly, Kat said, 'Stop. Seriously, Morgan. Don't clean anymore. This is a crime scene. I'm calling the police now.'

Kat got on her phone and punched in information because she didn't want to call 911. I mean the first question would be, 'What is your emergency?' Kat would then say, 'The kitchen is filled with pigs' eyes.' That didn't even sound right to her. No way could she utter those words to an emergency responder. Kat calmly called the local police station's number and hesitated when they answered. She still didn't quite know what she was about to say. She introduced herself, stated she and her daughter and grandchildren were staying in a friend's home at Pickwick for Christmas.

The nice woman listened and asked, 'And, how may I help you?'

Kat stammered. 'Well, my daughter is going through a dreadful divorce, and someone left a jar filled with pigs' eyes at the front door with a note on the inside of the bag that says: I SEE YOU.

'Do you or does anyone know who left the bag? Did you see anyone?' the responder asked.

Kat replied, 'No, but we really wanted someone to write out a report and maybe they could speak with the neighbors about any cars they may have seen in the area.'

The woman hesitated only a moment. 'We know how to do our job, ma'am. This is Christmas.'

Really? Kat was not impressed.

'We're short-staffed. What's the address?'

Kat didn't know and couldn't think properly.

'I need the address, ma'am.'

'Morgan, my darling, the police need the address.'

Morgan had not moved from the floor and her eyes were glazed over. She reached for her phone and read the address to Kat.

The officer replied, 'I'll send someone to you, but I can't give you an exact time. I'm sorry for this incident. Someone will be there soon.'

Kat grabbed Morgan's shoulders and took her into the sitting lounge, sat her gently in a huge leather chair, headed to the kitchen, got a crystal cocktail glass down from the cabinet, and went directly to Ash's bar. She poured Morgan a nice, smooth Chevas Regal Extra Blended Scotch and handed it to her. Morgan didn't look up. She kissed her daughter on her forehead and placed her hands around the whiskey. Morgan put her head down and wailed. Kat stroked her hair.

'Not now, my darling, please. You're over the worst of it right now. You are the bravest woman I know. I need to return upstairs to Ollie and Opal. Please, for us, I would never ask you to pull yourself together if it weren't for the children. I know how important it is to let this madness, sadness, and insanity out of your body but, please listen to me, I know better than anyone how strong you are. Breathe and don't let the bastard eat you alive.'

Kat's last words did it. Morgan lifted her head, wiped her runny nose with her sleeve, and said, 'I'm alright, Mom, really,' and gulped half the glass.

Kat went to tend to the children. She was upstairs for what seemed to be hours, but Morgan was floating in and out of reality. Her mother was right. *When I go down, the monster wins. I will not go down.*

Nanna-Kat returned downstairs, but only to fix a small treat for Ollie and Opal as she had promised. She placed strawberry Jello with whipped cream and sprinkles on top in lovely red and green dishes, hoping this gesture would restore their spirits. Kat took Dixie out first for a good sniff of fresh air and let her do her duty. When Kat came back inside, she could see Morgan looking outside the front door glass. Morgan opened the door, and an officer stood before her.

Kat quietly climbed the stairs as quickly as possible. She wanted to remain behind closed doors with the children. They had seen enough of police officers. Not here. Not in this home.

Not at Christmas, if possible. She carried a tray with the treats she prepared and an extra plate of M&M cookies. Finally, smiles on Ollie's and Opal's faces.

The officer introduced himself and kindly enough, apologized to Morgan for having to visit her on Christmas Eve. *How sweet.*

She invited him in. 'We must go through to the kitchen first.'

The officer shocked, exclaimed, 'Good God, what happened in here?'

There was a smell, a wretched odor, which was quite repugnant by now, too.

'A gift bag was left at the front door.' She shared that she thought it may have been a gift from one of the neighbors. At this point she didn't advise the cop that the home belonged to her attorney. In her mind that sounded a bit weird, so she refrained.

She went on to explain, 'My precious family followed me into the kitchen, excited to watch me open the gift, and then...my mom and I read the note aloud and it became blatantly obvious to me what objects were enclosed in the jar. I screamed. I dropped the jar. Eyes. Everywhere. Glass shattered. That's about it.'

The cop said, 'Do you know who did this?'

'I have a good idea.'

The cop rephrased, 'Well, that don't count. We need proof, not ideas. I mean, did you actually see who did this?'

Morgan was irritated. The cop knew it and she reiterated that she saw no one or anything. 'I was hoping you would canvass the neighborhood and see if anyone saw strange cars or visitors.'

The cop took off his cap and scratched his head. 'There aren't too many people out this way. Most people are staying in the condos by the marina for Christmas and I know for a fact that the people who owned the homes on either side are away overseas for the time being. The people who own the biggest properties contact us at the police department when they're going away for a while, so we can drive by every now and then.'

Great.

He got out his big pad and asked Morgan for her details, the usual stuff, best contact numbers, numbers of nearest relatives, best time to contact her, blah, blah, blah.

Then he asked, 'Are you the owner of the home?'

The strange thing is Morgan knew instantly by looking into his eyes that he knew she didn't own it, and it was the way in which he asked the question and the tone of his voice she didn't care for. She curiously asked, 'Why do you need to know that?'

'Well, there's been a crime or at least an incident. And if it was your house, wouldn't you want to know?'

'I assure you I'm going to be in touch with the owner and fill him in on the details.'

The cop looked down and said, 'Well, honey, that ain't good enough. I have a report here that has blanks in it and I've gotta fill 'em in.'

'My name is Morgan, not honey, and the owner is Samuel Ashley Downing.'

The cop's belly started jiggling first as his laugh gathered momentum. 'Well, see now? That wasn't so hard, was it?'

What was it with cops? Was she paranoid? Were they all in a hidden society together? Did they hate women? It could not be. One of the cops she dealt with from the very beginning of this diabolical disaster was nice, calming, and respectful.

She had had enough for the day, for the evening. And it was Christmas Eve. She honored her mother's wishes and performed her civic duty by dealing with the police. Nothing was going to come of this. She wanted back in the fold of her children and family, so she took hold of the reins again.

'Officer, is that it? Will you need anything else from me? I don't know what else I can tell you and I would like very much to finish preparing for Christmas.'

He said, 'Oh wait, I better take photos. If we end up in court, I'll need to provide 'em with lots of pictures.'

When he finished, he remarked, 'Well, you'd better get to this mess before you do anything. Them little kids I heard upstairs are gonna be scared when they step through the kitchen door.'

Morgan wanted to slap him. *If he only knew.* Before he could even get the words out, Morgan walked him to the front door and said, 'Yes, of course, if I think of anything you might need to know or if something else should come up, I'll phone right away.'

He tipped his hat while a toothpick hung from his lips and winked at her. *Unbelievable.*

CHAPTER FIFTEEN

Morgan discovered a pair of brand-new kitchen gloves and returned to her hands and knees to clean like she'd never cleaned before, tossing out all those beady, little, foul smelling, nasty eyes. While down on her knees the bright, white Hollywood *LOSER* lights began flashing.

EMBARRASSED. HUMILIATED. SAD. DESPERATE. PATHETIC. LOSER.

'No,' Morgan called out loudly, 'No. I am none of those things. I did not commit this desperate, cowardly act. I am not the loser. I am not pathetic. STOP. This is not who I am.'

MOTHER. DAUGHTER. FRIEND. LOVING. GIVING. KIND. LOYAL.

She spent a tremendous time kneeling trying to make the floor sparkle and the kitchen smell inviting. She felt, too, that she was scrubbing evil out of her system, out of her head. As much as she tried to picture the good words, the positive ones in her mind's eye, they would not remain fixed. The good descriptive words weren't permanent – only fleeting and flashing for a second.

'It's only a matter of time and practice,' she assured herself. She would turn those hurtful, horrible words into loving ones as soon as she rid herself of the monster. She reminded herself, too, any time she spent thinking of him and his sick, demented ways, was time that was stolen from her and from her children. No more stolen time.

She found a tall, fat, cinnamon cylinder candle in the cupboard and a shorter, wide, round evergreen candle, too. They looked brand new and had been placed there just for her family – she knew it. When Kat and the kids returned to the kitchen, the candles would be burning and there would be no remnants remaining of the monster and his evil deed. Morgan grabbed her phone and her Google Home speaker and found upbeat, lively Christmas music on Spotify. She turned it up a bit louder than normal and turned the spiffy looking oven on to bake. She grabbed her mother's lasagna from the refrigerator to allow it to reach room temperature.

She lit the fire. She opened the doors to the kitchen so you could peer in from the sitting lounge. As bad as the last sight and memory was of Ash's kitchen for Ollie and Opal, she was going to turn that vision around. Kitchens were meant to be filled with the best and sweetest of memories and new ones were going to be made in their kitchen tonight. Any kitchen is the heartbeat and soul of a house. *And so this shall be.*

Kat entered the downstairs with Dixie, Ollie, and Opal in tow. They all looked filled with trepidation. In her best act so far, Morgan walked briskly towards her children and hugged them so tightly they began to complain, grabbed their hands, and walked them into the kitchen.

'Yummm, Mom, something smells really good,' said Ollie.

'Cinnamon and you love cinnamon buns,' Morgan replied.

'Mmmm, cimmanim buns, Ollie grinned. 'Mom, are you making them?'

Morgan chuckled. Ollie had never been able to pronounce that word as hard as they had practiced!

She was about to respond when Opal asked, 'What happened to the rubber balls?'

Morgan softly held Opal's shoulders.

'Ollie, the beautiful scent is produced by the red candle and Opal, Mommy has cleaned the balls out of the kitchen so Santa can visit us tonight.'

Kat nodded approval while Opal asked, 'What are we having for dinner?'

Morgan shouted, 'WHO WANTS NANNA'S LASAGNA?' as only a professional cheerleader would and the two angels responded loudly with their hands in the air as part of the cheering squad, 'WE DO!'

Morgan found her footing and was on the right path.

Lasagna in the oven baking, fresh bread wrapped in foil warming in the lower half of the oven.

'Mom, why don't you be in charge of the wine choice tonight? I think I remember seeing a nice Spanish Merlot somewhere but whatever you like.'

Morgan popped over to the kitchen barstool and perused her phone. Eleven. Eleven missed calls and most numbers were different and certainly none she recognized. Morgan wanted badly to speak with Ash, not desperately, but strongly, yet told herself no matter what had transpired Christmas Eve was not the time to discuss madness or cruelty. The day after Christmas would suffice. If she, on the other hand, heard from Ash first, she would still refrain from sharing the sheer horror. It was the proper thing to do.

Morgan's phone began vibrating and buzzing around the kitchen countertop. Kat looked at her.

'No. No, Mom, not getting it. You and I both know who it is.'

Kat turned white. Then she turned red.

'I'm right, Mom. Answering the phone would just start another avalanche all over again.'

Kat prepared the table beautifully for Christmas Eve. The lasagna was hot and tasty, and Morgan had buttered the toasty bread, grilling it with just a touch of garlic salt and Parmesan cheese. She didn't fool with a salad. They had quite enough food and the kids would be too excited to eat very much. Kat poured the wine and even Ollie and Opal joined in the toast with their milk glasses.

'To Our Family, Merry Christmas.'

'Almost,' Opal added grinning.

The kids ate more than Morgan imagined they would. Their tummies were full. She could see their attitudes had changed. They were genuinely calmer and more relaxed and were super excited over the anticipation of Christmas morning. Happy. Morgan was appreciative that children appeared much more resilient than adults. She would keep a watchful eye over them.

Kat said, 'I'll escort the bubs upstairs.'

Morgan asked the children, 'Please take Dixie out first.'

Opal professed, 'Mom, It's my turn!'

Morgan attached the lead to Dixie's collar and reminded Opal, 'Please stay close and don't linger outside.'

The temperature had dropped vastly. Morgan could feel the cold as Opal fiddled with the doorknob. Kat kept a watchful eye over her grandchild through the paned-glass door until she returned to the safety of the house.

Morgan went to work cleaning the kitchen...again. Then she went upstairs to find the wrapping paper, collected the boxes, and the few gifts that were to be wrapped. She wanted to get these tasks completed so she could spend quality time on her Christmas letters. Kat had the children upstairs helping them into their pajamas. She had told Morgan she would read a nice, long story to them tonight. Before they went upstairs the four of them went through the ritual of leaving Santa a nice plate filled with cookies and brownies and a tall glass of milk.

'Don't forget the napkin, Mom.' Opal said.

Did I make my children like this?' Opal most definitely liked to cross her t's and dot her i's even at her tender age.

Morgan felt proud.

She collected scissors, scotch tape, ribbons, bows, and wrapping paper, spreading them along the large kitchen table and went to work immediately.

Kat returned to the kitchen later hesitantly. 'Understandably, the children want to sleep with me.'

Those words made Morgan wince because she thought they truly seemed better at dinner.

'Please don't worry. They're both already fast asleep in my bed and I know they simply need to feel safe.'

Morgan understood the children loved to be close to their grandmother. Kat had brought the dressing robes down that she had hidden in her closet and a special watch for Ollie and a locket for Opal. Kat had a knack for finding items that intrigued her children and had longevity. Now both women were busily wrapping and chatting away with peaceful and calming Christmas carols in the background. It was a pleasant moment in time.

Morgan's phone was buzzing away. She glanced at it and saw Antonio's name. Morgan picked up with scissors in hand, 'Merry Christmas, Antonio.'

He chuckled. 'You beat me to it. Merry Christmas, fabulous gal. How's it going?

'Fine, happy to have my mother with us and Ash's place looks like it belongs on the cover of Southern Living.'

Antonio was silent for a moment.

'Now, tell me how you're *really* doing because I have a friend who has a friend who knows a friend who knows a butcher. The butcher told his close friend that a tall, thin, cocky well-dressed man came into his shop at the beginning of last week and said he needed one hundred pigs' eyes. The guy told the butcher he wanted them for his kid's science class. Idiot. The kids are on school break. He's making it up as he goes along. Anyway, an incident report from Hardin County has been shared with the East Memphis Precinct and Ash's team was alerted. I don't know exactly what's happened, but I have a feeling that it's something rotten. I'm sorry. I want you to know that you can call me morning, noon, night, Christmas Eve, Christmas Day, New Year's – do you understand? Ash won't call you tonight because he says you're wounded and too proud and he doesn't want to interfere with your family time. I'm doing it instead.'

Morgan's head was spinning. *The monster went to a butcher and openly ordered pigs' eyes. Her colleague and dear friend knows something is wrong when she's trying her best to disregard the incident and finish Christmas. How does news circulate this rapidly? Memphis is not a huge city.* Morgan was confused. Pickwick Lake district is small with Hardin County population only approximately 7,000 people and it is Christmas Eve. She took another breath and another sip of her red.

'Look Antonio, it doesn't really matter what happened because the monster doesn't get locked up. He doesn't even get his hands slapped and the attitude of the cops, any cop lately, has become condescending towards me. I understand that Ash is in my corner, but no one is stopping the monster. Plus, Ash is 'spot on'. This is not the conversation I want to have tonight or probably ever again. It was awful; simply dreadful. The thought of him being in this area makes my skin crawl, but we are moving forward. You told me once, 'This too shall pass.' Another tragic episode of my life has just slipped by. I appreciate you for caring. It's wonderful to hear your voice.'

Antonio gave the impression he did not comprehend Morgan. 'I can be there by midnight.'

She smiled over the phone, 'Not necessary, but I'll always remember the offer. Merry Christmas, sweet friend.' Morgan disconnected.

Kat finished the wrapping. She had no clue the last large box she wrapped was her very own present. Morgan placed the pretty, bright packages underneath the tree and put the milk back in the fridge. She would have to remember to take a bite out of a cookie and leave brownie crumbs on the plate before the kids came downstairs.

Kat studied her very tired looking daughter's face. 'Do you want to talk?'

Morgan squeezed her hand and thanked her. 'Really, no, Mom, I'd rather think about tomorrow morning, but I'm so happy you're here with us. You were such a superstar today for the kids and me. I won't forget it any time soon.'

She held on to Kat for a while, then went about turning off the lights, locking up the house, and they scaled the stairs together with Dixie at their heels.

Morgan washed her face, took a good long look in the mirror, and scared herself. *Who is this woman peering back?* It was an exhausted, overly tired, sad, and angry, worn-out version of herself. *How will I ever get my former self back?* Morgan laughed. Antonio would tell her to go and discover her essence again. She didn't want her former self. *No. A new, healthier version would be preferred – a monster-free rendition.*

She pulled out three sheets of nice, linen stationery from a box in her luggage and her favorite Cartier writing pen and sat down in front of the exquisite French antique desk. The night now belonged to her, and she needed to form the words in a meaningful way so, if anything happened to her, Ollie and Opal and her mother would know, without any doubt, they each meant the world to her. She was enormously proud to be Kat's daughter and even more appreciative to be the mother of Ollie and Opal. Morgan closed her eyes to think a bit and she pictured the people whom she loved the absolute most.

Dear Mom,

Ever since I can remember, my entire life, you have loved me as all children would dream to be loved. I do not think I have ever felt judgment from you, I have only felt and received love, support, and loyalty. I know it was your dream to have more children, but it is my biggest wish that I have never disappointed you. Mom, you have been my rock. You have been a teacher of many subjects. You have been the best listener, and you taught me how to listen. I know that I am and have always been stubborn. You are tough and you stand your ground when you fiercely believe in something. You have instilled that same characteristic in me. I treasure the fact I am enormously proud to be your daughter, and my biggest hope is that I will grow to be half the woman you are today. I remain forever grateful to have you as my mother. Please know, always, how very much you mean to me.

Merry Christmas and all my love,

Morgan xxo

Dearest Ollie,

You are my little man of whom I am most proud. You are strong. You are kind. You are willing to help me, your sister, or your Nanna-Kat, or anyone whenever you see they need assistance. Ollie, please, no matter what life throws your way...remain as you are. Putting others before yourself will give you immense pleasure and your heart will be filled with gratitude for the rest of your days on Earth. Continue to be kind to others. Remember to set your sight on a goal that means a great deal to you and a goal that will, hopefully, make this world a better place. Remember to be thoughtful along the way. Remain strong when others are pushing you to go in an opposite direction. Stand your ground like the fine young man that you are already today, my sweet Ollie, and you will go the great distance. I could not ask for a better son. I could not be more proud of you as I am at this very moment. I have been blessed and fortunate to be able to call you my son, my first born. You, dear Ollie, mean the world to me.

I love you to the moon and back.

Merry Christmas, my love,

Mom xxo

Dear Sweet Opal,

In the morning when you open your eyes it will be Christmas. On this morning and every single morning thereafter, I want you to know just how much I love you. For a more precious daughter I could never have wished. You are my shining light, my little sparkling ray of sunshine and your sweet laugh is music to my ears. I love the way you smile. Remember to always be kind to others, love with every bit of your heart, and remember to be giving along your journey. Be true to yourself. Be honest. Most of all listen to your heart, follow your gut instinct. Once you are a little older you will know exactly what this means. Help others when you can. Follow your inner compass and set your goals high. Find something in your life that you enjoy doing tremendously. Live everyday as if there will be no tomorrow. Know always I will be your biggest supporter no matter what road you choose to travel. Travel far and wide because there is a great, big world beyond Memphis. Do not let others choose the path that you want for yourself. And know, always, my darling one, that I love you to the moon and back. You are my shining star.

Merry Christmas, my love,

Mom xxo

Morgan stopped and thought there was more she could say, but was there? Her children were still quite young. She hoped they would keep these letters for years to come, but, she knew, too, how she was as a child – wild and free. Didn't matter. Her heart was filled with love and she shared a bit of it through her pen this evening.

Exhausted; she was painfully tired. The house was eerily quiet, and it felt strange to her. This was a bit disconcerting. As gorgeous and enthralling as the house was, it was not home. It was, however, a grand place to spend this Christmas. *If only...*she pushed it out of her mind and refused to think of the disgusting afternoon again. Morgan marched into the bathroom, turned on the shower, and rinsed the day away. There was that alluring aroma again and it made her feel relaxed and peaceful. It was going to be amazingly easy to fall asleep tonight.

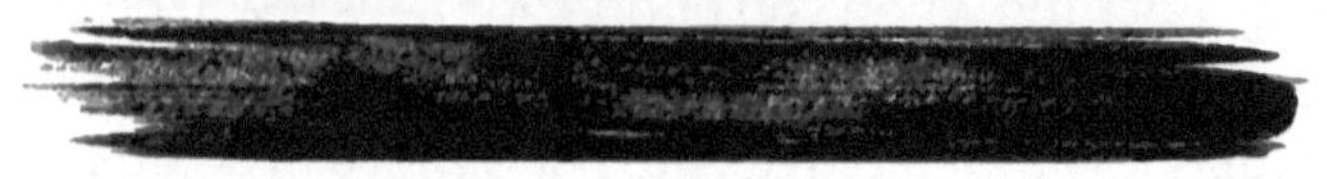

CHAPTER SIXTEEN

Her phone was buzzing on the bedside table, but the sun was barely peeking in the windows from over the lake. It was terribly cool, too, almost cold. She picked up her phone with one eye barely open and did not recognize the number. No. Nope. It was Christmas morning, and she was not allowing any negative thoughts to creep in or to hang about. She thought to herself that it was good the phone woke her because she had Santa duties downstairs. She needed to place an empty glass next to the plate filled with treats and stuff the stockings with her Christmas letters because she did not have the chance to place them on their pillows last night and fill the stockings with a few of Kat's homemade goodies, too. This was her favourite time during Christmas.

She was longing for something, Morgan didn't know what, but she felt a tinge of sadness and her tummy had sharp pains. Many Christmases are filled with glee, and some are nostalgic while others, she now knows, are painful. She had her wonderful mother and her two extremely sweet and healthy children by her side. There were thousands of people in the world who would long for what she had. She bowed her head for a sweet moment to give thanks, and she went about lighting candles, turning the music on softly, and preparing the stockings.

She was grateful for her five or six minutes because before Morgan knew it Dixie was bounding down the stairs first, full speed ahead, and almost tumbling. Kat had Ollie and Opal, hand in hand, and it was the prettiest picture Morgan had seen in a long while.

Morgan announced 'Merry Christmas' to all and said, 'Please. Stop for one second. I want to catch this precious moment on my camera.'

The kids groaned. It was over in a flash!

Kat said she would take Dixie out while the children were hugging their mom, kissing her cheeks, and telling her 'Merry Christmas'.

'Santa didn't eat very much,' Ollie commented.

Opal added, 'But he was very thirsty!'

Morgan watched as the children began investigating the name tags on the gifts. She gently bent down and handed Ollie and Opal a couple of presents. They were squatting on the floor with their legs crossed right next to the tree.

'Santa would want you to start opening those now.' Morgan made certain the first two packages she handed over were from Nanna-Kat because they would come in handy this cold Christmas morning. Ollie was the first to get his open and he looked overjoyed to see a nice, soft textured cobalt blue robe. Kat was back inside by this time and Dixie was right in the middle of the kids and the action. Opal's dressing robe was a lovely emerald green which was her favourite colour, so she was the first one to hug Kat's neck, followed by Ollie.

They sang out, 'Thank you, Nanna-Kat!' and put their new robes on instantly.

Morgan snuck out to make coffee and she got the hot chocolate started, too. She was truly proud at how poised her children were. They opened the presents gently and they didn't seem to be in any hurry at all. Perhaps that was due to the fact there weren't as many presents under the tree this year. *But it didn't really seem to matter to my kids. They are genuinely happy to be together and in peace.* More ribbons and bows were sliding off the wrapping paper and Ollie was excited.

'A guitar!' he exclaimed.

Opal opened a small keyboard to her complete amazement – she really didn't know what it was. They were both good singers. Morgan didn't know how they came by that talent, but she thought this year she would explore their hidden secrets and purchase musical instruments. Time would tell. They would either be enthralled and keen to practice as they should or they wouldn't. Her belief was that they would love to learn to play.

After the gifts were opened in Morgan's family, they would save the stockings for last. Most families, she learned, did it the other way around. *Who made Christmas rules anyway? Were they even rules?* She thought of them as family routines or rituals passed down through the generations. Morgan handed Kat a cup of coffee and sat cross-legged on the sofa.

She pointed to a large thick, square package under the tree, looking lonely, and told the children, 'I think, I'm not quite sure, but perhaps Santa has left that one for both of you!'

Ollie and Opal looked at each other and they both reached for it at the exact same time. They eagerly gazed at their mom.

'Go ahead. You can both open it.'

The big and awkward box was the National Geographic Map of the World 300-piece puzzle and the kids clapped their hands together. Morgan wondered again how they were truly her kids because she had never been into puzzles the way they were. She placed her mug on the coffee table and got up to get her mother's gift from under the tree. Kat opened the beautifully wrapped box, the one that she had managed to wrap herself, to the most gorgeous, cornflower blue cashmere sweater. It matched her eyes perfectly.

Kat smiled her trademark smile, held the sweater against her. 'I've never owned cashmere before. This is lovely. Oh, darling, it's quite impressive and you shouldn't have.' Morgan hugged her.

'Nanna-Kat, you'll look beautiful, and you must wear that all day for Christmas!' Opal exclaimed with Ollie adding, 'You always look pretty, Nanna-Kat.' Kat gave them each a huge hug.

This time Kat got the stockings down for the children and took Morgan's stocking over to her.

Morgan whispered to her mother, 'I know what's in each one because I filled them myself.'

Kat winked. 'Well, you may want to take another look.'

There was a tiny box wrapped in gorgeous, deep cherry red paper with a sparkling silver slender ribbon tied around it. Morgan certainly did not put *that* there. Morgan looked up and Kat was smiling from ear to ear.

'Go on. Open it.'

Morgan slipped the ribbon off and opened a black leather box. It was her mother's engagement ring that had belonged to her mother prior. Morgan looked up at Kat and couldn't say a word. The tears started. They streamed down her face and wouldn't stop. Ollie and Opal began to worry. They had no clue what was happening.

'Your mother is fine. She's simply overwhelmed by the gift,' Kat reassured her grandchildren.

Morgan couldn't speak. Kat went over to her and sat by her side.

'Why should you wait until I die to have something that means the world to me? I would love to see you wearing this on either hand or better yet, get it re-sized and wear it on any finger you like. You'll always have a part of me and your grandmother with you, by your side.'

They embraced and Morgan kissed Kat's cheek.

Opal found the exceptionally special locket in her stocking and in it was a picture of her mother, her grandmother, and her great grandmother when they were all younger. Kat tried to explain the locket, but Opal thought it was a wonderful treasure and she wanted it on...right then.

Ollie found his watch and stated quite loudly, 'I'm a grown-up now because I already know how to tell time, and I have a watch to prove it. I love my watch, Nanna-Kat. It's the best gift of all.'

Nanna-Kat knew how to make Christmas magical.

Morgan had Ollie reach in his stocking, and he pulled out his letter. Opal followed.

'Look, Santa wrote us letters,' Opal claimed.

'No, Opal, I wrote you each a letter.'

'Will you hand Kat's letter to her, too, please?' Morgan asked her daughter.

Opal jumped up and presented Nanna-Kat with an envelope.

Kat read hers, closed it, and walked over to Morgan, 'This letter will do for the remainder of my Christmases spent with you. Thank you, my love.'

Ollie was concentrating hard on his letter.

'Please will you help me read this?' Opal asked her mommy.

They got through the letters and kissed Morgan.

Ollie announced, 'I would like to read my letter every Christmas from now on.'

'You'll need to find a special spot to keep it and remember that spot.'

Opal started giggling. 'He'll forget. That's what boys do.'

Opal gave her letter to Morgan. 'Will you keep mine in a secret place for me?'

Morgan agreed and placed the letters back in their stockings for the time being. It was the perfect Christmas morning. Dixie was rustling through the Christmas paper and having the best time.

Kat lit the fire in the grand fireplace and its warm glow and crackling sound made all the difference in the world. The house had the genuine look and feel of a Christmas card. The weather was doing something strange outside regarding precipitation, but nothing was sticking. White, miniscule flakes dangling about in the air. That would do. It felt as if they were living in a snow globe.

CHAPTER SEVENTEEN

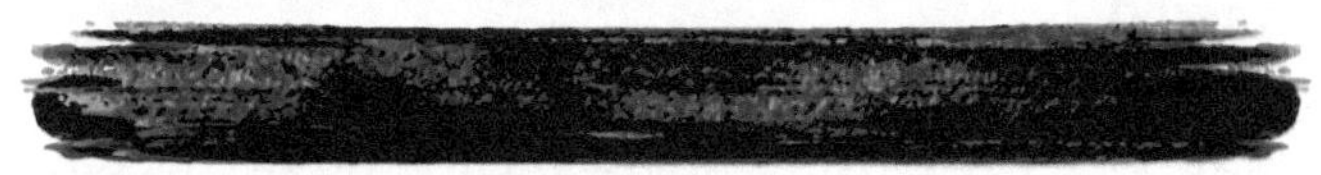

Morgan connected her phone to her JBL speakers and found sentimental Christmas morning music. The family was still hugging each other when Morgan's phone began ringing. She ignored it and got a couple of small mugs down from the cabinet for the hot chocolate. She sat the children at the kitchen counter and started to make a small bit of breakfast. The remainder of the day would be about delicious food, good cheer, merry music, and far too many desserts. She presented bowls of fruit and a plate of muffins for everyone to nibble on while they enjoyed their hot beverages. Morgan wanted more coffee – lots more. She had slept quite well. It was one of those deep, dark sleeps where one can't remember even the slightest portion of a dream. She couldn't shake off the harsh tiredness though that was permeating throughout her bones. Her phone kept buzzing, so she glanced and saw it was Lee.

Morgan instantly responded, 'Merry Christmas, my darling. We miss you and love you and have thought of you so very much. Oh, Lee, I truly wish we were together.'

Lee echoed Morgan's sentiments. Then she said, 'Come home. I mean it. When you do decide to leave Pickwick, come back to me. It was great having you here and I think you'd be much safer.'

Morgan wasn't going to entertain any thoughts about future living spaces or safety. For goodness' sake, it was Christmas day. They sent kisses through the phone and Morgan promised, 'I'll ring you soon.'

Kat got up from her comfy cushion. 'I'll manage the turkey – consider it my job!' It was a small one so there wouldn't be that much effort involved and at least, for the first time in years, no one was up at 5:00am basting the turkey bird. That was a small relief! Kat started bringing out pots and pans and sea salt, olive, oil, onions, and the chopping board, too, to prepare the dressing.

Morgan loved her gravy and Kat's dressing was still the best she had ever tasted.

'Why doesn't my dressing ever taste like yours?'

Kat laughed, 'Don't you know everything tastes better when someone else prepares it?' 'Right, that's it.' Morgan watched Kat go to work.

Ollie and Opal were still eating and they gave Dixie a piece of muffin. Morgan shook her head. She began to tidy the sitting lounge. Everything looked cheery and inviting. It was if they were caught in time and it wasn't as if Morgan wanted to stay there, but she didn't feel as if she were ready to move forward either. Her phone was going off. Ollie got it from the counter and took it over to his mother. It was Antonio again.

The very moment Morgan clicked the green answer button, Antonio shouted, 'Merry Christmas, sweet friend; go to your front door.'

Morgan's voice sounded shocked. 'What? Did you have something delivered? I hope it's far better than the last gift.'

Antonio replied, 'Indeed, now go and open your door.'

Morgan did and low and behold, Antonio stood before her with the biggest white poinsettia plant she'd ever seen held right in front of his face! It was gigantic.

Antonio's smile matched it. 'Please don't be angry. I wanted to be with family, and I know I'm naughty for inviting myself and I'll leave, I'll go right now if that's what you really want, and...'

Morgan cut him off. 'Stop, Antonio. It's wonderful to see you and I'm genuinely happy you're here. I would have said something, she lowered her head...but.'

Then Antonio picked her up and hugged her. 'It's all good and Merry Christmas.'

The kids ran up and grabbed Antonio, dragging him into the house. Kat was singing out from the kitchen while she chopped. It became apparent Antonio's appearance was exactly the lift the family and the house needed. Dixie was overly enthused, too. Morgan felt genuinely happy on the inside again and, perhaps, a tiny bit safer.

Antonio handed out precious trinkets for the children and he gave Morgan a serious best-selling book about how to quickly move beyond divorce.

He slyly remarked, 'This isn't to start now, but tomorrow might be good.'

They both chuckled. Then he presented her with a hand-dyed silk scarf with deep greens, and vivid blues, and purple hues that was simply brilliant. Morgan hugged him again.

'Your present is back at my house. Sorry, but the good news is I have a unique bottle of red here we'll be sharing today.'

Morgan placed the poinsettia on the first rung of the stairway, but it was far too large. She placed it on the floor next to the stairs and it looked as if it were custom made for that specific space.

'Magnificent!' Kat exclaimed.

Antonio presented Kat with a box of Godiva chocolates and Morgan thought she saw her mother actually turn crimson. Kat kissed his cheek and gave him a thank you hug.

The next minute Antonio put on an apron and looked like a master chef in the kitchen. He was guiding Kat more than assisting her. Morgan thought this would be a suitable time to get the children upstairs to change and she would put a little effort into her appearance, too.

POP! Antonio called out to her, 'You cannot begin this day without a few bubbles in a glass.' He had not only started to prepare for the Christmas meal, but he had perused the wine stock and found a terribly nice, chilled vintage of Champagne tucked away in the corner of the wine fridge. Morgan hadn't even had a chance to look there.

'Different priorities for different people,' she chuckled. She took her glass with a smile and a wink and instructed Ollie and Opal to follow. 'Come now, up the stairs.'

The happy mob of three with Dixie in tow, wagging her fluffy tail, each scampered to get ready for the day. Morgan would go back downstairs and relieve her mom and pick up where Kat left off so she could freshen up, too.

The day was off to a soft, sweet beginning and Morgan was counting her blessings. She should have reached out to Antonio. Yes, she most certainly should have invited him to Pickwick, but this was to be their private family time. It didn't matter now. Antonio felt very much like family. He was such a kind man, an extremely intelligent person, and a perfect gentleman on top of it. *Good combination. Why hasn't a woman latched on to him by now?*

In no time at all Morgan had freshened her face, slipped on slate grey wool pants and put on a soft, cranberry red sweater with a white, silk blouse underneath. She slipped on low, comfortable charcoal grey heels just to feel a bit dressy. There. She felt more like Christmas now. Ollie was doing brilliantly dressing himself. Opal was struggling to get her favourite dress over her head. Her hair needed a little assistance, too. Morgan adored her little ones. Her heart swelled as she watched them.

Ollie walked out and asked, 'Well, what do you think, Mom? How do I look?'

'Like a million dollars.'

Opal got the giggles and asked, 'What exactly does a million dollars look like?'

Morgan quietly whispered under her breath, 'My most sensible and level-headed child. What did I do to deserve these charming beings?'

She offered to put Opal's hair on top of her head in a beautiful Audrey Hepburn bun.

Next, Opal wanted to know, 'Who is Audrey Hepburn and I want to see a picture.'

Morgan reached for her phone to Google Audrey Hepburn.

Opal clasped her hands together! 'Oh, she's so pretty and yes, I want her bun.'

Bun done. The three found their way downstairs and Dixie, somehow, someway, was sporting a brand-new green bow with bits of fake holly berries around her neck. Morgan looked down at Dixie, then over to Opal.

Opal's eyes were wide. 'Well, you know it's my best colour and Dixie looks so good in it, too.'

Christmas music. Christmas smiles. The aromas of turkey and stuffing and goodness only knows what else, wafting through the air, plus the candles had been lit. Antonio must have found a hidden stash of candles because the place was now looking closer to a fire hazard than a home, but it was a spectacle to behold. Magic surrounding their family. The family is in a cocoon again. Morgan's French Champagne was depleted, but Antonio was on it and had her glass filled in a flash.

Morgan gently reminded him, 'It's still early and I'm going to take it slowly.'

He smiled and took her for a twirl in the kitchen. *Cheeky guy. He's going to be the Christmas entertainment without a doubt.*

Morgan slipped up behind Kat and hugged her, 'I'm taking over, please give me any needed instructions.'

Kat insisted, 'I'm fine,' but Morgan pointed.

Kat turned around. 'My darling, you look beautiful. Yes, I'd better go upstairs and see what I can do for myself.'

Morgan kissed her and she felt that warm trickle of happiness run through her again. Antonio was watching. The weird thing was that she was literally on the verge of tears but would be unable to explain why if anyone asked. Antonio must have sensed this because he put his glass down on the counter and placed his arms around her waist and held on gently.

He whispered in her ear, 'This will be over soon and you're going to land in a better spot than you could have ever imagined in your wildest dreams.'

Morgan only wanted safety and shelter and an abundance of love in their lives – *not a whole lot to ask for.*

She looked up at Antonio and said, 'I'll settle for normal and monster-free.'

Antonio was now in charge of the music selection and kid beverages and adult beverages. He commented with a broad grin, 'That's a lot for one guy!'

Morgan was beaming.

'Mom, can I take Dixie out for another walk?' Ollie asked. Opal looked at her mother, 'Me, too, please?'

Morgan gave this some consideration and looked at Antonio. As he nodded, she said, 'Rightio, but make it a fast one and wrap up, okay?'

They leapt up together, fighting over Dixie's lead, and the three of them attempted to go out the back door together. What a sight.

Morgan sang out, 'Remain close where I can see you.'

She didn't like the sound of her voice when she gave commands, so she lightened the sound and told them, with a smile, 'Don't linger.'

Antonio made the choice to stand guard at the kitchen bay window.

Morgan placed the finishing touches on the sweet potato casserole filled with pineapple pieces and chopped pecans, heaps of real butter, and copious amounts of brown sugar. It smelled like a dessert, and it looked more like one, too. The kids only ate sweet potatoes at Christmas simply because they're topped with a kazillion miniature marshmallows. Morgan ate sweet potatoes any way she could have them – not Ollie and Opal nor Antonio, she now learned. The stuffing was baked separately, not like everyone else's. Morgan discovered through past Christmases many people prefer the stuffing stuffed inside the turkey as its namesake suggests! Kat had never liked it that way and habits and tastes get passed down through generations. Kat once said the stuffing was lighter, fresher, cleaner, served away from the interior of the bird. *Cleaner?* Oh well, Morgan enjoyed the stuffing on its own now, too. She imagined this was the way Ollie and Opal would prepare stuffing for their future Christmas dinners, also.

She noticed her mobile vibrating back and forth on the counter while Antonio was helping the cherubs return inside with Dixie. It was nearing time for Christmas dinner and she didn't feel the need to peek at her phone.

'Ollie, Opal, will you help set the table, please?'

They decided against using the formal dining room. There was no need for that. The large, dark, mahogany round table situated in the cozy corner of the warm and inviting kitchen was more than perfect. It sat six guests, too, so space was not an issue. Morgan did find a lovely bronze, cream, and rich ruby tablecloth with matching napkins in a kitchen cupboard and a gorgeous place setting for six guests. There was an assortment of slim crystal vases tucked away in the corner, too. She had an idea.

'Kids, do you think you can manage this fabulous tablecloth for me?'

Morgan walked over to the magnificent floral arrangement and carefully, gently pulled out the delicate white flowers, hibiscus, wild, white irises, snowballs, snowstorms, sweetly, scented white jasmine mixed with the creamy-white striped, bold yucca accents. She found scissors in a kitchen drawer, cut the different florals to varying lengths and placed them in a tall, slender cut glass vase. Simple. Splendid. Ollie and Opal were busy placing the cutlery where it should go. Opal directed Ollie when he was unsure of any placement and in a moment's time, the table transformed into a Christmas work of art. Morgan discovered a crystal water pitcher, and she placed crystal glasses at each place setting. She was only a tiny bit concerned about her children using fine crystal, *but for one night, one meal, and for this Christmas holiday, why not?* Besides, Ollie and Opal were growing and learning, and this would be a useful experience for them.

Kat descended the stairs looking exquisite. Antonio even stopped. 'How gorgeous you look, Kat.'

Kat had slipped black satin trousers on and was wearing her brand, spanking new cornflower soft blue cashmere sweater with her own mother's strand of genuine pearls, earrings matching. Kat took Morgan's breath away because Kat was the quintessential figure of composure and classic beauty. It was as if for one moment, everyone was in their element – their own space of peace and contentment. Blessings in abundance.

It was real. The evening was genuine. But, for every second that passed Morgan felt as if she were play acting. *Why?* She thought about this for a moment and reflected it must be because every single time she feels good about something, the monster arranges to destroy those positive feelings. The monster had to stomp on any thing sweet in her life and that thought continually kept her on a sharp and uncomfortable edge. *Was it the monster? Or was she allowing herself to imagine it was the monster? No. It was the monster.*

Antonio had been most observant. He had refrained from filling her glass too often. This time he swept over her and presented a fresh, new glass filled to the brim. He was such a grand host. He never missed a beat. Kat announced she was ready to begin serving and the three adults set up an appealing and luscious buffet on the kitchen countertop. It was easier that way and the table wouldn't be overloaded with hot dishes. Morgan prepared the children's dinner plates while Antonio lit the candles on the table.

'How elegant everything looks,' Morgan observed. 'Yet somehow humble, too.'

Kat brought fresh, delicious homemade monkey bread out from the oven. The wonderful scent alone of the hot bread was making everyone's mouth water. Morgan fixed Antonio a plentiful plate while Kat placed the bread in a basket in the center of the table.

Morgan encouraged Kat, 'Please sit down,' as she prepared another two dinner plates.

Antonio offered to say grace. 'Praise God for whom all blessings flow. Loving Father, we thank you for this food, and for all your blessings to us. Lord, Jesus, come and be our guest, and take your place at this table. Holy Spirit, as this food feeds our bodies, so we pray you would nourish our souls. Amen.'

Well, Morgan learned something new again. She had no clue Antonio was religious or a practicing Christian. There were a few things she probably didn't know about this man. Either way a proper blessing was delivered upon a proper Christmas meal. She couldn't remember the last time she or her children had attended their family church. Her children needed to be exposed to organized religion so they could make decisions for their own futures. It shouldn't be up to her to make their minds up for them. The monster had been brought up in a different religion from Morgan's and every Sunday seemed to start a war in their home. Now, there was nothing Christian about that! *She now understood these were the real topics that required a discussion prior to any marriage or committed relationship.*

Morgan's mind raised the word *DESPERATE*. The Hollywood lights began to form in her head, and she slam-dunked them back to the dark recesses of her psyche.

The guests watched Dixie as she sat excitedly by the table, practically under it, obviously wishing any guest would get a bit sloppy. Everyone was chatting and Kat was receiving rave reviews about her cooking. The meal was close to perfection and far too much had been prepared. Morgan cooks the same way Kat cooks. *Why do they both prepare enough food for fifteen people? She had no clue.* But it always happened.

The precipitation outside was becoming thicker and there were signs the dust of snow was making proper attempts to stick. Shocking! Would they have a white Christmas after all? The kids were enchanted. Everyone was full and looked as if they were going to be stuck in their chairs for life.

Antonio offered to take Dixie out for a bit. Only Ollie and Opal raised their hands for Christmas dessert. Kat was removing dishes in the blink of an eye. Same old story. The cook prepares for two or three days, and dinner is consumed in under forty-five minutes.

Opal raised her hand, 'May I have some red velvet cake, please, because it looks so much like Christmas?'

'May I have a big bowl of sweet potatoes all to myself? I don't know why Nanna-Kat puts dessert on the table while we're eating dinner,' Ollied added!

Morgan laughed and followed the requests. Kat had the biggest grin on her face and certainly seemed to be in her element.

Antonio returned to the kitchen. He looked different. He went about the motions of releasing Dixie's lead and even picked her up and toweled off the bottom of her paws. She had bits of ice stuck between her toes and she didn't look so happy about it either. Antonio began chatting, but he wasn't looking at Morgan. This concerned her. Something was up with him. Morgan continued clearing dishes and helping Kat to tidy up while the children ate their desserts with gusto. *Where were they putting all the food?*

Morgan asked Antonio, 'Would you like a bit more red in that glass?'

'Most certainly.' Still, his eyes did not meet hers and this made her feel uncomfortable.

Then Antonio looked up, 'Initially Morgan I thought I was coming to surprise you, but to be truthful, I needed or rather, wanted to be with family more than I wanted to surprise you. I wasn't truly planning to stay the night. Well, at least, I hadn't thought things through thoroughly, but now the weather is beginning to turn a bit nasty, and I don't want to be driving in it.'

'And that you will not be doing. You're not going anywhere. I still haven't been in every room, but there will be another bedroom, no doubt, or at least a dozen places we can find for you to place your sweet head. No need to worry about anything.'

There. It was out in the open. He was staying and Morgan could see absolute relief in Antonio's face.

CHAPTER EIGHTEEN

Morgan and Kat made the kitchen shine again and with the soft glow of the lovely candles, it felt like the truly special place it was.

'I'm going to run upstairs and get changed, but I'll be back down in a bit,' Kat said.

Morgan leapt at this opportunity to assuage her niggling doubts and asked Antonio, 'What's up? What's bothering you?'

'Nothing. Not a thing.'

Morgan went up to him and knocked the back of his knees with hers, 'Now, tell me the truth.'

'Look, Morgan, it may be nothing, but I could have sworn I saw shoe tracks in the snow to the right and the left of the back deck. They could be from a neighbor, they could be from anybody walking their dog, but they didn't look right to me. They weren't small prints. They were large – definitely noticeable, most assuredly a male's footprints.'

Antonio saw immediately he had made a mistake. 'See? This is exactly why I didn't want to say anything.'

Morgan snapped, 'Stop protecting me.' She grabbed her purse and re-read the instructions to Ash's alarm system. She hadn't secured the place last night because she figured locking each door was more than enough. Plus, she didn't think in her wildest imagination the monster would be stupid enough to come back two days in a row. *Stupid. Right. Yes, he would. The monster does anything that brings him satisfaction.*

Morgan asked Antonio, 'Please don't share anything about what you saw with my mother, okay? And we'll discuss a plan later.'

See? The night had been too perfect. There can be no room for positivity or happiness in my world right now. STOP. Don't do this to yourself. Morgan began her usual self-chatter.

The kids looked as if they might burst, plus they also acted extremely sleepy, and Morgan wondered if they would make it up the stairs together.

'Tell Antonio good-night and kiss Nanna-Kat upstairs and wash your faces and brush your teeth.' She promised them, 'I'll be up in a matter of minutes.'

Antonio attempted to pour another glass, but Morgan raised her hand for him to stop. 'I want to be on my toes, Antonio,' she quipped. 'I've had enough and as enjoyable as it is, I need no more.'

Antonio nodded. 'You're probably right.'

'Please tell me this is not happening. What person in their right mind is out on Christmas day in blistering cold weather lurking around a house?'

'You said right mind. The monster's mind does not operate like anyone else's, and I didn't say the prints belonged to him. We must not get ahead of ourselves.'

'Bullshit, you know they do.'

Kat returned downstairs to say goodnight and shared, 'Ollie and Opal are back in my bed, but it's completely fine. We'll return home soon enough, and I enjoy having them close to me.'

Morgan knew there was nothing truly to argue about. The kids were happy. Kat was overjoyed. They may be a bit crowded, but not much. Kat kissed her daughter and gave Antonio a hug and poured a glass of water in the kitchen. 'I've enjoyed this day immensely.'

'Night, Mom.'

'Good-night, Kathleen,' Antonio added, 'And thanks again for such a splendid Christmas dinner.'

Antonio and Morgan simply sat. They looked at the flickering candles and each became lost in their own thoughts. Pictures of the past, questions about the future, but mostly they were attempting to soak in the moment and everything there was to be treasured. *Mindfulness. What a great concept. What a contemporary and often over-used word. How does one reach that simple place of clarity and mental peace?*

Morgan said under her breath, 'I'm unable to reach any place of peace until the monster disappears and it doesn't look as if that will happen any time soon with footprints scattered about in the snow.'

They fell asleep. Antonio and Morgan never made it upstairs to check out the additional bedrooms. The warmth of the fire was too comforting, too settling, too inviting and obviously too demanding for them, so they stayed; they never moved. The fire must have gone on burning ever so slowly for hours. How could anyone leave the heat of a good, wood burning fire? Antonio and Morgan apparently could not.

CHAPTER NINETEEN

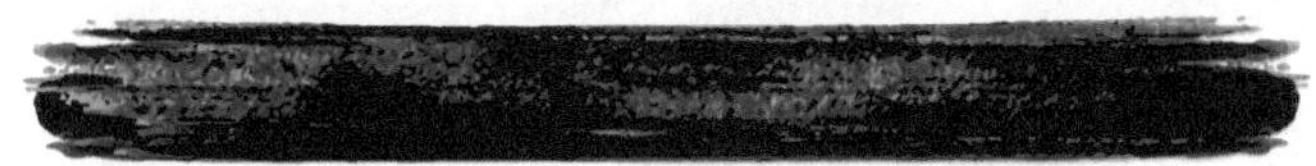

Opal shrieked. Morgan burst up from the overstuffed sofa, tossing pillows out of the way. The sun was beginning to filter soft amber and delicate peach rays through the sitting room's massive windowpanes.

Antonio spluttered, 'What the Hell? Where the Hell am I?'

He too was stupefied. Morgan ran upstairs to Opal as Kat was coming out of her bedroom with Ollie holding on to her hand. Opal was pointing to the floor in front of her mother's bedroom door. Dixie was acting curious and anxious.

A dove. A white dove. One white dove on the dark, thick wooden floorboards directly in front of Morgan's bedroom door with a broken neck. A white dove in her holiday home at Christmas – dead. *How? How could this be? Why? Oh My God.* Morgan remembered now she fell asleep…they fell asleep. She never set the alarm. *How stupid of her. How dreadfully inept. How utterly irresponsible.*

Antonio was holding Opal while Morgan paced, looking like a zombie. He snapped Morgan out of it and handed Opal to her and said, 'I need to make some phone calls in private.'

Morgan pointed him to her bedroom and directed everyone downstairs.

Shakes. Uncontrollable shaking. Chills. She kept telling herself to stop. She forbade her body to be weak. She willed the trembling to cease. It seemed to be working. Kat got the hot chocolate and coffee going. Kat couldn't speak. Enough was enough was enough days ago, weeks ago. Everyone had reached their limit of adrenalin surges and panic and by the look on each face there was nothing left to feel.

That's worse, isn't it? Not being able to feel is far worse, right? She was confused.

But Morgan was not thinking of herself. She could only imagine, fathom, the damage being done to her children. If she and her mother were incapable of taking anymore, how on Earth could they be asked to do so? She wanted out. She wanted to scoop up her family and leave immediately. Then an epiphany! That's exactly what the monster wants her to do. She would be playing right into his hands. She wasn't going anywhere and if she did what she was supposed to have done in the first place they would not be in this predicament now. The alarm system was a state of the art high-functioning system. Ash had explained to her that he purchased the best money could buy. They would be safer to remain. These thoughts were running rapidly through her head, and she was pretty pleased with herself for coming to a decent conclusion.

Morgan picked up her phone and was about to ring the monster, when Antonio reappeared, reached for it and asked, 'Who are you calling?'

She looked sheepish.

'Don't even think about it, Morgan. You haven't made one wrong move so far. Do not give that disgusting person the satisfaction. You had a restraining order put out on him, remember?'

She snarled, 'Yes, and what good did it do?'

'Right now that doesn't matter. You call him and it will undo everything you're trying hard to preserve. No. It's not fair. You're right, but please. You've come this far. Hang on and let's see this thing through.'

He held her tightly against his chest and she could feel her heart pounding rapidly.

Kat handed Morgan and Antonio cups of coffee. The children were already seated at the table with their hot chocolate and they weren't talking.

Antonio leaned into Morgan's ear, 'The cops are on the way.'

That made her laugh.

Then, what was that? What did Morgan see out of the corner of her eye? Slight footprints. The shape of at least half a foot on the lounge room floor – making their way to the spiral staircase. She almost shrieked out loud! She knew then the monster, most certainly, walked right past them in the dead of the night. *Unbelievable. Not acceptable. Not fathomable.* But to see with her own eyes, actual footprints, made her physically ill. Morgan had the usual urge to make the floors tidy, to make them shine again, but she had learned by now not to touch any evidence from any incident.

'No crimes ever seemed to be committed,' she huffed, 'only incidents.'

She called Antonio to her side and whispered to him, 'Can you see what I see?'

'You better believe it. I'm getting my camera now. Try your best to keep your family away from these spots.'

Kat, Ollie, and Opal sat in silence, looking defeated.

There was a knock at the front door, a hard sound. No doorbell ringing this time. Antonio called out, 'I'll answer it.'

Morgan mustered up the most genuine smile that she could. 'Ollie, Opal, if you climb the stairs carefully and get dressed, I'll drive everyone over to the Dae Break Café for lunch later on.'

Kat got the message and rustled the kids together. Morgan hated that they would have to pass the unfortunate dove again. Kat caught Morgan's eyes and Morgan knew she'd do her best to steer the children as far away as possible.

It was a different police officer this time. He was younger. He was broad and round. He seemed to Morgan to be most impatient. As a matter of fact, his demeanor did not mask the fact he simply didn't want to be there.

Antonio glared at the young policeman. 'You work for the people, and you have a job to do. Your job is to protect and serve.'

The police officer smirked, 'Remove a dead bird, sir? Yes, I suppose.'

Antonio flew into super alpha male form. He demanded, 'What is your full name, rank, and attending supervisor's name? You better believe I'll be entering my own report, and it will go higher than Hardin County. I'll also be sharing details and descriptions of your behavior with Downing, Carruthers, Xavier, and Worthington.'

Curiously, those words got the policeman's attention. He gained interest. 'I've heard the name Downing, not sure where or why, but I know it. Now, tell me exactly what transpired here.' He pulled out his notepad and pen.

Morgan began speaking. She didn't recognize her own voice. She stood taller and began acting as if she were in control again. She shared the story beginning with Opal's terrified scream. Then she led the officer over to the position where Morgan and Antonio saw the vague images of shoe prints on the floor.

Morgan turned to him and asked, 'Do you see those prints on the floor?'

The officer only replied, 'Nope.'

Antonio said, 'Look again. Here I have already taken a collection of photos, but no doubt you'll do the same. Stand exactly where I am standing now.'

The police officer looked like he wanted to smack Antonio in the face, but he did as he was told. Reluctantly he stated, 'I may see something, but I can't make out what it is.'

'Perhaps you need to start wearing glasses,' smirked Antonio.

Smartass, grumpy looking, lackadaisical, and most unconcerned officer responded, 'I'll get my camera, and you need to take me to the bird, too.'

He would not look at Antonio or Morgan. Pictures snapped. No words spoken. Morgan knew it was another police officer, uninterested in domestic disturbances, going through the motions and believing he was unnecessarily bothered during the holidays.

The police officer finished filling out the report and said, 'With no witnesses or any description of the intruder, rest assured, I wouldn't have hope anything is going to come out of this episode. I'll turn in the paperwork and report it to the proper people, but I wouldn't hold my breath.'

Antonio reminded him, 'Make certain it's filed with the other business that recently occurred.'

Morgan sensed the officer really didn't like to be reminded how to handle his job and he was seething right now, practically spitting.

Antonio asked, 'Aren't you forgetting something?'

He spat out, 'What?'

'There is a deceased bird upstairs on the landing. The bird is evidence and needs to be dealt with the way Hardin County deals with evidence brought about by incidents.'

Clearly agitated, the officer, put on a fake smile and said, 'Yeah, we'll deal with it.'

Antonio retrieved a couple of small plastic rubbish bags from the kitchen and said, 'No, you'll deal with it and remember, I have photos already in my camera, date and time stamped.'

The officer snatched the bags from Antonio's hand and marched upstairs.

'Unbelievable,' muttered Antonio.

Morgan sighed, 'I thought it was just me or only women, but the police officers must not have a great deal of action here at Pickwick and they, understandably, prefer it that way. I would, too.'

The officer headed towards the door announcing, 'Someone will be back in touch if we receive any further information concerning this matter. I'll let myself out.'

That was it. Antonio and Morgan mused over how much more effort would have been placed into the incident investigation had it been a human body instead of a precious little dove.

CHAPTER TWENTY

Antonio motioned Morgan into the kitchen. He poured two small glasses of a fresh, crisp, New Zealand Sauvignon Blanc. 'Don't be coy. Drink up. We both deserve this. Dreadful business this morning, but once again, Morgan, it's behind us.'

Morgan didn't need any encouragement regarding the wine. It was the phrase 'once again' that made her twitch. She was attempting to muster a little enthusiasm and a kind spirit in order to maintain some decorum for the children and her beloved mother. Her body did not respond kindly to being delivered to the mountain top of happiness and dropped back into a deep, dark abyss of madness. It was beginning to show.

Kat must have heard the police officer's quick departure, so she and Ollie and Opal came back downstairs with Dixie hard on their heels.

Ollie asked, 'Can I take Dixie for a walk?'

Opal perked up. 'May I come, too, please?

But Ollie wasn't happy, 'No, Mom, can I be alone with Dixie for a bit?'

Morgan hesitated and looked at Antonio. Then she glanced over at Opal and softly said, 'Opal, you can walk Dixie the next time.' Opal pouted the tiniest of pouts.

Morgan's voice showed concern as she advised Ollie, 'Please don't stay out long. We'll be heading to the Dae Break Café with Antonio as our guest.'

Morgan couldn't get any smiles. Faces and spirits were down-trodden. She felt powerless. Awful, disgraceful feeling. Kat and Antonio each kept a watchful eye over Ollie through the plantation shutters.

She pushed the Hollywood signs in their big, bright white lights to the dark crevasses of her mind. Once again. Morgan felt far older than her real age. That feeling needed to leave her body as quickly as it appeared.

Dixie was tucked safely inside the kitchen in her warm, cozy bed and Morgan locked the house. Everyone was piling into the Lexus. Antonio with his long, lanky legs sat in the rear seat in between Ollie and Opal. It was a funny sight, but the kids adored having him right in the middle and they were holding Antonio's hands. It was a sweet picture to observe in the rearview mirror. She began the descent down the driveway and the world looked normal. That was the first good sign. It was peaceful and bright with traces of snow amongst the leaves on the trees and flakes scattered about the hard, cold ground. The sun was providing her best efforts to grace them with her presence. It was still extremely chilly, and the ride was uncomfortably quiet. Morgan couldn't help but wonder how much her children could be mentally and emotion-ally damaged by the trauma that had descended upon them over the last few weeks. Once she returned to Memphis, she would make an appointment with a child psychologist. If there *was* something going on, any real fear or deep concern that Ollie and Opal were not sharing with her, perhaps they might share their worries with a sensitive, kind professional. Morgan would ask Kat, too, if the kids had voiced any opinions before they went to sleep last night.

The Dae Break Café was hoppin' again. Here it was the day after Christmas, but the people arrived in droves. Morgan didn't think they would get a table, but she caught the eye of the last server they had, and the hearty woman beckoned them over to a table in the corner.

'Great!' said Morgan, 'You're a super star!'

The server grinned from ear to ear and said, 'Ya'll hold on a minute and I'll be right back for your orders.'

Antonio asked Morgan, 'Where have we landed?'

Kat giggled. Good. First chuckle of the day. *Please, God, let there be more.*

Antonio was genuinely studying the blackboard and began to lick his lips. 'Mamma's cooking. Well, kids, aren't we in for a treat today?' He let out a 'Yahooo' a little louder than he anticipated and Ollie and Opal burst into fits of laughter. *Rightio. This is the atmosphere we want.*

The server came back and said, 'Lordy, everyone must be tired of bein' in their own homes and they shorely don't want no more turkey. We gonna' be servin' some meals today in this little place. What can I get ya'll to drink?'

The children ordered a hot chocolate each and lo and behold, Kat, Antonio, and Morgan asked for Blue Moon beer. They each ordered the same beverage without conferring with one another!

Antonio announced, 'We're in rhythm and that's all that counts.'

The server put her hands on her hips and said, 'Hate to disappoint, but we don't do alcohol.'

Sad faces. Morgan lightly kicked Antonio and her mother under the table and replied, 'Tomato juice all around for the adults, please.'

Ollie ordered the chicken spaghetti and as he did, he explained to their server, 'I've never heard of such a thing, but I just have to try it and I hope I like it.'

The server's belly was bouncing up and down as she chuckled.

Opal asked, 'May I have some chicken and dumplings, please? And, please may I try your purple peas because I love that colour and I might like them a lot. I do not like green peas.'

The server was getting even more tickled. Kat went for a small vegetable plate and said, 'I'm looking forward to lima beans, mashed 'taters,' and fried okra.'

Antonio motioned to Morgan and she eagerly ordered 'Two serves of fried green tomatoes, devilled eggs, and cabbage, please'.

Her lunch order cracked Antonio up and he smirked, 'Remind me not to sleep anywhere in your vicinity tonight.'

More giggles. Antonio went for the country fried steak, mashed taters, fried okra, and green beans *and* mac & cheese.

Opal piped up and said, 'Oh, Mommy, we forgot about the mac & cheese.' Ollie agreed, 'Yeah, Mom.'

Morgan ordered one small side plate they could share. 'Whew!' the server retorted, 'Ya'll must not have eaten much fo' Christmas. This order's gonna be enuff fo' a small army!'

Their table roared with laughter and the people seated next to them did, too.

Morgan, Kat, and Antonio made small talk while the children took in the scenery of the café and its Christmas decorations. There were plenty of lively conversations occurring in one small place. Morgan thought the children looked especially relaxed, but that was probably because they were away from the house. Perhaps she should pack their belongings and leave sooner rather than later. Perhaps not. She needed to make more happy memories for this year's Christmas in Ash's home - nothing bad could happen there again. It was against all odds. She felt her mood lifting and a calmness landed over her.

Servers surrounded the big, family table with plates coming in from every direction. A little clanging and banging and lunch was delivered. Not one single item missed or overlooked. Pure country cooking joy.

Exclamations of goodness and Ollie elatedly exclaimed, 'The chicken spaghetti is the best spaghetti in the whole, wide world.'

Opal, however, was not sold on her purple hull peas. 'Mom, the colour doesn't matter because they taste the same as green ones.' Nope. Apparently, peas taste like peas no matter the colour.

Antonio stretched back with his arms over his head. 'I have discovered true heaven and it resides in the country.'

It was turning into an extremely pleasant afternoon at Pickwick Lake.

The server came back and cleared the plates. She suggested, 'No one can leave without trying Dae Break Café desserts.'

Kat, Morgan, and Antonio groaned with their hands motioning 'No,' but Ollie and Opal were keen.

Opal chirped, 'Cherry pie for me, please.'

Ollie chimed in, 'Please may I try a big piece of pecan pie?'

'Ice cream on top, too, please?' Opal pleaded.

And their sweet server asked them with a wink, 'Does pie come any other way?'

Good Lord. My kids might burst on the way back home.

Dessert devoured, well, almost. Opal couldn't finish and Ollie almost looked a bit ill, but he seemed happy. The adults finished their coffees.

As they paid their bill, Morgan stepped over to the server and said, 'Thank you. You truly made our day, our holiday here. You've been an absolute delight.'

She slipped an additional $50.00 note in her hand and said, 'Merry Christmas.'

The server hugged her. It was a big hug and it felt fine.

Antonio led the passengers in Christmas carols on the way back home. *Normal. Normal. Normal. Smile. Act. Encourage small talk. Normal things.* This was Morgan's mantra on the ride back to Ash's house. They ascended the long, winding, and spectacular driveway when Kat noticed a car at the top of the drive.

'Look, a man is standing outside a car next to the driver's side, checking his phone.'

'Ash,' Morgan exclaimed, 'Ash!'

Morgan knew instantly her mother thought she sounded a bit more excited than maybe she should. She had barely placed the car in park and didn't truly pull appropriately into the garage. She was hurried and popped out of the car and ran towards Ash. She wasn't thinking. She felt the gaze of her mother's eyes watching carefully and regained a bit of composure, stopped running, and simply put her hands up for a hug and to welcome Ash.

Morgan giggled, 'I'm welcoming you to your own home, Ash. How does that feel because it feels especially foreign to me!'

Everyone came in closer.

The kids were the first to surround Ash. 'Oh, our Christmas has been wonderful and we love our beds so much!'

Only when they slept in them.

Antonio escorted Kat up to Ash and properly introduced her. Ash bent over to give Kat's cheek a slight kiss and declared, 'How enormously pleased I am to meet you.'

'It's lovely to finally meet you in person, too.'

Morgan ushered everyone inside and took their coats, their wraps, their scarves, and hats and placed them on hooks in the mud room.

Ash commented, 'The home looks warm and welcoming and very much in the Christmas spirit.'

Opal popped her head around the corner and said 'Yes, everything was wonderful until the bird died.'

Ash looked at Morgan. He had been driving for almost two and a half hours and he had spoken to no one. He had rather planned it that way. He shot Morgan a fast look with a question in his eyes.

'Opal, you are absolutely correct,' Morgan replied, 'but let's not think of that now, and remember, it's your turn to take Dixie for a stroll. Nanna-Kat told me she felt like a brisk walk, too.'

Kat understood and grabbed her coat.

That changed the subject. Dixie heard her name and even brought the lead over for Morgan to clip it on. 'Smart Dixie,' Morgan quipped and out they went.

Morgan was about to say stay near the house, but instead Opal announced, 'I know, I know, we won't go far.'

Still, she couldn't move away from the windows and observed her gals closely while Ollie headed to his room to change clothes.

Antonio was already at the bar, reaching for red wine glasses, white wine glasses, champagne glasses, and stocky, bold cocktail glasses. He was busying himself and putting ice in the stainless-steel bucket but *also* keeping an eye out for Dixie's walkers. This host was going to be prepared for a variety of beverage orders. Antonio seemed just as thrilled to see Ash, and maybe, a tad bit relieved.

Morgan appeared calm and confident, relaxed, and grateful, too. She wanted her mom to like her attorney, but Kat seemed a bit stand-offish when Ash arrived. Morgan noticed herself staring at Ash...but with a great deal of respect. She liked looking at Ash's eyes as they were kind and gentle and filled with stories. She hoped her mom would see what she saw in his eyes – compassion and kindness. This was her attorney and the only seriously important concern was that Ash perform a proper job representing her and Kat's grandchildren. That's all that mattered to Morgan and she presumed that's what mattered to her mom the most.

Morgan sighed comfortably and inwardly as Opal and Kat returned to the warmth of the home with Dixie panting by their sides and settling right in the middle of the excitement. Dixie was such a lovely little being. She never demanded much - only heaps of love, fresh food and water, and yummy treats every now and then. She just had an 'I was put here on this Earth to be loved' look about her!

Ollie excitedly suggested to Opal, 'Let's start our new puzzle!'

'That's a great idea!'

Morgan sat them at a tall square table with high, comfortable bar stools featured at the opposite end of the main sitting lounge. It was perfect because it was a big and wide space for the puzzle and the children could chat away as much as they liked while the adults enjoyed their surroundings. It was a fabulous home with very clever and well-designed spaces.

Kids settled and happy. Dixie curled up in a little furry ball in her bed. Antonio began taking drink orders. He was right on top of his game. Ash looked concerned, but Morgan almost always thought Ash looked worried because it was his natural, resting face.

Antonio raised his hand. 'Now, I'm not pushing, but this is a special moment because we're all together and I think we should begin, at least, with a glass of cold French Champagne.'

'I'll probably have only one, but that sounds delightful to me,' Kat said.

Antonio popped the cork and the bubbles began flowing. Morgan was observing. *I could easily live like this surrounded by people I love and respect.*

The afternoon lingered with small talk and the brilliant sun melted away any traces of snow or footprints. Kat even seemed to relax and enjoyed conversing with Ash. Morgan knew, too, Kat had always had a soft spot for Antonio. She was about to get up and pour a tiny bit more of the bubbles, but Antonio beat her to it.

'Could we speak privately? I'd like to have a word,' Ash asked Morgan.

Kat heard him. Morgan began to wonder if Ash had been hoping since the moment he arrived if he could have a word. If so, he had been a superbly patient man because he had arrived hours earlier.

Morgan responded, 'Certainly.'

Kat piped up, 'Antonio is going to help me prepare a very light dinner for the evening with an abundance of tasty leftovers.'

Antonio raised his glass. 'Absolutely.'

CHAPTER TWENTY-ONE

Ash led Morgan to his study. She hadn't been in this part of his house before and she gasped when Ash opened the double doors to the paneled room lined with bookshelves from the ceiling to the floor and the exquisite light fixtures, two of them, hanging from the twenty-foot ceiling. The room smelled of wonderful old leather. Ash gathered firewood from a tall and stately antique brass box in the corner and lit a fire for them. The crackling sound, the dancing flames, and the sheer size of the fireplace left her in awe. Ash looked most comfortable in this room. He pointed to a paprika coloured upholstered chair with thick, wooden arms and said, 'Please, have a seat.' Ash looked as tired as Morgan felt.

He began by saying, 'I'm not going to kid you. This monster of yours likes to lay traps. He's been in front of the cops in the East Memphis precinct and in Hardin County of all places sharing a description of you that is less than desirable or kind. Most cops, Morgan, see through people like this but, there are always one or two willing to listen, bend a few rules because they think they're helping a poor bloke who's been deserted by his dirty, double-timing, evil wife. We know the truth. That's what matters the most. In the meantime, the priority remains to keep you and the children safe. That has been top of the list since we first met.'

Morgan sat with her ankles crossed, continued to sip tiny amounts of her champagne, and listened.

'What I would like from you, if you are up to it, is to hear your story – your version of the melt-down of your marriage from your lips, from your perspective. If you want to share your entire life's story that's perfectly fine with me. You decide where you would like to begin and end with the story of your marriage. From what has already transpired it is important, to me, that I get a better sense of the monster. No one knows him better than you.'

Morgan found herself shaking again - her entire body trembling. *Why?* She was certainly not being threatened in any way. She was with a friend, an educated man, who had helped her tremendously and was fighting for her.

Ash saw her body physically trembling. He got up from his chair, came around his desk, and gathered a nice, dark grey woolen throw that was draped over the top of his office sofa and placed it around her shoulders.

Morgan thanked him and sighed. 'I want to share. I do. I want to purge myself of many stories, but even when I replay them in my mind, I begin to feel physically ill.'

Ash softly commented, 'You don't have to divulge every single instance today. We can do this over days in separate blocks of time. This, in the end, will help you, too. I'm not medically trained or sophisticated in that area as you know, but I do know from personal experience that bottling sad or unsettling memories inside can be harmful in more ways than one.'

Morgan nodded her head in agreement. She unconsciously looked down at her empty glass.

Ash pointed, 'Let me have that and I'll return shortly.'

He returned with a bottle of Australian Pikes Traditionale Reisling on ice and two fresh wine glasses. 'You're understandably very emotional, so take this slowly. I meant the wine, not your story - either way, I'm not telling you what to do. You can consume the entire bottle if you wish. This is my feeble attempt at being the wise one.' He smiled tenderly.

'Thank you.' Morgan took the glass from his hand and slowly began to recall.

'Snippets, little pieces of incidents or parts of a day enter my head at the strangest times and once the episode starts re-playing, it is hard for me, exceedingly difficult, to get it to stop. This, Ash, is the thing I work on most every day for myself and for my children.'

'I think you should be commended for recognizing that fact.'

'The bizarre aspect is that I truly can't remember how most arguments began, only certain ones. How words can escalate into the monster becoming physical with me is quite astonishing. Whenever these episodes happened it was as if I were watching it happen to someone else. I think I really did black out the harshest memories.'

'In all likelihood that's exactly what you did. This is the way your mind and body fights to survive. You know, Morgan, it would never hurt you to talk to someone specialising in this field. No one would think less of you. It might help tremendously.'

'I'm definitely getting counselling for my children. Once I get Ollie and Opal set up with a person who might be able to help them, I may investigate seeing someone myself.'

Her body was not shaking as hard as before. The wrap Ash had placed on her shoulders seemed to help, but Morgan knew instinctively her body was not responding to any temperature. It was reacting to the thoughts and images conjured in her head while recalling the monster and his evil tricks.

Morgan drank a sip of white crisp, cold wine and thought it was close to perfect.

She began to speak slowly. 'Ash, I thought it was time that Ollie and Opal were part of a real family again. That is the least these two precious children of mine deserved. After the first divorce, their father moved on quickly and not long after, began having more children. It was a terribly challenging time. I was young when I had them, but I never wanted to terminate a pregnancy. I wanted Ollie. Then, I planned Opal to prove to myself and the world that we were a stable and connected little family. It was never going to work. We were both too young. Attempting to raise Ollie and Opal alone was the single hardest job I had ever done in my entire life. Getting out of a loveless and unhappy marriage is one thing but raising two young ones under the age of five is outrageously difficult. I met a man. I met a man who appeared kind. He did not seem especially keen to have stepchildren, but he was nice to them when we first met. He talked with them, bought them treats from time to time, but he never genuinely wanted to be with Ollie and Opal unless I was around. Ash, there were all sorts of triggers that I should have noticed and paid attention to, but I looked the other way. I made that choice, too, didn't I? Putting my head in the sand put us right in the middle of this mess. I don't know how long their little lives might be impacted by these dreadful scenes.'

Morgan felt deep pain, sadness, and shame.

Ash gently replied, 'I've never met a person...yet...who has made no mistakes.'

'My closest friends were trying to warn me away. I heard multiple horror stories, but I'd never seen that side of the monster and there was no way I was going to believe any of them. Looking back, now I believe every story that passed my ears prior to our marriage must have been true. His actions then mirrored most of his antics now – scary, threatening, controlling, evil, and violent. I distinctly remember we had discussed the fact I had a few more college courses I needed to complete to finish my bachelor's degree. I recall the monster telling me to return to college as soon as I could because the degree would increase my earning power, and he said he would like that. The monster was constantly reminding me how much Ollie and Opal were costing him, so I made the necessary arrangements and entered the local university. I was proud. I soared through the first semesters taking business and management classes, working, trying to keep a proper home, and looking after my children. It felt as if I were thriving.' She paused and took a breath.

'I'm not saying anything about it was easy. I remember, too, the monster didn't want me returning home from class, discussing anything concerning my studies. He instructed those conversations were off limits in our home. Third semester came around, it was the initial stages, and I was sitting in the middle towards the front of class listening to the professor. I was taking microeconomics. I had already surprised myself and aced macroeconomics. Suddenly, the classroom door swings wide open, the professor was in the middle of his lecture, the monster parades in dressed in his work suit and tie, walks over to my desk, looking at no one but me, instructs me to collect my books, pick up my briefcase, and announced we would be heading home. The students were staring with their mouths wide open. The professor was shouting, "Excuse me, excuse me, I'm conducting a class." The monster shouted back, "Go right ahead. You're one student down." I recall he was squeezing my right arm tightly. I was barely managing to hold on to my briefcase and my books. Once outside, the monster turned me towards him with the look I am all too familiar with now and said, "I didn't marry you to become your baby-sitter. You're finished."

By this time, he was screaming in the parking lot like the mad man he is, "You're through. Do you understand me?" I remember telling him he was hurting me and to let go. He pushed me towards the car. We got in. We drove home in silence. And when we entered the home, I was already worried because Ollie and Opal had been left alone, he said, "See? I told you I would bring your mother home. Now she can cook dinner for us." As always, I tried not to scare the children. I kept my voice low, put my things away, changed clothes and went downstairs to make a meal.'

Tears were streaming down her cheeks, but she pressed on. 'We had discussed school, Ash. We had several conversations regarding college before I committed to the task and then...in a heartbeat, on a whim...he forgets what words had passed between us and imagines all sorts of things in his head. No doubt he thought I was out having an affair and may have even been completely surprised to find me in class. He thought the worst of most people except for his mother.' Morgan's body was outwardly shaking again.

'Take a break and have more wine if you like. Can I get you anything? I'm going to go check on Antonio and Kat and have a word.'

Morgan shook her head.

———

Antonio and Kat had fixed an enticing buffet that spread along the kitchen countertop. They were both in great spirits.

Ollie and Opal grabbed Ash's hands. 'Come and see how well we are doing with the puzzle. It's really big and it may take us years to finish.'

Ash couldn't help but laugh and eagerly walked over to the table. 'By golly, you are two little strategists. You've worked a storm out of one corner.' He seemed most impressed by their efforts.

Their little blue eyes beamed right back at him with the broadest smiles.

Ash said, 'No, sir, this is not going to take you years. You'll have this puzzle completed before you know it!'

They both jumped up and down and clapped their hands together.

Kat quietly asked, 'Is Morgan okay?'

Ash thought it best to be truthful and explain what information he was seeking at present. Kat immediately looked concerned. 'So much pain, Ash. It's going to take a lot out of her reliving it again.'

'I understand, perhaps not how monumentally dire the situation has been, but I assure you we'll be working through bits and pieces, not the entire chunk at once.'

'Chunk, one big, fat chunk of my daughter's life fed to the monster. You don't get pieces of your life back, but you do learn how to maneuver towards a better and healthier future. My daughter will be stronger than ever once she moves beyond this horrifying time she and the children have endured.'

Kat touched Ash on his elbow. 'If you both want to take a break there are goodies available to nibble on. Antonio and I decided we would do a bit of grazing tonight. Whenever we feel a bit peckish, we're heading to the buffet. Ollie and Opal have already eaten properly. I'm going to wait a while before I offer desserts.'

Ash realized he hadn't eaten a thing the entire day. 'Suddenly, I'm ravenous, Kat.'

He went back into his study and announced, 'Come and let's grab a bite.'

Morgan stared, 'I couldn't possibly eat.'

'I think you'll change your mind once you see what Kat and Antonio have prepared for everyone. It looks sumptuous!'

CHAPTER TWENTY-TWO

What a sight to behold! A Christmas dining experience two days in a row, but this sampling was very relaxed and casually presented.

Morgan was smiling again. 'What a divine job you've done! Surprisingly, she began filling a plate with turkey and cranberry sauce and Dijon mustard. She added a few raw veggies and sat down at the corner kitchen table again. This time Ash joined her with a full dinner plate that Kat had insisted on preparing. Antonio poured more wine for Ash and Morgan, acting like the maître d, then he and Kat slipped into the sitting room. Dixie sat calmly below the two diners looking from side to side. She was extremely polite when it came to begging. She had no doubt that one of the humans sitting above her would drop a nice, juicy, tender bit of turkey. It always happened.

Morgan felt more relaxed and the colour was returning to her cheeks.

She turned towards Ash. 'Why is the monster able to get away with everything he does to me? Why hasn't anyone been able to stop him? We all know too well there is a restraining order against him, yet he still does as he pleases.'

Ash sat silent for a moment. Then he looked at Morgan directly in her eyes. 'It's a difficult job for police when there are no fingerprints or witnesses. The only reason I knew about the incident on Christmas Eve is because I have a friend, a good cop inside of the East Precinct. I advised him if any report came through their computers and your name appeared, to please contact me. He conducts simple searches for me every day or recently, every hour, and contacts a member of my team. I was angry beyond description and I wanted so terribly to communicate with you, but I knew you were trying to manage a normal Christmas. I could not stay away today.

Morgan thought Ash's face looked genuinely concerned as he stopped to take a sip of his wine.

'These local guys do not deal with enormous crime and many of the good, ole boys want to postpone handling anything that is not serious until after New Year's Day. I'm sorry, Morgan. It's the way of most small towns across America. Police officers steer clear of domestic issues if they can. They certainly don't want to put energy into them. Emotions run high. People want to press charges. Couples kiss and make up and cases get dropped. It happens time and time again.'

'Not good enough,' Morgan replied. 'And this case is not getting dropped. He was in the house, Ash - your house. Antonio and I saw what we knew to be images of shoe prints on your floor, leading up to the bedroom. It's not right. He had the balls to enter the house and walk right past us. Oh, God, if he got a good look at Antonio, you better believe he'll be using him against me any way he can. He killed a precious being and left it at my bedroom door. How did he know that is where I slept and not my mother?' Her voice was high and filled with a combination of rage and fear.

'Please try and stay calm. He probably had already stuck his head in the other bedrooms and realized the one at the end of the hall was for you or for you both.'

The thought of the monster slithering past them while they slept made Morgan squirm.

Poor, precious dove.

'Try your best not to think of it and if you do, try to replace the sad image with a positive, happy one.'

Morgan did the eye-roll thing. 'I don't have any energy left to be angry. I feel depleted of heart, spirit, and soul. That's it. I feel empty. I'm walking around with nothing to give.'

Ash retorted, 'Nonsense...you have more left to give in your little finger than most people on the planet.'

Antonio heard the conversation as he strolled back into the kitchen. 'Oh yeah, essence, baby, the essence of Morgan will be back in no time.'

Morgan groaned as Antonio laughed!

She cleared their plates and washed and tidied the kitchen.

Ash commented, 'How wonderful it is to have life at the Pickwick House.'

Morgan hesitated, but she wished to know more about this amazing man. *So, how will I know unless I ask?*

CHAPTER TWENTY-THREE

Morgan turned as she was wiping the kitchen countertops. 'Ash, where is your family? What happened? Do you mind telling me?'

Ash looked bemused. 'No, not at all. It's a fairly regular story. Still makes me sad, nonetheless, but it is nothing out of the ordinary. Remember though I need to hear yours; we are not here to talk about me.'

'Well, c'mon then – be fair. Plus, I need a bit of a break.'

Morgan was seated back at the popular kitchen table and Ash took another sip of his wine.

'Morgan, she was beautiful. She was the single most gorgeous woman I had ever laid eyes upon in my entire life. She was tall, her arms and legs were lanky, and I would later discover she was not comfortable within her own body. She said she had felt awkward as a young girl and was continuously teased due to her height. She was a red head, too, but the red turned more strawberry as she grew older, and her freckles only came out when the sun was at its harshest. The way she moved was what attracted me to her in the first place and the way she tilted her face when she listened to me.'

Ash was staring at his wine glass and closed his eyes for a moment. 'Morgan, she was exquisite, and she wouldn't agree with me, but she's still incredibly special today. Her eyes are like no others. They are pale blue and with her pink-red hair she had an ethereal look about her. Striking. That's probably the best word I can construct. You were either drawn to her or she intimidated the Hell out of you. I was captivated and once in her fold I never wanted to leave. We were young, too. We were total strangers attending a law conference at the Memphis Peabody Hotel. The place was packed. There was much to be accomplished in two short days. We were seated at the same table. Most law firms had enough representation whereby they could fill a table of ten, or two tables of ten, or more. We were both representing small firms and only starting our careers. As you know the Continental Ballroom is huge and attorneys from all over the South were packed in like sardines. When I first glanced at her, when she sat across from me, and introduced herself, I couldn't speak. I thanked the Lord, then I tried to regain my composure. I'm not shy. I am not easily intim- idated, but a sophisticated, gorgeous woman had been assigned to sit across from me at our table. I kept my cool. I was myself. I was kind. I behaved as any proper gentleman would do and that's what she noticed. I wasn't gushing - wasn't falling all over her. God only knows I wanted to. At the conclusion of the first session when people got up to stretch their legs, it was she who came to me, sat in the empty chair next to me, introduced herself, and handed me her business card. We trotted off to have a cup of tea and water and by the end of the day she had agreed to dine with me that evening. My life changed for the better. I was the most fortunate man on Earth and I loved her with every part of me. Eight months later we were married.'

Morgan found herself enthralled and she was imagining the two young lovers at the Peabody Hotel. She smiled at Ash. 'What was her name?'

'Alexandria,' Ash said looking off in the distance, 'but everyone called her Alex.'

Alex and Ash – how lovely.

'Where is she now? What happened? Do you have children? How long were you married?'

Ash put his hands up in the air! 'Whoa, now, only an hour or so ago I was inviting you to share your past, but I didn't bombard you with questions.'

'Sorry, I'm really interested. You are an extremely kind man, Samuel Ashley Downing, and I cannot perceive how anyone would want to leave your...essence.'

They both laughed like little kids.

Antonio must have heard the childlike laughter and thought it might be a suitable time to reenter the kitchen. He took it upon himself to top up their glasses. Kat followed and fixed a small dessert that Ollie and Opal could enjoy at the kitchen bar.

You could see faces and bodies were winding down and the house had a certain feel to it as if it were yawning, too.

Antonio called for Dixie and she immediately hopped up and started doing her little Dixie dance. She has enjoyed copious amounts of attention from everyone these last few weeks. She might not ever be the same again. How grand is it that people simply take care of business and help when and if they can.

Morgan announced, 'Hey everybody, I cannot remember the last time Dixie and I traipsed outside together. Tomorrow will be my day to show my fur baby around Pickwick.'

Laughter erupted and Kat told her grandchildren to tell everyone 'Good night.'

Ash received big hugs and a thank you from both children. When Antonio came back in the rear door, he was almost tackled. Ollie ran over to his mother and held on tight this night, followed by Opal and her big smooches.

Ollie commented with a frown. 'Yuck, Opal. Your kisses are too loud!'

Morgan popped their little bottoms, 'Sweet dreams, my precious cherubs.'

Both replied, 'Sweet dreams, Mom.' Kat and the kids climbed the stairs and disappeared into their bedrooms while Dixie seemed to bark 'Wait for me!'

Antonio stood up and announced, 'Okay, you two. I want a chance to chat with you both and share a glass, but I'm going to be heading to bed soon. By the way, Ash, the copper here this morning really had a snarly attitude and was no more interested in investigating than the man in the moon.'

Ash shook his head. 'So, I've heard.'

Antonio continued. 'Opal was completely distraught and it was most disconcerting that the monster invaded your house.'

Ash nodded again.

It certainly seemed to Morgan that Antonio needed to debrief. He looked like he desperately wanted to purge the madness he witnessed and have someone listen to him because it had indeed been an unusually nasty morning.

Ash and Morgan encouraged Antonio to rave on because it was the exact medicine he needed. *When people's lives are turned upside down and drama and trauma become the norm – that's when people must voice whatever they're feeling deep, down inside or they lose a bit of their humanity.*

Antonio looked better, refreshed, after he replayed the early hours of the morning and stated, 'My, I got the toxic, sinister poison out of my system. It feels as though I've released the pain and the ugliness.'

Then he asked Ash, 'You're staying tonight, too, right? I mean, it *is* your house.' Morgan, Ash, and Antonio burst out laughing again.

Ash stood up, scratching his head. 'Well, I came to pay Morgan a necessary visit, but I hadn't thought beyond my original plan.'

'I was in that very same boat only a day ago, Ash.'

More chuckles. Ash was going on about work he needed to do at his computer and for Antonio to take any bedroom upstairs he wanted.

Morgan looked at them both and smirked, 'Except for the ones that are currently claimed!'

Antonio kissed Morgan on her forehead and pointed upstairs to the lovely Dixie looking longingly downstairs at the gang. Morgan knew where Dixie would be sleeping tonight. Antonio sauntered up the stairs for the evening.

Ash smiled over at Morgan. 'Did you select this wine?'

'As a matter of fact, I did. I'm a huge, unapologetic fan of big, bold Australian reds. They're much softer than they used to be. I enjoy how they taste and feel in my mouth.'

'I'm most impressed and inclined to agree. I think I'll finish the evening with one more glass. How about you?'

Morgan couldn't produce a real reason why she shouldn't, so she held out her glass. 'Yes, please.'

Then Ash's blue eyes regarded Morgan and he asked, 'Are there any other moments in your marriage which struck you as especially bizarre that you might want to share with me now?'

Morgan felt her tummy tighten. 'There are several but...there is *one* evening, Ash. Parties were terribly difficult for us. The monster never felt comfortable in crowds, and I quickly learned after our marriage that he suffered frequently from panic attacks. As a matter of fact, everything about the man I thought I knew changed after we said the words 'I do'. The vows we spoke held no meaning. I couldn't hold up my end of the bargain because of the person he revealed himself to be. He couldn't keep up the façade once the ceremony was over. We were truly tragically and forever doomed. Anyway, I brought several dear close friends into the marriage. He brought one so-called friend, but he talked down to him, and he talked behind the guy's back, so I have no real clue why they referred to each other as friends. The monster trusted no one, including me, or especially me.

Morgan felt her grip on her wine glass tightening and she drank from it. My friends had especially nice homes in Germantown, and they were well established so there was always a reason for a celebration. The sweetest part about my closest friends is that they didn't approve or willingly accept that I chose the monster, but they did their best to make him feel a big part of their lives, too. They did a brilliant job to be certain. Once he and I were married the monster was in the fold of the gang.'

Morgan took a deep breath, 'I cannot tell you what started the argument. I've mentioned before that I can't recall most fights we had or the motivation behind them. We attended lots of parties. I began to dread them because they ended the same way. He would become angry. He would accuse me of drinking too much. More than likely, I had. As much as you may not believe it, I prefer people in smaller groups, too. I would normally connect with an old friend, male or female, and chat away the night. The nights I chose an old male friend to chat with were problematic. The moment the monster felt the slightest twang of insecurity or jealousy or whatever uncomfortable feeling he was experiencing he would rev it up.'

'What do you mean by rev it up'?

'Well,' Morgan continued, 'He would become louder, talk faster, stand taller, dance more, grab any females standing next to him, and pull them closer and it got to the point that he would forget I was there – didn't remember he had a wife. I'm not talking about kissing or sex, but he would choose to completely ignore me. Now, most of the males I chatted with knew him and a bit of our history and they tried to be friends with him, but the monster, I later observed, made no new real friends.' Morgan shuddered.

'He wouldn't allow anyone in public or at a private party to see what he was really like at home, so the moment he was up to his ears and had had enough of me enjoying a conversation or smiling too much, laughing or relaxing, feeling comfortable in my own skin, he would bend over, tell me to say good-bye to our host and to do so immediately. Those would be his last words I heard prior to departing every party we ever attended.'

'Did you comply?'

'Most certainly. I knew what it was going to be like once we arrived home. I never wanted to create a scene or a public ruckus either, however, there was no reason for him to behave that way. I never, ever played around on him. I was the one who desperately wanted my kids to have a family again. I didn't marry this man to run around and cheat on him. Since the first day of our marriage, I believe those were the thoughts he was having about me. Now I know he was so terribly insecure, mentally and emotionally ill, that he couldn't fathom how anyone could love him, so he pushed people away - everyone - except for his mother.'

Morgan sipped more of her big, bold wine.

'This particular weekend my children were with their father, and they were away until Sunday afternoon and we had attended another party. The monster said nothing on the drive home. We got inside and he threw his keys onto the tiled kitchen countertop, and I remember they made a crashing noise. Then he screamed, "Why do you always do this to me? Why are you so Hell bent on making a fool out of me? Why? Why? Why? If I ever see you touch another man on the arm...the shoulder...anywhere, I'll cut your hands off! Answer me, Damnit. Why do you do what you do?" This is when I became accustomed to the new look – the different face. This is when his voice went up an octave and his eyes looked like they belonged to someone else. The face, the frothing at the mouth, the glazed eyes, became the 'other person' who lived in the same house with us. That time he picked me up. He's tall, you know. He lifted me above his head with his arms straight out and begin turning around in a circle as fast as his feet would move. He was screaming how much he hated me and yelled he was going to make certain that I never did that again.' Morgan felt her body tremble.

'The screaming, the twirling, it seemed to last for hours. I know it didn't, but I was holding on for dear life to the top of his shoulders and the ceiling fan was on, I do remember that, and I was thinking my head was going to be sliced any minute. I was trying my best not to scream. My screams only ignited more anger. I was crying - pleading with him to please put me down. The only reason he did was because he became exhausted, and he dumped me on the rug below. The sofa was there, but he dropped me like a rag doll on the floor. I ran to the bedroom. I never locked the door because he gets into any space he wants to enter. I learned the only way to deal with his other side was to let it run its course. He had to cry, moan, scream, pitch a fit, hit his head against a door, or put his fist into a wall and talk incessantly until he had no more gas. I became familiar with this process within thirty days of our marriage. After his mad and insane performance, he would fall asleep across the bed, and I would finally...breathe.'

Morgan's hands were visibly trembling. 'Sometime in the middle of the night, without fail, he would say he was sorry, and he would cover my face and my lips with kisses, but mostly he wanted to hold me while he was in the fetal position. This was well and truly 'the process'. Not too many months later, the apologies stopped, the waking in the middle of the night asking me what had happened, ceased, too. He developed into one angry, sorted machine and you did not want to stand in his way. There was a point where I thought he tried his best to temper these episodes when Ollie and Opal were with us, but that effort was too hard. When a person is mentally unstable or has a personality disorder, they're not really in control, are they?'

'Morgan, does he have a personality disorder?'

'That's what the psychiatrist at St. Frances Hospital told us and the monster became enraged and stood up and shouted to the doctor, "How dare you utter those words in front of my wife?" That was the last time he or I visited the doctor in his office. He was a kind and caring man and rang me a week later to check on me. I don't think he was supposed to do that, Ash, and I do believe the doctor would have hung up the phone had the monster answered. He pleaded with me to get him help. He understood if my husband was not pleased with his efforts or his bedside manner, but stressed it was most urgent to seek help from another doctor. Then he said to please consider carefully what he had told me and that it could be a matter of life or death if I did not. Whose life? Whose death? I often wondered what he meant, but I certainly know now.'

Ash looked at Morgan differently. Morgan realized Ash was studying her face while she was seriously hurting recalling the trauma – no doubt the pain was showing. She felt Ash was going to push her to go further, but he must have decided against it. She had returned to her past and it was not a pretty picture. She suddenly perceived the room as heavy and dark.

Morgan knew as much as she felt anger and fear towards the monster, she realised she must have a bit of compassion left in there, albeit diminishing, because she was smart enough to know the monster was seriously ill. Seriously ill human beings can still inflict an incredible amount of damage. Morgan's deepest desire was to continue to keep her children safe and she believed Ash thoroughly understood.

Ash sighed a deep breath. 'Thank you, Morgan, for your brutal honesty. I do think you signed up for a marriage you didn't ask for or even expect. Let's try to get this divorce finalized as soon as humanly possible and get you and Ollie and Opal to a healthy, happy place.'

Morgan tried to manage a smile. 'I'm all for that, Ash. Why do I suddenly feel as if I've been hit by a Mack truck?'

Ash gazed at Morgan sincerely. 'That's what dredging up ghosts can do. Now, I bid you good night and I assure you every crevice, front, back, sliding door, and the garage has been securely locked. Since the alarm is turned on and the house monitored, please remember, don't open the back door for Dixie in the morning until you've turned it off or the racket may give Kat a heart attack – any of us actually!'

'Rightio, Ash. Thanks for that reminder. Good night.'

As Morgan dragged herself up the intimidating staircase, she remembered she had barely noticed her phone the entire day. Heaven again.

CHAPTER TWENTY-FOUR

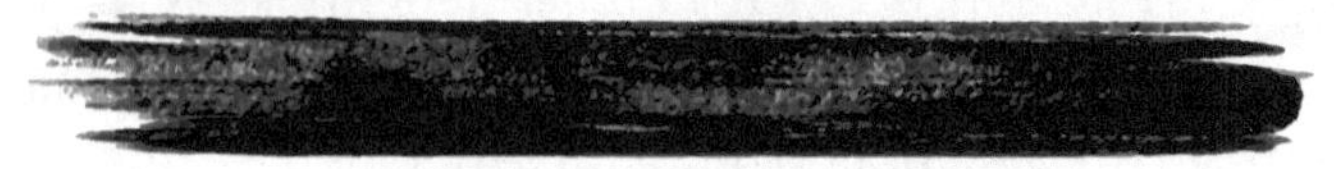

The house guests slept like babies, each and every one. Morgan was awakened by Dixie scratching on Antonio's door.

'Oh,' she yawned, 'That can't be good.' She pulled herself out of the oversized, luxurious, dreamy bed, slung on her dressing robe and cracked open the door to Antonio's room. She heard deep breaths and copious amounts of snoring and that made her snicker. She collected Dixie in her arms, travelled down the winding staircase, and right before grabbing Dixie's lead and her heavy coat, remembered the alarm.

'Well done!' she exclaimed aloud and Dixie wagged her fat, poofy tail. Morgan and Dixie went out the back door together. She took her furry family member down the stairs of the deck to the right, then back to the left, over a little ridge and they just stood there, the two of them staring out into nowhere. 'Sweet Dixie, I could get used to this. I never knew I would enjoy lakeside country living, but I'm growing very accustomed to this place.'

Dixie sat on the cold, crispy leaves and looked as if she had approved of Morgan's words and agreed with her.

A crackling sound. What was that? Morgan looked at the bottom of the ridge and there he was. Just like that. The monster was standing tall in a deep, black overcoat with one hand in his pocket and the other holding...*whaaat? The briefcase? What in the Hell is he doing out in the middle of the woods with his briefcase? Who does this sort of thing?* And he was staring. He stood there and gazed, not moving an inch. Dixie stood up. She must have seen him, too, even though it was a substantial distance. Dixie was managing a low, deep growl. *Can dogs recognize faces from that far? Did her tiny, button nose pick up his scent? I don't know – I'm not sure.* Dixie appeared frozen, too.

Morgan decided not to shift her feet. She made a conscious decision to stand firm. She was not going to scream or make a fuss as she was certain this is exactly what he expected her to do. She stared, too. She glared back. She didn't do anything nasty or alarming but remained stationary. In a flash, he was gone – vanished. She searched beyond him and looked east and west. No person in a black overcoat to be seen. Okay. *Had I imagined him? No, I had not.* She has been married to him long enough to know and recognize his silhouette. This time Morgan would not share the sighting. This time she would not tell a soul, not even Lee. Upsetting Morgan was the game and pushing his limits on the restraining order was the one thing he enjoyed most. Calling the police, telling anyone, has never brought about any change thus far. He did not care for the government. He did not care for rules. At least, as she had often said, no written rules pertained to him. She would leave this alone and not mention a word. Morgan would, however, make a fast cup of coffee, run upstairs, and write down what she saw, or what she thought she saw. *No, damnit, I know that was him.* In any event, Morgan would jot down her version of the morning in her private journal - just in case.

Dixie and Morgan walked up the slight hill back to the wooden deck and Morgan thought somehow, someway she had just waged a war and won. She did not back down from the monster. It felt good. She felt that surge of empowerment once again.

They entered the house and Morgan heard the patter of tiny feet and Kat was standing in the kitchen taking wonderful blue-berry muffins out of the oven. The mugs were already out with a fresh pot of strong, black coffee brewing. Antonio and Ash, no doubt, would be up soon once the coffee aroma made its way wafting through the house. Kat and Morgan hugged one another then Ollie and Opal joined in. Dixie appeared in the middle of all feet. Their furry confidant simply couldn't miss a group hug.

Kat was peering intently at Morgan. 'Are you okay?'

Morgan said, 'Better than ever.'

'I'm not so sure about that, but I want to believe you.'

Morgan thought Kat certainly didn't miss much. Ollie and Opal were sipping their hot chocolate and they asked Kat for cinnamon toast or as Ollie says 'cimmanin' and Kat was busy preparing it, frying crispy bacon, and slicing fresh fruit.

Antonio with his lovely, wavy, mahogany brown tousled hair was sauntering down the stairwell and Morgan squeezed his hand on her way up. 'Hey, he said, I'm having a cuppa and I'm hitting the road.'

Morgan stopped. 'Really, why?'

Antonio looked surprised. 'Morgan, the office is reopening today. There won't be much going on, but Mike is expecting me. He already knows that I'm driving in from Pickwick and I'll be a bit late. We texted earlier and he asked how you were. He told me to tell you he hoped everyone had a Merry Christmas and he'll contact you on New Year's Eve or before.'

She walked back down the stairs with Antonio. 'Please tell Mike thanks again for everything.'

Morgan made the announcement. 'Antonio will be departing after his coffee,' with a sad, funny face and you would have thought someone said Christmas would never be celebrated again to hear Ollie and Opal's reactions. They didn't want their pal to leave.

She gave Antonio another big bear hug. 'Your visit has meant the world to me and the children.'

Kat piped in. 'Don't leave me out.'

Antonio finished his coffee, grabbed his hat, coat, and scarf from the mud room, thanked Kat and kissed the cherubs. 'Morgan, please tell Ash I'll be in touch later in the day. Being here has been splendid. Ciao!'

Gone. In a flash. Antonio had left the Pickwick Lake House.

CHAPTER TWENTY-FIVE

The tribe would have to adjust to Antonio's absence. He was the glue or so Morgan interpreted. She already missed him and he wasn't even down the driveway. Back upstairs, Morgan checked her phone – too many strange numbers, but a tremendous number of missed calls from Lee. She took a moment to ring Lee before her shower. 'Hey, what's up?'

Lee grumbled, 'Is your phone broken or are you simply not talking to me?'

'Oh, no, I've been genuinely slack, and I've left my phone alone on the kitchen countertop for the last two days. Lee, there are too many numbers coming through that I'm not familiar with. What's going on?'

'Well, I'm not sure. For a start, strange cars drive by slowly in front of my house throughout the day and the evening. When I boldly walk outside, I admit I don't recognize the faces, but it's unsettling.'

Morgan asked the obvious question, 'Have you telephoned the police?' She knew instantly what Lee was going to do.

Lee laughed, of course. 'I have no plans to contact the police. I did, however, contact your Mr. Samuel Ashley Downing at his office because I thought he may have the slightest interest in what I had to say, but his office advised me he was staying at his holiday house. Now, what am I to presume? Is he there with you at Pickwick or does Mr. Downing own a dozen or so holiday houses?'

Morgan blushed and stammered. 'Lee, Ash *is* here, but he didn't know, and I didn't realise he was going to stay with us. He arrived yesterday early afternoon because he said he needed to discuss the case and he wanted to meet Kat, too.'

Lee didn't respond immediately. After a deep sigh, 'Morgan, does he think this is a good idea? Do you...really?'

Morgan thought for a moment, 'It is all above board, Lee. This is his house after all.'

Lee interjected. 'Yes, it is, but he loaned it to you for a retreat and a private, family getaway. So, he's sleeping there, too?'

'It's not like that. He's not like that. He may be one of the nicest men I've ever met, and we have had quite a bit of drama, even here, since our arrival.'

Lee's voice was sincere. 'I'm sorry to hear that.' She sounded unimpressed that Ash had been there and Lee was never one to hide her honest opinion. 'Firstly, are you and Kat and the children okay? Are you safe?'

Morgan reassured her dear friend they were. She also mentioned that Antonio had been a surprise visitor for two days and he had left to return to the city early in the morning.

Lee gasped, 'You've had a Christmas party without me?' – mocking shock and inserting a laugh.

'No party, I promise, but a sweet and informative time and I must say, Lee, Antonio's presence and Ash's appearance made the kid's Christmas that much better. Mine, too, if I'm to be completely honest.'

Lee's voice reflected relief. 'Good. You seem rested and happy and that's what I wanted to find out. Would you mind terribly giving Ash my mobile number and asking him to phone me? If there is anything specific I should be doing besides trying to read number plates, I'd like to know. I still have a house filled with terribly needy people. Gotta run. Love and miss you.'

'Yes, I'll certainly give him your number and I miss you, too.'

Morgan was about to turn on the shower then she remembered her journal. She pulled it out of her purse and sat at her favourite unfamiliar writing desk. Date. Check. Time. Check. Yes, Morgan knew when she took Dixie outside. Then she began to describe the exact sight she and Dixie had viewed at the bottom of the ridge. Morgan tried to think how long they were out there; probably no more than six or seven minutes. There. She had recorded her early morning discovery of the lurking monster. If only Dixie could talk. *And would anyone ever need to read this entry in her private journal? Who knows?*

Next on the agenda was a hot, steaming shower with that enticing and gorgeous scent covering every square inch of the bathroom. Morgan felt as if she needed no perfume after that experience. She stayed in the shower much longer than usual and it rejuvenated her body and her spirit. The luxurious shower made her lighter in step and she looked forward to whatever might unfold throughout the day. Morgan took a little extra care with her make-up and paid more attention to her hair. She'd been piling it on top of her head too much lately and had almost forgotten what it looked like down. Natural, pretty, wavy, and tiny light blonde streaks introduced and scattered amongst her real colour, but it was longer than she remembered, too. *Must get a decent trim, soon, and Ollie and Opal are due. Must do that during the holidays.* A trip to the hair salon may be exactly what they needed within the next couple of days. Durn. She forgot about New Year's Eve. She even wondered if there were a salon around Pickwick, more than likely, they would already be booked due to the holidays. 'Oh well, something to Google later this afternoon,' she muttered.

Morgan was descending the stairwell while Kat, Ollie, and Opal were ascending simultaneously! They giggled and said 'Hello' to one another as if they were greeting strangers. Ollie got especially tickled.

Opal stated proudly to her mother, 'Ollie and I are going to work very hard on our new puzzle today and you need to make sure no one goes near it, please, or it might get messed up.'

Kat winked at Morgan. 'You look terrific!'

Morgan beamed and mouthed 'thanks' and headed for a huge, hot steaming mug of coffee.

Ash was already in the kitchen reading the paper. *I don't remember the last time I read a genuine newspaper!*

He stood up when she entered the kitchen and Morgan smiled.

'Morgan, you look stunning. What a beautiful sight you are this morning.'

She could feel herself beginning to blush. 'Honestly, Ash, showers work wonders and sometimes a girl has to let her hair down...eventually.'

Ash quipped back. 'So, I've heard.'

She poured strong black coffee and asked with her eyes if he would like more, he nodded yes.

Morgan read the national and local news on her Samsung. Ash continued reading and they could both hear the hustle and bustle upstairs of Kat, Ollie, and Opal preparing for the day.

Ash put his paper down and looked up at Morgan. 'I have an idea. It's been a while since I've been here. Would you like to take a drive around the lake with me and spend a bit more time together? I do have further questions.'

'That sounds wonderful. The children want to work on their puzzle and my mother is probably wishing she had a bit of quiet time for herself. Oh, and I have more questions for you, too.'

Ash folded his newspaper. 'Yes, Morgan, I bet you do.' His eyes were twinkling.

'I'll pop upstairs and have a word with mom.'

After speaking with Kat, Morgan made her way back down the winding stairs and shared with Ash, 'I think my kids are incredible. Honestly, Ash, they told me it was okay if I went out because they were going to be extremely busy with their puzzle and they needed to concentrate. Opal told me, "Hard!" Sometimes, I can't believe they're my children. They're kind, smart kids, and they make me laugh almost every day.'

'It's been terrific to be around them and to get to know them. You're a truly fortunate woman.'

Morgan nodded contemplatively. 'Well, indeed, yes, I am.'

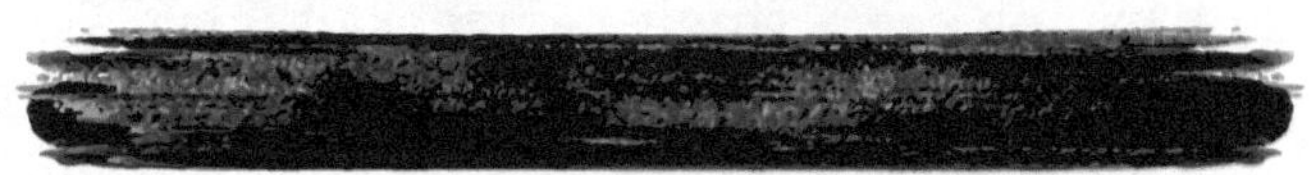

CHAPTER TWENTY-SIX

Morgan and Ash collected their warm coats and scarves. Ash added his wool hat, and she slipped red leather gloves into her pocket just in case they went out for a walk somewhere. They got into Ash's car which happened to be another Lexus only the 'Big Daddy,' ultra-luxurious model. Morgan just looked at him squarely. 'Your friend?'

Ash managed a huge grin. 'Yes, he offers me well-looked after demo cars and I have fallen in love with the way these cars handle. I'll be driving one kind of Lexus or another until I can no longer drive, I do believe!'

They slowly made their way down the grey, winter pathway with the lean, naked trees and entered the main road towards the marina. Ash and Morgan took in the gloomy and somber winterland views as he continued navigating the twisty, winding roads. They weren't saying anything, but it wasn't an uncomfortable silence. Morgan wanted to understand Ash. She genuinely wanted to know about his past. She was not trying to be nosey. She was extremely interested in this particularly intriguing and kind human being. *That was all*. So, she took a deep breath.

'Ash, will you please continue your story about Alex and your family?' she asked gently.

'Well...exactly what is it you want to know?'

'Everything.'

'That's a tall order.' He told her again, 'There's not a lot to tell – nothing out of the ordinary happened to me that hasn't happened to a million other men.'

'That may well be true. But it was your wife and it's your story, so it's different to everyone else's.'

'If you insist, Morgan.' Ash sat up a little straighter in his seat. 'I still hold Alex in high esteem. As many couples do, we simply drifted apart. Alex is an immigration attorney and she is Hell bent on saving every single refugee out there. Her grandparents migrated from Czechoslovakia, when the country was known by that name, decades ago and worked hard and became proud Americans. You would never meet a nicer or more giving couple than Alex's own parents. I was told her grandparents tried diligently to learn to speak English properly early on and they worked multiple jobs to get Alex's mother through school and higher education. Alex's mother was a stunner, too, but she kept her head down and became the first child of her family to graduate from college. She insisted from an early age that her children would follow in her footsteps without fail and they did indeed. Alex is exceptionally motivated and lets nothing stand in her way. She instilled the same character and work ethic in our children.'

'There. I just learned another nice little nugget of pertinent information. You have children. How many and what are their names?' Morgan felt smug.

'I'm beginning to think you prefer listening to other people's stories.'

'Yes, far better than sharing mine.'

'Well, our first born, Samuel, is finishing his master's degree in architecture with Yale presently. He has combined his architecture with a management program and will be looking to work in the private sector soon. I fly to see him rather frequently and we are quite close. I adore Connecticut. For a reason I can't quite explain, I feel extremely at home in New Haven. I refer to Sam as my 'fine son' and he hates it! We missed each other this Christmas, but we were together this past Thanksgiving and he's doing rather well.' Ash paused momentarily.

'Go on,' Morgan coaxed.

'Well, then we move on to Anastasia, whom we affectionately refer to as Tassie. Sam named her that. He could never pronounce her entire name correctly, so he dubbed our little darling, Tassie. Anastasia refers to herself as 'Tas' now she is older. Tas is completing her PhD at Emory university. She was able to skip her junior year in high school – always had her nose in a book and seemed to prefer her studies over people. She's very artistic, too, but has never devoted any energy to that area. You'd love her, Morgan. You'd like both of my children.'

Morgan wondered why he said that, but then again, Ash had been watching her swoon over her own kiddos, and she could feel from the conversation how proud he was and how much he loved his own two children.

Ash changed gears as the car traversed a steep hill. He continued, 'Tas wants to save the world, too, especially women. She wants to empower them. So, she's been focusing on women's studies concerning racism, gender, and sexuality. I fear she is going to land in politics. I don't know why. She's never voiced it, but people gravitate to her and look to her for guidance. I think she'd make an excellent professor, but I have grave doubts that she will ever go down that path. Whatever Tassie chooses to do, she will excel. She is an outstanding human being. She and her mother are together this Christmas in Atlanta and Sam was going to fly down for three days to be with them. I spoke to them on Christmas day and everyone is fine. I most definitely miss them...especially during the holidays.'

Morgan inhaled a massive deep breath. 'Alex, too?'

'Well, no, I meant I miss the kids. Alex and I are over. We weren't living as a true couple for about two years prior to divorcing. There we were, two attorneys living under the same roof, and neither of us could get the paperwork or the procedures started properly. It's a wonder we are divorced now, but I took the bull by the horns and began the process, advising Alex, along the way what was to be expected. We got there in the end. We sold the house in Germantown, and both purchased smaller houses, and we each got a holiday home. I kept the one in Pickwick because it was such a close and quick getaway and Alex chose the one in West Palm Beach. I don't care for West Palm, but it was Alex's go-to spot when she desperately needed a break.'

'But you loved her so...'

'Yes, Morgan, that's true, but she was away a great deal of the time. Her clients were scattered throughout Tennessee. She took on hundreds of cases knowing she would never be compensated adequately. That was okay, of course, and that was her choice, but the workload was never-ending, and we saw less and less of one another. The children knew we were divorcing before we did. We weren't even faking it as a couple. We went about our day as two separate individuals and I was the one missing the intimacy. I missed my wife and Alex only appeared to care about her clients. It was her caseload. The work tore us apart and turned her into a machine. Looking back, I could have voiced my concerns sooner and perhaps louder. I could have reminded her of who we once were and what we had and how much we would lose if we gave up, but, quite frankly, she wasn't around that much for me to express my greatest fears.'

Morgan was listening intently, 'Was anyone sad when the marriage ended?'

Ash just looked over at her with a question mark while he adjusted the heat in the car.

'I mean, it sounded as if everything had been over for quite a while. I can't even imagine how you would have said goodbye. Sorry, Ash, I have a habit of over-thinking things.'

'No, you hit the nail on the head. I think we grieved privately and separately for the end of our union, but we did that long before the final divorce decree came through. I dealt with the realtor because Alex was rarely around. When it came time to relocate, we scheduled our moves separately. I told her to take anything she liked or wanted. I was not going to have our relationship reduced to any level of bickering over material items by that time. Looking back, we went through the motions and did the best we could. We are both fairly sane people, Morgan, and we acted the way most adults do who loved one another a great deal at one time.'

Morgan peered over at him, then glanced down, and looked out of the passenger car window reminding herself this moment – living in the present – was a gift. She suddenly felt tremendous sadness and longed for a different time and place for herself and her children. The mindfulness exercise was not producing its charm.

'Where does Alex live now?'

'Downtown Memphis. She adores it there. She especially loves the Mississippi River, the bluffs, and the views from the very top of the Bass Pro Shop. Any client, new friend, or family member visiting Memphis gets the "Alex Downtown Tour" of Beale Street, The Lorraine Motel, The National Civil Rights Museum, breakfast at The Arcade, lunch at Central BBQ, or dinner at The Rendezvous, and champagne at the Peabody Memphis lobby so they could gaze at its opulence. It's amazing the lengths this woman would go to in order to share 'her city' with others. Alex was born in Chicago, but you would never know it. She is a true Memphian at heart. Any time she would come home after escorting a new friend to downtown Memphis, she would recall the experience as if she were seeing everything for the very first time. There was always something a little bit new, a little bit different, she would claim.'

'You must really miss her.' Morgan was watching Ash's face. 'I personally can't imagine loving someone that much, then losing them.'

'I count my blessings that we had our years together that were absolute magic, and our union produced two fine human beings. That is what I choose to think about now. She has moved on. There is a man in her life. We have not met, no doubt, we will, and I wish her complete happiness, Morgan. She truly deserves it.' Ash looked genuinely sincere.

Suddenly Ash's face was smiling from ear to ear! 'Look ahead. Viv's Barbeque. I haven't been there for years, and I know they used to serve breakfast. I've lost all track of time but talking has made me hungry!'

Morgan reached for her gloves in her coat pocket. 'Well, I've never been to Viv's before and I'm eager – let's go in.'

They entered and heard a server talking about how she'd been there since 6:00am. It was quaint and cozy and guests were chatting away, laughing, and drinking big fat mugs of coffee. Morgan had no clue what time it was, but she was thinking breakfast. Ash had other ideas.

'Best burger you'll ever have, right here.'

Morgan was astonished! 'Oooh, I'm not ready for a burger, but you go right ahead. I really need more coffee and I'm feeling like hot, delicious, scrambled eggs, and hash browns. She added, 'Loaded hash browns, I think!'

The server came over to their table and she was super friendly and eager to help. She poured coffee into a big, heavy ceramic mug and Ash nodded he would like the same. Ash continued to describe the burgers so vividly, Morgan relented.

'Make that two burgers, please with extra pickles and mustard for mine.'

The server smiled directly at Morgan, 'I'll be back in a jiffy, and you won't be sorry you changed your mind!'

Lord. Two burgers arrived. They were not huge in size which was good, and they were cooked to perfection and crispy on the edges.

'The taste is out of this world – delectable!'

They were both extremely hungry and didn't say a word for a while, only smiling at one another.

Morgan finally looked up from her meal. 'Did I just eat a hamburger for breakfast?' 'We both did,' Ash chuckled! 'Wasn't it a fine breakfast though?'

Their server appeared with her hands on her hips. 'I told you so!'

'Ash, it feels as if we've been driving around in circles for the last hour or so.'

'My trip down memory lane may have taken me off the path, but I didn't have a real plan. I think we landed where we were supposed to be at this point and time in our lives on the planet.'

How lovely it is to not have a fast-paced schedule and how difficult it's going to be to get the kids back in a routine and immerse myself back in my work. Reality. Right around the corner and Morgan could feel it in her bones. Once again, she thought she was saying these last few words in her head, but they were coming right from her mouth. So, Ash's response surprised her when he agreed.

'Reality is going to be a harsh slap in the face.'

⸻

They returned to the car and Ash continued to drive through the lake area slowly and methodically. It was pretty and serene, and Morgan knew from past memories, Pickwick was especially green and glorious in the summer. This had been a genuinely nice retreat despite the ugly episodes, and she was most grateful Ash had offered his holiday home to her. Morgan wondered again what sort of situation she and her children would have experienced if she had decided to stay at home this Christmas. She felt fortunate to have her mother staying with them, also. Kat was an added bonus, not only for Ollie and Opal, but for her own spirit, too.

Ash was being a good host and driver and pointing out some houses that belonged to a couple of his good friends, some were attorneys he had known a long while, and others were business owners, and there were friends he had met from Alabama and Mississippi, too. One couple living in California purchased a large home so when they flew to Memphis to see their grandkids everyone could stay in one place and have outdoor entertainment. Ash commented, 'They're a terrific couple and I'd very much like to see them.' He continued, 'Pickwick is a friendly community and no matter how long I go without seeing some people, they always act as though they're happy to see me again.'

Morgan suggested to Ash, 'It feels more like a village to me.'

'Exactly, Morgan. That's how it seems at Pickwick.'

Ash stopped the car for a moment. 'I don't want to return to the house yet. I genuinely came here to get your story, Morgan, yet I've been telling mine. How did that happen? You have exceptionally savvy techniques of persuasion, but I do need to get this part of my job accomplished. Knowing your side of events will help me in preparing to do the best job I can possibly do for you, Ollie, and Opal. I'll be leaving early this evening and heading back to Memphis, so tell me, honestly, are you up for it?'

CHAPTER TWENTY-SEVEN

Morgan felt shocked for a moment. Leaving. *Ash is leaving this evening.* Suddenly, she didn't want him to go. First, her dear friend, confidante and colleague, Antonio, departed, but now, Ash? She was experiencing real uneasiness but did not want Ash to pick up on it. Plus, she wondered...*why? Why was Ash's mention of leaving feeling her with dread?* He was her attorney, for God's Sake. He will be representing her in court and doing the job he is meant to do and paid to do. *What's up with that?* Morgan could not explain it herself. Holding it together, she did what she was used to doing. She smiled. She faked a big, fat smile.

'Certainly, Ash, I'll answer any questions you have for me.'

Ash now appeared to know exactly where he was heading. 'Well, I could use a nice, cold beer. I do enjoy a cold beer in the winter even if that sounds a bit odd. Now, I'm taking you to another place I haven't been to in a while. I do know they serve wine, but I can tell you right now, it will not be the kind that you are accustomed to drinking. Will that be okay with you?'

Morgan laughed a little, 'I'm not posh. I'm certainly no wine snob, but when I can afford to buy a nice drop, I do. Yes, whatever they have on offer will be fine.' Her attitude in the moment appeared to agree with Ash.

They pulled into the parking lot of the Pickwick Sports Bar & Grill. Morgan already imagined what it would be like inside, and her mental image nailed it. She felt comfortable and relaxed when they became settled and Ash looked relieved there weren't too many people about. It was still early in the day. Serious pool players and avid sports' lovers frequented this establishment. Morgan was neither, but that didn't matter. They were someplace quiet, dark and very much alone. Ash went to the bar,

'May I have a glass of your best white wine?'

A bartender with a chiseled face and broad shoulders shot him a look. 'Okay, coming up.' He smirked.

Then Ash ordered an ice-cold Corona beer on tap and the guy perked up saying, 'Well, that's more like it.' Next the bartender asked, 'Do you need a couple of menus?'

'Not at the moment, but here's my card and if you can, run a tab, please.'

The handsome, dark-haired bartender took his card and Ash returned to the table saying, 'Sorry, I have no clue what's in your glass.'

Morgan raised hers to his and said, 'Cheers.'

The atmosphere felt edgy. Morgan knew that once she continued with her story that it was going to take a chunk of her soul and she did not feel particularly strong, but knew she needed to at least make a good attempt.

Ash had a notepad and a slim, grey-metallic writing pen he slipped from the interior of his jacket. He placed them both on the table and, additionally, hit the record button on his phone. Morgan recognized Ash's routine once she began recalling her memories.

He only remarked, 'Thank you, Morgan, for doing this.'

Morgan closed her eyes and looked towards the ceiling. 'There was another night that caught me totally off guard, but it was the monster who suffered the most. We were on our way home, yet again, from another party in the heart of Germantown. And, as you are probably aware, the Germantown police are vigilant and always seem to be out in abundance - they don't miss a thing, do they?'

Ash nodded in agreement.

'We were only minutes away from our house - probably less than two miles, when suddenly, there were flashing blue and red lights behind us, right on top of us. The monster started cursing under his breath, his shoulders tightened, his eyes turned into small slits. He was hissing he was so furious, and we had not even pulled over yet. Once he complied, the police officer motioned for him to roll down his window, which he should have already done, but he wouldn't give any person in authority an inch. Then the officer flashed his light in the monster's eyes and told him he would prefer it if he drove into the church parking lot across the street because it would be safer to do so. The monster didn't say a word, entered the massive church lot next to us and the cop pulled within an inch behind our car – literally. The cop then came back to the window, instructing him to get out to which the monster asked, "Why?" Questioning never sits well with cops. So, the cop did not respond and repeated his instruction, "Get out of the car" and added the word, harshly, "Now." He huffed and puffed, and I heard the officer ask him if he had been drinking. The monster replied, "Yes, we've been to a party and that's what most people do at parties, sir, (placing a big emphasis on 'sir') and my wife has been drinking, too."

The cop demanded the monster walk with him to his patrol car and to get in the back seat to take a breathalyzer test. Monster refused. I couldn't make out the exact words that were being spoken or rather yelled, but in a matter of sheer seconds, two more patrol cars had moved in on us. At this point, I decided to step out of the car. My only thought was I needed to be a witness. Immediately two or perhaps three officers were screaming at me, "Ma'am get back in your car – GET BACK IN YOUR CAR NOW." They scared me to bits. They made me angry, too, because I didn't know what I had done wrong. I certainly was no threat, and I didn't know why they were so concerned with my actions. Anyway, I was scared. I sat back down in the passenger seat and craned my neck to watch the action. Hands and arms were flailing about. The monster was acting exactly like a caged animal and was not complying with any request, refusing to cooperate at every turn, screaming his bloody head off, and the next thing I saw was his head being protected by a hand or two and he was pushed into the back seat of the first patrol car.

'Another officer came over to me shouting, "Get in the driver's seat and go home now."

I remember I just stared at him. He repeated, shouting, "Did you hear me?"

I answered, 'Yes, Sir' and fiddled for my keys and got out of the car and walked over to the driver's side, got in, locking the doors immediately.

'This same police officer followed me to the door of our home and when I say followed – I mean if I had accidentally hit the brakes of my car unexpectedly, he would have been on my roof of my Volvo. He did this purposefully and I promise you I felt his wrath from his car behind me. The driveway to our home went up a steep hill and then you had to turn sharply to get into the garage. He pursued me up the driveway and when there was no real room for him to be there, I decided to get out of the car before I drove it into the garage.

'Once I exited, he got out of his car and held out his thumb and forefinger about an inch apart and said, "You were this close to being arrested. Have a nice night." I asked what was happening to my husband and the cop shouted back he'd be spending a nice, long night in jail until he learned how to behave. The monster was now in the Germantown Hotel Motel Jail and it was going to be all my fault.'

'So, what did you do then?'

'I don't remember sleeping. I had the same clothes on in the morning. I quickly showered and changed when the morning sun began to rise. I didn't know what to do. I had never been in this situation before. I got my keys and purse and drove to the jail. When I arrived, I saw him. The monster was pacing in a cell and, Ash, he was seething. He had worked himself up into a complete rage only suppressing it on the inside. He was smart enough to know that any further outbursts would have kept him there a good while longer. I was pointed to a reception desk and a police officer stood up and said "He's a real piece of work. I suppose you want him to come home?" He asked me this as a question and not a statement. Then the guy said slyly, "It would give me immense joy to keep him here. All you need to do is say the word."

'I didn't say a thing and signed the paperwork. Another police officer unlocked the cell. The desk officer gave the monster his personal belongings and, of course, he had to have the last words on his way out, so he announced proudly and boldly, "I will see you all in court." He grabbed the keys from my hand and pulled me by my elbow. He didn't say a word on the way home. He waited until we were inside and unloaded.'

'Unloaded how?' Ash asked, 'Did he hurt you?'

Morgan looked into Ash's eyes. 'It wasn't always about physical pain. Every time he was upset with the world or angry with me, he certainly didn't twirl me above his head or grab me by my throat, but the words that he unleashed were toxic, painful, and dreadful to hear. He would scream in my face so loudly that I thought his head was going to burst. I would end up cowered in a corner with my hands covering my ears and he would remove my hands to make certain he remained in control, and I was paying attention. Nasty. Horrible. Frightening.

'My children were away that weekend, too, and it gave me great consolation that they didn't witness him. The first words out of his mouth were, "It should have been you. I bet you drank more than I did. Now, I have a record. Now, I'll need to pay attorney's fees. You're going to cost me thousands of dollars. LOOK AT ME. This is going to cost me a fortune and too much of my time and it should've been you. YOU DISGUST ME. Get out of my sight. Get out of this room. I don't want you near me. Do you hear me?"

'His screaming went on for hours. Whenever I left his presence and attempted to get away because he yelled he couldn't stand the sight of me, he'd follow and repeat everything he had previously said a hundred times over only getting even louder and telling me what a piece of shit I was. He continued to come towards me with steam and voluminous rage, then back away, and repeat, trying his best to threaten, intimidate, or scare the Hell out of me. Ash, when the situation was this bad, I could only remain calm and wait for the energy, the anger, and the madness to slowly withdraw from his body. It would. It did and then, the pattern would follow. He would climb into bed, get into the fetal position, and pass out from the torture his body just experienced.'

'Morgan, you just voiced the torture his body experienced. That makes me think that you don't hold him responsible.'

'I've already told you it felt as if I were living with two different people - two entirely separate personalities. Slowly and surely, I did learn and recognize he was seriously ill. I cannot forget any of these horrific episodes, but I do think in my heart of hearts that he didn't want to feel the way that he did. The intensity of the feelings the monster was experiencing was the root cause of his thoughts, words, and deeds. No person would choose to feel the way he felt. I'm quite certain of that. What I cannot forgive or forget is that when told time and time again that specific medications could bring relief, he refused and resisted taking anything except medications his mother would bring to the house for him. It was mind-boggling and the situation we were in was life depleting. It was soul destroying. It was utterly heart breaking.'

Ash gently responded, 'How wise you are, Morgan.'

She was reading something terribly kind in Ash's eyes and she wasn't quite certain if she saw sympathy or empathy. Morgan thought her wisdom had been gained through great pain and she felt like she wanted to be held, more than anything, at that moment in time. She also felt as if she were growing closer to this amazing human being. Morgan didn't want a protector, but she knew she would like Ash to become a part of her life, her children's lives – *but how?* Well, most certainly, she did not know. Morgan considered Ash, possibly, treated her differently from other clients but this could be her imagination working overtime. She thought he was an angel living amongst real people and a brave and strong warrior. She decided she would need to keep those thoughts to herself - perhaps forever – and she wanted to learn how to become her own warrior.

Ash peered over at Morgan noticing tears streaming down from the sides of her eyes. He handed her a napkin. 'Are you alright?'

'I had no idea I was crying. Sorry.'

Ash replied with a sweet smile, 'There is absolutely no reason on the planet to apologise and you can stop at any time when you feel as if you need or want to do so.'

'I suppose it helps to talk about it. Several episodes I haven't even discussed with my dearest friends because the scenarios were so eerie and bizarre. I would go over what had happened in my mind and decide there was no way I could share. Plus, Ash, it's embarrassing. It's another failed marriage – a broken commitment – and painful to relive. I want the past to be miles and years behind me. It will give me the greatest security of all when I know that Ollie and Opal are in a sturdy, sustainable, dynamic, and loving environment. I can give them that, I know that I can, but it's hard to accomplish when the monster is lurking over our heads.'

'Hold that thought and I'll be right back. Are you hungry at all?'

Morgan was. Ash was right about talking – it can ignite an appetite. She felt the excessive barrage of words she had just spewed out into the atmosphere had burned a whole lot of calories.

It took energy and effort to recall memories, especially rotten ones. When Ash reappeared, he had one very full glass of white wine and another Corona.

'The beer is so cold and refreshing that I had to have one more glass.' He was managing two small packages of mini pretzels for them, too. 'I'd like you to know, the bartender commented they didn't get too many beautiful women ordering white wine at this time of day, so this glass is on the house.'

Morgan grinned from ear to ear. 'How sweet.'

Ash opened the pretzels for them. 'Morgan, you're doing a splendid job. And, I am under the impression you have more empathy and compassion for your husband than you are willing to acknowledge.'

Morgan stared straight ahead as if she were announcing to the universe, 'Oh, I wouldn't be too sure about that.' She was munching on her miniature pretzels and thinking how nice it would be if people could be fixed. If they could go away to a place, distant and unfamiliar, and come back changed – more kind, more calm, more peaceful, more understanding, more tolerant, softer spoken, more giving of their time, energy, and efforts, more grateful, more relaxed, more mindful. There was that word again.

Ash snapped her out of it and asked, 'Where are you?'

Morgan shyly looked down, 'In a place where all people can be fixed.'

Ash recognized the afternoon had been difficult for her and raised his glass to hers. 'Cheers.' He glanced down at his watch. 'We'll have to be heading back soon, and I'll need to pack quickly and make a couple of phone calls to my office. Morgan, how long do you think you might be staying at Pickwick? It makes no real difference to me; I'm only curious.'

'I, too, will be contacting my boss this afternoon and I've decided to stay until the day after New Year's Day. We'll leave at a decent time on the 2nd of January, if that's suitable for you.'

'Not a worry at all and you're more than welcome to stay as long as you like.' He grinned and reminded her, 'The longer you stay, the harder it will be to get back in the saddle!'

Morgan huffed. 'Don't I know it.'

He looked at her tenderly as if to ask how many further horror stories were inside that head of hers.

Morgan suddenly felt extremely exposed and began to envision those vivid Hollywood signs in harsh lights.

'Is there anything else you feel like purging? I told you I was a good listener, and I meant every word of it.'

'Only a few general things. Oh, and I forgot to mention Lee urged me to tell you to contact her. Unfamiliar cars have been driving by the front of her house during the early afternoon and evenings. She refuses to call the local police, but she did say that she thought it might be something you would need or want to know. Then she asked me if she should be doing anything other than jotting down license plate numbers.'

Now Ash looked concerned again. 'May I have Lee's number?' He jotted it down on his pad with the rest of his copious, scribbled notes. 'I'll call her before I depart for Memphis. Leave this with me. The monster is probably paying someone to conduct intimidation tactics, and it could even be an undercover cop under the assumption that you're the baddie, Morgan. This guy has spun a story that makes *you* sound like the monster, keep that in mind.'

'No doubt,' Morgan looked away.

'What general things were you thinking of before you remembered Lee's request?'

'There have been a couple of afternoons in the past month when I've felt, rather, I've known someone has been in my home. You know when you draped a jacket over a chair. You know when you placed the magazines and newspapers back in the stand. You know, at least, I know, when I have definitely not made my bed in the morning, yet I return home and it's been made, and the bedroom is nice and tidy. It's quite disturbing, Ash, to think he is roaming around our house, sitting in it, and doing as he pleases. I could never get away with something like that, nor could you. We're still married so is he thinking that because the divorce is not final, he has a right to be wherever I am?'

Ash huffed. 'I wouldn't have a clue what this guy is thinking. May I strongly suggest a high-tech monitoring and security system, one that includes interior and exterior cameras? The police value and appreciate that type of concrete evidence.

The company that installed mine at Pickwick Lake works out of Collierville and they are extremely reliable. For you, for your children, and for your current situation, I strongly recommend it as your attorney.'

'Yes, I should consider it.' She also said, with a small laugh, 'In order to afford a system like that I'll have to return to work a lot sooner, concentrating on attracting more clients.' *Anything was possible.*

Ash drank the remainder of his icy beer and Morgan finished her glass of white.

'Think hard. You may not believe something to be out of the ordinary, but if anything at all strikes you as odd on the way back to the house, tomorrow morning, tomorrow night or in the middle of the night – do not hesitate to call me. I'm serious. You understand, right? Sometimes monsters make a mess of the trivial things – that's when they get caught.'

Morgan assured Ash, 'I will, and yes, I do understand. There are dozens of phone numbers on my phone I've left alone. If I don't recognize a number, I do not answer it and I'm most certainly not returning any of the phone calls.'

'Perfect. Good, but don't delete them either. At this point we don't know if they could be evidence.'

'Promise. I've not deleted any numbers.'

They drove back quietly and Morgan was lost in her thoughts. The sun was setting quickly, leaving behind a dark and violent looking sky. It appeared a thunderstorm was ominous. Morgan welcomed the rain. Their Christmas company would be departing, and her family could do more nesting again. She felt a strong bond forming with Ash. She felt a new friendship developing, a deep and lasting one, and that note was comforting to her.

CHAPTER TWENTY-EIGHT

When they entered the front door Ollie and Opal almost knocked them over. 'Come here, come here! Look what we have done! Oh, Mom, we worked so hard, and the map is really pretty!'

It looked as though the children had completed almost half of their new spectacular puzzle and National Geographic did a superb job with the colouring of the pieces. It was a stunning sight to see.

Ash commented, 'You two are the most accomplished children I've ever met. You did an excellent job today. You should be pleased and proud.'

Ollie and Opal squealed and Kat was beaming.

'Hi, Mom, and how was your day? Did you get to catch up on your reading?'

'Yes, and baking, also.'

Morgan was in awe. 'Oh, Mom, you didn't! You made more goodies?'

Kat shot back, 'Nanna's rights. I get to spoil my grandchildren especially at Christmas. I baked the small ham, and it's already sliced and covered in the oven in case you two have not eaten. I've prepared a cheddar cheese, potato and onion bake, and made a creamy spinach casserole, too. There is a luscious lemon pie for dessert that looks dreamy if I may say so myself!'

Morgan looked at Ash and said, 'Sorry, but you're eating before you leave. You don't have the option of dismissing my mother's grand efforts.'

Kat stared at him. 'Ash, you're leaving us so soon?'

This brought complaints and whining from the little people department. Ollie joined in, 'Oh, please stay with us!' and Opal added, 'Please...just a few more days?'

'I'll return soon, kids, I promise you. Ladies, I need to get in touch with various clients, pack my belongings, and I'll be back to enjoy Kat's fine cooking before you know it.'

Morgan thought she would decant a bottle of red wine. She picked out one of the last purchases before the Christmas madness from her most fav wine shop, Buster's on Highland. She didn't have a big budget, but she had an excellent idea what her Christmas bonus would be, and she'd made a decision to buy at least one special drop of red. She purchased a beautiful Cabernet Sauvignon from Bordeaux, France. Her mates at Buster's helped her decide on a 2014 Chateau-Ducru-Beaucaillou Saint Julien 2014 and she had never paid that price for one bottle of wine. It was her one Christmas present for herself and, hopefully, it would be shared with people she cherished. Unfortunately, Ash could not have much, he already consumed two beers and would soon be on the road again, so the rest of the bottle Kat and Morgan would eagerly savour when they got comfortable in front of the fire later that evening. She looked forward to that.

Ash retreated to his study and made the necessary phone calls to clients. He saved Lee for the last. When he rang her, she seemed a bit aloof and cool, but he chalked that up to having unnecessary and unwanted drive-by visitors.

He advised her, 'Please continue to write down the date and time if any suspicious car drives by, the make of the car, the colour, how many passengers, and of course if you could read the license plate number that would be superb but keep your safety in mind first.'

'I've tried to do exactly that, but they do speed away once they see me come out of the front door.'

Ash reiterated to Lee, 'You've done the right thing by ringing my office and if anything, no matter how small it seems appears to be out of the ordinary, call me no matter the day or time.' He grimaced thinking he had said those same words not long ago to Morgan. He didn't give out his personal cell number to many, but he offered it to Lee. Morgan and her circle needed to be on high alert and life may continue this way for a while longer.

Ash passed through the kitchen again on his way upstairs to throw his personal items into his hand luggage. He motioned to get Morgan's attention.

'Is everything all right?' she asked.

He sighed. 'Lee was a bit abrupt when I first rang her, but as we continued to speak, she seemed to warm up and the conversation became more relaxed. I discovered how much she genuinely cares for you – more of a sisterly love than the love between two friends. I certainly got the impression Lee is seriously concerned, and she genuinely fears for your life. Keep her in the loop. It must be lovely to have a friend who thinks so highly of you. Anyway, I'm sure you realise how much she cares, but she is distressed.'

'Thanks for sharing, Ash.'

He assured the ladies, 'I'll be back down promptly.'

Kat announced to the kids, 'Please tidy the puzzle area as best you can and wash your hands because it's time for dinner.'

Morgan had already set the table and Kat spread the delicious meal over the counter buffet style again. She had even taken the time to make miniature, knotted, sesame covered bread rolls that were glistening with butter. Morgan reminded herself she would never achieve this level of baking.

'I feel as if I'm starving.'

Ash heard her comment as he approached the kitchen. 'I couldn't agree more. Kat, you did an excellent job. This looks amazing.'

Kat helped Ollie and Opal with their plates first and they were seated. Kat insisted Ash follow, then Morgan, then she fixed her plate. The children had big, tall glasses of ice-cold milk. When everyone was finally seated Morgan asked if she could pour the gorgeous red.

'I know you're driving, Ash, so I'll be careful not to over pour.'

Kat took a sip of the deep, burgundy coloured wine. 'This is an outstanding drop, Morgan. It's French, isn't it?'

Her mother was good – she was most observant and knew good wines.

'It's pretty nice,' Morgan winked.

Ash closed his eyes while relishing the flavour. 'This is not Australian, and this *is* very special. Was this a gift? Should I feel guilty about enjoying this or did you pick this one out yourself, too?'

Morgan simply laughed. 'Too many questions. No, it's not Australian. It is French. Ash, you can make a toast, please.'

Ash thought for a second and raised his glass. 'May this family have the most peaceful and prosperous New Year – Cheers to New Beginnings.'

Ollie and Opal raised their milk, and the adults clinked their glasses together.

Kat was busy wrapping the remaining food, and placing it in proper containers, returning it to the refrigerator. There would be volumes of leftovers. No one wanted her luscious lemon pie and Kat was a bit disappointed, but the kids asked if they could have a small piece before bed.

Ash came out from the mud room with his jacket, wool hat, and scarf around his neck. He bent over and kissed Kat on the cheek. 'It's been lovely to spend time with you, and I've never had better home cooked meals prior to this visit.'

Dixie entered the picture looking intrigued.

Kat blushed. They hugged.

Ollie came forward and Ash shook his hand. 'Promise me, Ollie, to take a photo once the puzzle is complete and to send it to me, please.'

Opal interrupted. 'Ollie doesn't know how to send pictures.'

'I do, too, Opal. You don't know everything I know how to do.'

Ash bent over to Opal. 'Your mother can teach you both how to send photos and Opal, I have no doubt you and Ollie will surprise each other at the speed in which you complete your puzzle. Be exceptionally good for your mother. I know that you will.'

Opal looked up at Ash and asked, 'Will you please stay for just one more day?'

Ollie added, 'Yeah.'

Morgan wondered if the kids felt safer with Ash or Antonio in the house and this thought made her feel a bit squeamish.

Ash responded with regret, 'I must return to Memphis.'

He stopped before Morgan and put down his case and put his hands on each side of her shoulders. 'You're not indestructible. Please know you have a huge group of people on your side, and you're doing an exemplary job under complicated circumstances. I'll be in touch soon. Call if you need me.'

He kissed the side of her cheek. Morgan knew...right then...it was as if an electric charge soared through her body, and all she wanted to do was hold onto him. She and her highly honed perception skills sensed Ash felt exactly...the...same...way.

Ash said goodbye to all, placed his items in the Lexus, and traversed down the long, winding driveway.

CHAPTER TWENTY-NINE

Kat was upstairs helping the kiddos prepare for bed. They were a bit cranky with each other, but she understood they were tired and had been sad to see Antonio and now, Ash, leave. She perked them up by reminding them a very tasty dessert would be waiting on them downstairs, but they would have to brush their teeth for an extra good while if they ate their pie.

Ollie said, 'That's a good deal. I'll do it.'

Opal got excited. 'Yum, Nanna-Kat, I love your pies.'

Kat told them to carefully walk down the stairs, and she would have their treats waiting for them. When she got to the kitchen, she heard Dixie barking furiously outside. Kat looked out the door to the deck. Dixie must have heard or seen a possum or something that didn't agree with her. Morgan was with Dixie, so Kat didn't worry too much, however, Dixie continued to bark loudly and aggressively, and that made Kat open the door. She called out, 'Morgan?'

'Mom, I don't have a clue what Dixie is going on about, but something has her out of sorts.' They stayed out a little longer and when they returned to the warmth of the kitchen the skies unleashed tremendous thunder, white, bright lightning bolts, extreme winds, and heavy, pelting rains with a fierceness that they hadn't witnessed in quite some time.

Kat shook her head. 'Morgan, you know how dogs instinctively know things before we do. Perhaps Dixie was trying to tell you to get your silly butt in the house before all Hell breaks loose!'

'You're probably right. This is a bloody bad storm. I hate Ash has to drive in it.'

Kat stopped in her tracks. 'Oh, my, yes, dreadful.'

The kids were attempting to run down the staircase. Morgan stopped them.

Opal excitedly exclaimed, 'Mom, our entire room lit up like it was daytime.'

Ollie chimed in, 'Yeah, and the room shook, too. Nanna, you're going to want us to sleep with you tonight because you're going to be very scared in this storm!'

Morgan whispered in her mother's ear – 'Where do they come from? They crack me up, Mom.'

Kat's shoulders were jiggling up and down from laughter. Then she winked at Morgan. 'I do sleep much better in a ferocious storm knowing somebody is close by!'

Morgan kissed her forehead.

The kiddos ate their pie with glee. Morgan thought the combination of the sugar and the savage storm would most certainly keep them up half the night. The violent weather was relentless.

'I'll read you a bedtime story in the lounge room and after that we'll turn down the lights really low and watch the electrical storm together,' Morgan said.

Opal asked, 'Like a magic show, Mom?'

'Something like that. Mother Nature *is* magical so let's watch her perform tonight.'

Ollie said, 'Mother Nature, show us what you've got.'

Kat and Morgan roared with laughter and Ollie got tickled watching his mom and his nanna. They were huddled together as one and would exclaim with sheer awe when the bright, white lightning showered over them. This went on for about another thirty minutes, but the storm was not showing any signs of slowing down. The winds sounded wicked and fierce. Ollie and Opal drifted to sleep wrapped like a safe cocoon next to their mother and grandmother with Dixie nestled firmly in the middle of her family. Morgan moved to the other side of the sofa closest to the fire and Kat opted for the chaise lounge. They could still hear one another and not disturb the little ones.

'If this continues,' Morgan said, 'I'll get warm blankets for the babes and sleep downstairs with them. Now, we deserve the remainder of that gorgeous French drop, don't we?

'You better believe it.'

'Mom, please remind me to try to take Dixie out one more time if Mother Nature calms herself and to remember to set the alarm.'

'Ash taught me how to do it anyway, so if or when you forget, I'm capable of setting it.'

Morgan realised then Ash really did think of everything.

The ladies kicked back, relaxing, and were over the moon with the taste and feel of the French Cabernet. Morgan put on some B.B. King, Isaac Hayes, and sprinkled in a little Booker T. & the M.G.'s, Al Jarreau, and they let the music of years past wash over their bodies. The music selection was superbly eclectic – all over the place! *Perfect, exactly like my life.*

CHAPTER THIRTY

Ash was not comfortable. He knew it looked like a storm was brewing before he got on the main highway, but he certainly didn't expect anything this powerful. He could barely see a car's length in front of him even with the high beams on. It had been a long time since he had driven in weather conditions this massive and angry. He thought about pulling over to the side, but there were very few cars on the road and Ash considered himself to be a cautious and hyper-vigilant driver. It looked later at night than it really was due to the extreme cloud cover. Ash could not remember when he had this much difficulty seeing US-72. This was the easiest ride in the state of Tennessee, but not tonight. He knew he would lose travel time, but better to be safe than sorry.

Ash had a podcast playing. One of his partners had advised him to take time to listen to one of the most bizarre stories he had ever heard before called S-Town. Ash remembered Worthington telling him, "Look, Xavier's wife told my wife, and she told me they both agreed it was a damn good bloke's story, too. My wife said she stopped doing what she needed to do for over eight hours just to listen to S-Town. I'm telling you, Ash, you should have seen her face. Well, Hell, I started listening and was late for an appointment. I don't listen during the day now. But I'm telling you that you need to do hear this." So, S-Town had been playing on the way over to Pickwick and Ash picked up where he left off. He had no idea how or when he was going to fit in the remaining hours of the podcast.

It was difficult to concentrate – hard to listen because the winds and the rain and the lightning were not going to give him a break. And there was a car that should have been keeping a safer distance in Ash's mind, and it was getting on his nerves.

Ash said aloud to no one, 'Look, idiot, we practically have US-72 to ourselves, move the Hell on and give me some room.' Not happy.

The rain pelted down on his windshield, the wipers did their best to keep up with the job, but the storm was winning. Ash looked in the rearview mirror. Hells bells, the car was easing up on him, practically on his bumper. *What the Hell is going on?* He told himself the first chance he had when it felt safe and he could see more clearly, he would pull to the side. Maybe this person had an emergency. Then he felt bad for feeling so angry. He talked himself into a calmer state.

The car felt as if it were being pushed from side to side by the weight and sheer force of the outrageous wind. Then, BOOM! Ash felt a push from the rear. A huge scraping sound and BAM again, Ash's head jolted forward, and his car lunged ahead! Was it the storm? No! It was the 'other' car. It looked like a white car – hard to see with the rain battering down. He saw the lights in the rear get brighter and closer to him again. He tried not to stiffen and held the steering wheel at the proper places while this time the car plunged with its might into Ash's rear. The tires were screeching. He heard that much over the storm. The car behind him appeared to be stuck or attached to his Lexus. There was a bloody awful sound, then both cars were propelling forward, only now, Ash was losing control of his. His car was turning inwards, towards the opposing lane and he could not for the life of him get it back on track. WHOOOSH! His car spun and spun around again and the next spin Ash realised he was air born! The speed at which his car was travelling when he was rear-ended did not give him the chance to regain control. He was holding on for dear life and the last thing he remembered was the airbag exploding. His head was pounding, and his ears were filled with sounds of steel tearing apart, metal on metal, and then, eerie silence.

Ash felt as if he were floating. His eyes were wet. His hair and his ears felt drenched. There was a wretched smell of burning rubber and oil. He could easily move one arm but was having trouble getting his right arm to do what he was directing it to do. Then he heard a smash, another loud bang and he instinctively covered his face. The front windshield was now completely shattered, and he saw a dark glove and a black coat reach in through the window. Ash tried to utter words.

He attempted to say, 'I'm so damn glad to see you,' but nothing came out. He didn't know if he was dreaming this or if it was reality and he couldn't get his bearings either. Was he upside down or was he on his side? He attempted to speak again. Nothing.

Next, the arm reached in through the front, broken window and extracted Ash's cell phone from the roof of the car. Just like that. A hand came in. His phone was stolen! No words were spoken.

He was not the kind of man to panic. He knew to remain calm. He thought he may have heard footsteps walking away, but he knew, without any doubt, he heard a car drive off. He began to breathe slowly and calmly. He tried to reach his legs with his one good arm to see what kind of shape he was in, but he could not get through the twisted dashboard, gnarled wires, and tangled panels that were pinning him down. He composed himself the best he could. He was not afraid of dying. He was not quite ready, he told himself, so he began to think of his two bright children. He tried to breathe deeply repeatedly, but it hurt. Then his thoughts turned to Morgan. He remembered how bright and happy she looked earlier in the day, and he tugged hard on the fresh, lingering, new memory of how she looked at him when he departed. Ash must have drifted off because the next thing he heard was emergency personnel trying their best to get his attention. Strange. The voices sounded miles away and he could not focus. He wanted to, but his eyes simply did not work properly.

The sound of the sirens was now terribly loud – too loud. *Could someone please turn the noise down?* In his mind he was asking the kind soul, working diligently above him, this question but nothing was coming out and the man did not seem to be paying any attention to him.

Ash was told it was over twenty hours since he left his Pickwick house. He had been taken to Baptist Memorial Hospital in Collierville. Two of his partners were in the room when he woke up and Antonio was outside talking on his cell in the lobby.

Morgan was shocked and horrified and was desperate to see Ash, but Antonio assuaged her fears and told her, 'It's probably better for everyone if you stayed back until we understand the whole picture.'

Morgan couldn't understand Antonio's request. She wanted to be there as a friend, by Ash's side, as he had been a friend to her.

Antonio promised, 'I'll relay every single word to Ash you want him to hear, but right now he is recovering from surgery.'

'It was him, wasn't it?

Morgan's voice sounded distressed and filled with anger. 'I am a danger to Ash because of the monster. I caused this. If Ash were not my attorney, if I had not agreed to stay in his holiday house, if...'

Antonio stopped her. 'That is complete nonsense, and you know it. Nothing that happened on US-72 is your fault. That section of the road is a crime scene now and you can bet your bottom dollar the police are searching it, investigating with a fine-toothed comb.'

Morgan huffed, 'Fat chance they'll find anything with the storm that went through. Fat chance they'll do anything because the monster's name is written all over this and now, it seems, he'll get away with attempted murder, too.' Morgan burst into tears. She was ringing from Ash's study and the stress had been far too great over the past hours. The cruelty, the harassment, the stalking had reached an all new high.

'Who is going to stop him? Is it up to me?' Morgan asked Antonio these two simple questions.

He snipped back, 'Stop it. Stop thinking that way. The police will find a clue. The law will stop him. The courts will stop him. He will have cuffs slapped around him so tightly and you'll not hear from him or see him for a great, long while, if ever. You must hold on to that, Morgan.'

'Antonio, please don't hide anything from me. Please tell me exactly what's happened to Ash.'

'Ash suffered a severe concussion, his legs are badly bruised, and his right leg has deep lacerations which have been cleaned and stitched, he has one punctured lung, and a severely broken right arm. The bones were basically crushed in his arm from the impact of the roll. He has vocal cord damage, but the doctors don't think it appears to be vocal cord paralysis.'

'I don't understand,' Morgan said through her tears. 'What does that mean?'

'The sharp turns, the flip, the position of seat belt, or even the airbag could have played a part in the vocal cord damage, but no one knows for certain. The doctors said Ash's voice sounded stronger and better this morning, but he's been advised to write notes and refrain from speaking for the next few days. The doctors would prefer limited visitors. Ash's body needs time to regain strength and to heal.'

'Does Alex know? What about his children?'

'His ex-wife, Alex, has been here this morning, but Ash asked her to leave after about ten minutes by his side. His children were notified, but Alex advised them to stay put and if Ash's condition changed for the worse, she would contact them.'

'Morgan, Ash is fit a fiddle and has the will of a fighter. He's going to make a full recovery. We must be patient. He knows you're thinking of him. Send him a card or a letter. Reading won't hurt his throat, and he'll get a kick out of it. He wrote me a brief note telling me to tell you he has an entire team watching over your case and he has assigned his most trusted partner, William Worthington, to you in his absence.'

In his absence...Morgan couldn't stand the sound of those words. She replied softly, 'Thank you, my friend,' hung up the phone and had another decent cry.

The only good thoughts to race through her mind were that the monster did not kill Ash. The monster did not win. And Ash was wrong about Morgan. She felt no compassion towards her husband.

Kat entered the study with a hot cup of tea and gave Morgan a hug. Kat had been most distressed by the news of Ash's accident and looked as if she had shed huge tears, too. They told Ollie and Opal that Ash was in the hospital, but the kids were under the impression that the wreck was caused by the severe weather. Morgan said nothing to set the record straight.

Ollie asked his mother, 'Can we make a get-well card for our new friend?'

'Yes, please, Mommy, we need to tell him we miss him,' Opal pleaded.

'That's an excellent idea.'

She and Kat would prepare a card to send with the kids' card, too. That might bring a small smile to Ash's face and his sad eyes. Oh, she cringed at the thought of Ash being in hospital because of her estranged husband. *Shocking. Unacceptable. Devastating.*

'I think I'd like to keep busy so I'm going to make another large pot of my chicken noodle soup,' Kat said softly.

'Good idea, Mom, and if you need any help chopping onions or celery, I'll be glad to join in.' Morgan looked down at Dixie. Dixie seemed to know that the house was sad. 'C'mon, sweet girl, let's go get some fresh air.'

It was still sloppy and muddy outside so Morgan put on a pair of tall rubber Wellington boots that were standing proudly by the back door, waiting for duty to call. She placed Dixie's tangerine coat around her fluffy little body because the temperature had most definitely dropped since the storm.

'We'll be back in a while, but I want to go for a good stomp around the area.'

Kat shot Morgan a look.

'Yes, Mom, I'll be careful – I always am.'

It appeared the neighbours to the east of Ash's house had returned home from their international travels. There looked like a flurry of activity, people shuffling back and forth from cars and unpacking multiple items, or the neighbours were being robbed. She hoped the latter was not the case. In any event, Morgan led Dixie in the opposite direction. The air was fresh. It was overcast and the gigantic storm had made a serious mess of the woods. She wondered where the forest animals hid during the storm. Her mind wandered every time she went for a long walk.

Dixie was leading her this time, and it seemed as though they were heading for a specific destination. Yes. A rabbit hole or a 'something or other' hole. Dixie stuck her nose deep inside and her tail behaved like it had been plugged into an electrical socket. Something excited her! It took everything in Morgan's power to get her distracted and interested in the walk again. Dixie made multiple attempts to persuade Morgan to take her back to the hole, the deep, dark abyss that held secret, furry animals.

The hour-long walk was exactly what she needed. Morgan made a definite decision in the fresh outdoors. She was finished with tears. *No more crying. Done. Over. Enough.* She needed a plan.

CHAPTER THIRTY-ONE

Morgan thought of the .38 caliber pistol, a Smith & Wesson she had purchased a while back from her friend, Stevie. Stevie had twins under the age of two with another bub on the way at the time when she told Morgan he didn't want a firearm in the house any longer. Morgan only paid a hundred bucks for it and Stevie gave her a handwritten receipt. She didn't think she ever registered the gun. She would ask Ash about the process and what she legally needed to do...later. She knew she needed to search for the receipt, too, because if she remembered correctly, it would have the gun's registration number on it. Now Morgan was a bit concerned she might be in considerable trouble. *But who knows I even have possession of a firearm except for Stevie? Authorities must need to know – her local police station?* Morgan had no clue, and she knew zero about guns.

She changed her mind about asking Ash anything. He didn't need to know her new plans - not now. Morgan and Dixie returned from their brisk and productive walk, and she headed straight to Ash's study with Dixie by her side.

Morgan searched Google and found an indoor shooting range that wasn't terribly far from her home. *Good.* They offered evening classes and the availability to practice on Saturday and Sunday mornings but only opened for limited hours over the weekend. She had played around with target practice when she was barely twenty years old and had a good eye at that time, but that was the only experience she had of ever holding a gun. With serious amounts of practice combined in a brief period of time, she knew she would be good. There was no choice in the matter. She had to be competent with the .38 and she had to feel confident. Once Morgan put her mind to anything she normally exceeded her own expectations. There was a need for her to get this done quickly and professionally. The monster was not going to hurt anyone close to her again.

She hoped when she contacted the shooting range, they would be able to answer any questions she had about gun ownership. First thing in the morning before the kids got up, she would make a phone call and take proper notes. She wanted to register for classes as soon as she got her family back to Memphis and settled. There were only a few days remaining. Tomorrow would be New Year's Eve. She and Kat and the kids would have a small and private celebration in front of the fire.

Lee was ringing. Morgan answered and before she could say a word, Lee spluttered, 'Thank God, I got you! All the guests have finally departed, and I have a mountain of laundry to do. I wanted to check in and see how you were and find out when you're coming back. You're staying with me.'

Morgan took a deep breath. She told Lee about Ash and there was a long silence over the phone. Lee got straight to the point.

'That was no accident, Morgan. Your husband is written all over this.' Lee's voice was beyond angry.

'How right you are, but they haven't found anything that could pin him to it as far as I know.'

'Hell, Morgan, this is terrible and the situation is becoming more dangerous every day. Who does he think he is?'

Morgan could only mutter, 'The man who does as he pleases.'

'Damnit, Morgan, you need to be on high alert all the time. Do not let your guard down for one minute, I mean it. I love you. That bastard has done enough damage for a lifetime. He needs to be put away. Now, when are you coming home?'

Morgan knew her words were not going to land well, but she needed to get it over with and convey her thoughts. 'Lee, when we return, we're not staying with you. You know how much I appreciate your offer, but we need to get back into our own house and our own routine. Ash has put a hard word out to the local precinct and I'm not telling anyone but you, I own a gun and will be taking lessons as soon as we settle back in the city.'

'Good God, Morgan, have you lost every brain cell in your head? You don't need a gun. The monster will get his hands on it and you'll be gone. Has he turned you into an idiot, too? You have two precious children, two very curious little minds, do you really want a weapon in your home? You need to rethink this. This is not the Morgan I know. I need to go. I feel sick inside.' Lee hung up.

Morgan felt nauseated, too. She didn't need her best pal to be mad at her. She completely understood what Lee was saying and feeling, but she had to do what she thought was right in her heart of hearts. Morgan pushed the conversation out of her head. She would need to depend on Kat to watch over Ollie and Opal while she took shooting lessons, so she thought it best to sit her mother down now and explain as thoughtfully as possible her plans. The children were as busy as beavers plotting away at their puzzle. They were quiet and content, concentrating hard.

'Mom,' Morgan said, 'I need to speak with you for a bit. Can we sit in the kitchen?'

Kat slid her book onto the coffee table. 'Of course.'

Morgan began slowly explaining her upcoming new plans and her exact, well-considered reasons for them. She thought she sounded quite calm, professional, and reasonable. Kat's eyes were enormous. The strange thing is that Kat did not fight her.

'I know you well, Morgan, and if this is what you have decided to do, I won't be able to change your mind. I do hope you speak with Ash and Antonio regarding your decision, and I also hope you will consider what real consequences can occur while having a gun in your house. Consequences come from expected and unexpected directions, Morgan. I'm quite certain you have not thought this through.' With those words, Kat got up, left the kitchen, reached for her book along the way, and went directly upstairs.

Morgan felt like she was two down. Two people she loved deeply were quite upset with her. They didn't have a monster on their back. *They did though, didn't they?* Anyone associated with Morgan had to deal with the monster in one way or another. She tried to shake it off. There was a nagging feeling. She wanted to remain confident in the decision she made, but Lee's voice and her mother's kept replaying in her head.

Her phone rang. This time it was Antonio. 'I left Ash's room about thirty minutes ago and he was in high spirits. He is still writing notes, but he is positive and I thought you would want to know ... and—'

'And?' Morgan asked.

'Well, I didn't want to surprise you again so I'm coming out with it. Morgan, I've been invited to a big New Year's Eve bash but, I'm not feeling up to it and, well, I was wondering if you and Kat and the kids wouldn't mind seeing my face again.'

Morgan was secretly pleased and relieved. 'Antonio, get your wonderful self here with us. We'd love to see you.'

'Great, because I'm half-way there now. I left the hospital and started driving towards you.'

'Fabulous, see you soon!'

Morgan called out to Kat and the kids. 'Antonio had so much fun with us that he can't stay away, so he's heading back for a couple of nights.'

The news certainly made a broad smile appear upon Kat's face on the upstairs landing and the kids were cheering and clapping their hands by her side! Fabulous, uplifting news! The house was happy again. She would take the opportunity to tell Antonio about her special plans. *Hmmm, perhaps not. He'll only go directly to Ash and then I'd have four people I adore against me.* She wouldn't be able to handle that. She would think about it later.

Kat returned downstairs and began shifting things around in the kitchen. *She's banging around in there because she's mad at me.* Morgan knew the kitchen was Kat's favourite spot to be and normally happy sounds were coming from this part of the house. The kids were chatting over the puzzle, furiously working with their tiny hands and the colourful pieces of cardboard.

Morgan went upstairs for a quick shower. She glanced at her phone a saw a text message with the word: URGENT. Morgan didn't recognize the number and there was no name. *No. No, I'm not going to respond. He's behind this.* Then she wondered if Ash had been hurt because she had not been responding. *Was this the monster's way of getting my attention? The more I don't answer his calls, the more damage he causes. She began to question everything.* Her head was spinning, and she began to feel quite ill.

She sat on the gorgeous, upholstered ottoman in front of the dressing mirror and closed her eyes to think. She felt herself squeezing her hands. Her heart was racing. Morgan considered options and then, came to her senses. She and her attorney had demanded the restraining order and if Morgan contacted the monster in any way, the entire case against him could be compromised. She knew that much. As hard as it was to do, she would remain tough and refrain from answering any texts. She felt immensely angry and completely and utterly worn down through and through.

She hopped out of the steaming hot shower then put on her nice jeans and a lovely dark green silk blouse. She went back downstairs and was heading towards the kitchen to check with Kat but could not shake the worrying feeling about the gun, so she went into Ash's study instead and got on his computer.

Then, it suddenly hit her. She knew damned well that the monster had been inside of her house on at least two, separate occasions. *What if he had already found her gun?* That thought was most disconcerting and seriously troubling. She felt she would have huge problems if that scenario occurred. Morgan felt the panic rise, then, told herself her imagination was working overtime and that's the last thing she needed. *BE WISE. STAY CALM.*

She did a quick search on gun registration and received the shock of the day. She and Stevie had not managed the transfer properly or legally. Stevie, Morgan recalled, was quite emotional when she had arrived at Morgan's home, explaining that her twin boys were into everything, climbing shelves, standing on cupboards, and going into rooms and closets that they were not supposed to enter. Stevie was concerned that her boys would get their innocent hands on the gun and think it was a toy. She wanted the gun to disappear. She wanted it as far away from her home as possible.

Morgan's eyes widened when she researched and discovered when a firearm is transferred from one person to another, the transfer must be witnessed. Someone such as a trained or authorized officer of a recognized firearms club or a public service employee, or a police officer, or a licensed dealer must complete a transfer form. So, no doubt, once Morgan returned home, she would have to alert Stevie to travel with her to the local police station and they would play act. They would speak as if the transfer was happening that very day, and the paperwork and registration would begin from that point. She read somewhere that it could take up to 28 days for the registration to be approved and she would have to pay a fee. The information she had discovered made her feel better. Though she could not help but picture in her mind the gun missing from its hiding spot and that thought gave her chills.

Morgan turned her mind back towards Ash's face and it made her want to rush to his side. She wanted to know for herself how he really was.

She went into the kitchen and told Kat, 'I must run to the local shop to get a proper card for us to mail. 'Ollie and Opal, would you like to come with me and perhaps we'll be able to find some crayons and construction paper for you to make Ash a special card of your own?' She had no idea what the store would have, especially this time of the year.

The kids seemed happy that their mother had asked them to join her. Fresh air and a small outing might brighten everyone's spirits.

Ollie was by Morgan's side in a flash. 'Yes, Mom. I want to go.' Opal already had her jacket on saying, 'Me, too. We'll make the best card ever!'

The Pickwick Supermarket looked tiny from the outside, but as they entered Morgan was surprised. It was much larger than it appeared and it was well stocked. She remembered Ash had told her that it had been there for a good while. The owners probably listened to the locals and their needs and did their best to accommodate. At any rate, she was impressed. They found a tiny stationery section and picked out a medium sized box of crayons and a thin pack of coloured construction paper. Morgan began reading the get-well cards and found one that was not too wordy, nor too sentimental, and it had bright, bold yellow sunflowers on the front. She selected two packages of child's scissors and picked up some more milk, fresh loaves of bread, bananas and more coffee, and extra vanilla ice cream for the children. They were in and out in a relatively fleeting period of time and Opal was chatting away in the car about her plans for Ash's card.

'Mommy, will we see him soon? Is Ash coming back to visit? He did promise.'

Ollie chimed in, 'Yeah, Mom, he promised.'

'Well, yes, it's true Ash wants to return for another visit,' Morgan explained, 'but he's had several surgeries and he can't help he had to break his promise because the doctors won't allow him to leave the hospital just yet.'

Ollie looked sad. Opal added, 'Ollie and I will make him the most prettiest get-well card he's ever seen.'

Morgan smiled and let that one go.

The kids tumbled out of the car with overloaded enthusiasm. 'Can we start making our card now?'

Morgan set them up with their new gift card making supplies at the kitchen table. Dixie made the decision to slip in under the table for a nap. She went over to Kat and showed her the card she had picked out.

'Oh, that's lovely, Morgan, perfect really. Let me dry my hands and we'll sign it right now.' Kat got the kitchen towel, and Morgan went off to get a writing pen.

Kat penned: *Dear Ash, the news of your accident was simply dreadful. My heart breaks that you were so seriously hurt. You are in our thoughts and I am praying for your speedy recovery. Please take good care of yourself. I hope we will see you soon. Warmest Regards, Kat.*

Morgan added: *Dearest Ash, I am filled with sorrow and distress. This would have never happened had we not become acquainted. I would do anything to reverse this tragedy. Not a moment goes by that you are not on my mind and I wish, more than anything, I could see you to know for myself that you are healing properly. My greatest comfort is knowing that you are alive and, soon to be well, again. Sending hugs and best wishes – Sincerely, Morgan*

She thought about writing 'xxo' and changed her mind.

There. Morgan sealed the envelope and addressed it for mailing.

Ollie and Opal were diligently working in the corner. Opal was attempting to cut out flowers when Ollie announced, 'I'm going to tell Ash how much more work we've done on the giant puzzle.'

She loved her little beings. There were moments like these when she felt her heart might burst from love and adoration.

Morgan ran back to the study. She booted up Ash's computer and searched through tons of on-line florists. She found one in the

Collierville area, rang them, and told them she wanted bright bold yellow and white flowers. The lady on the phone acted a bit shocked.

The clerk said, 'Those are springtime colours and we are still in Christmas season.'

'This has nothing to do with Christmas or the New Year. I want light, bright colours that will fill a room with hope,' Morgan said a bit anxiously.

The woman replied, 'Well, I can order some in, but it's gonna take at least 24 hours before they arrive.'

'Yes, please, I want a fresh, huge arrangement in a bold, dark wooden basket and it must have a 'wow' factor. Can you do that for me, please? Will $200.00 buy me something enchanting and enlivening?'

The clerk instantly responded in a cheery voice, 'Yes, ma'am, absolutely.'

Morgan gave her details and the address of the Baptist Hospital and Ash's room number.

'What would you like the card to say?'

Morgan thought for only a second. 'Sending the warmest wishes from the Pickwick Lake House Sitting Tribe. We miss you.'

Done! If she could not be by Ash's side, she would let him know how much he was thought of. Morgan missed his eyes, his voice. It overwhelmed her to realize exactly how much she missed the man himself.

CHAPTER THIRTY-TWO

The kids continued to chat merrily together while the glue, scissors, and construction paper were strewn about the kitchen table. Four tiny hands were flying back and forth, cutting, folding, and gathering coloured crayons and markers.

'I think you've made quite a little masterpiece. Fantastic job – you two!'

'Thanks, Mommy, but we're not quite finished,' Opal claimed. 'We need to colour in the background.' Ollie added, 'Yeah, and we need to sign our names, too.'

Honk. Distant honks. More honks. The kids began to scramble from the kitchen table with shouts of joy and Morgan couldn't wait to set her eyes on Antonio again, either. Her heart was racing as she eagerly headed towards the front of the house with a huge smile in place, she flung open the heavy front door to welcome Antonio.

'Oh, My God.'

Morgan immediately attempted to close the door behind her to protect her kids, but he grabbed her. Ollie and Opal gasped and screamed out for Kat.

The monster yelled at the top of his lungs, 'Get back inside and don't let me see your faces again! DO YOU HEAR ME?'

His was a terrible sound – a voice from a dark and vicious place. The door slammed and Morgan instantly heard crying. The monster had her by the top of her arms and was walking her over to the side of the house. He threw her up against the massive stone wall and it hurt. Her shoulder blade cracked with pain. She did not move. He had both hands around her throat and he screamed, frothing at the mouth, spitting over her face. 'You think you're going to get away with all this? Do you still believe you're leaving me? You're not going anywhere. Get that through your thick head. You married me. You're mine. I'm going to show you what trouble you've caused. I'm going to make you suffer like you've never suffered before, but you'll not have your divorce, you bitch. You'd better sever all ties with your friends. You'll have none left by the time I've finished messing with them. You need to remember – you need to know I am always watching.'

With these last words he shook her like a ragdoll. He shook her so hard she thought her teeth would fall out, pounded her against the stone wall repeatedly, then he pulled back his fist and bashed her in the face. Morgan heard a pop, and she couldn't remember to breathe. Everything fell silent.

Antonio was bending over her. Morgan was regaining consciousness, and she was having difficulty taking in the scene. Kat was behind Antonio and Morgan thought she saw a patrol car coming up the driveway.

Antonio held her head as gently as he could. 'My dear, sweet friend. An ambulance is on the way. Don't say a word. You're going to be fine.'

Morgan heard Ollie and Opal weeping.

Kat was shushing them, cuddling them, and loving them both while telling them, 'Your mom is going to be okay. I promise.'

'Where is he?' Morgan weakly asked.

'Shhh, I'm going to follow the ambulance. Kat and the kids will remain here and we'll talk once they get you settled.' Antonio kissed her lightly on her forehead.

The ambulance soon appeared and Morgan was whisked away on a stretcher. She didn't understand why she was being transported to the hospital. She wanted a hot, steamy bath – that's all. And she wanted the monster to die.

No. No tears. Morgan stuck by her guns. She would not allow herself to cry or to fall in a heap in any way. Not permitted. Her mantra remained: *If I fall, the monster rises. The monster will not win.* She had lost track of the score, but they were not to the finish line yet. She would make certain with every fiber in her body that in the end she and Ollie and Opal would win their freedom and their safety and their right to live their lives free from fear. If only it could be sooner rather than later.

She sensed she had been in and out of consciousness and felt horribly groggy.

A tall, very thin doctor with tortoise shell round rimmed glasses stuck his head in the room and introduced himself. He had a kind smile and a commanding voice.

His words were filled with compassion. 'You've had a tough time and not a decent ending to this year. I'm sorry you had to endure this, but I can tell you with absolute certainty you're going to be fine. I want to get a couple of X-rays of your back. You have serious bruising and, I'm not sure if you remember, but you were complaining dreadfully about the pain in your shoulder when you arrived.'

He continued, 'I glued the laceration on your cheek and your cheek bone may have a small fracture. It will, most likely, heal on its own but it will be painful for a while. These are my initial observations but I'm going to have a trauma specialist look at you later today, too. You don't appear to have any swelling or very little at the least, so that's a good sign.'

He paused, gave her a slight smile, and let her take it all in.

Morgan muttered, 'It's not the New Year yet, is it? I still may succeed in having a lovely introduction.'

Her response made the doctor smile, and he picked up her hand and patted it. There. Another pat on the hand. She sighed heavily. He looked at her with empathetic eyes.

'I'm not going to push anything on you, but I would like to have a counsellor visit you. You've been through a most unpleasant ordeal and a good friend of yours filled me in on a few of the nasty details. It never hurts to talk, it only helps.'

Morgan saw the sincerity and concern in the doctor's face, but she assured him, 'I'm okay.' It hurt her to speak.

FAKE. FAKER. LIAR. FAKE.

NO. STRONG. SURVIVOR.

Kat and the children popped in next, and she was shocked to see how puffy and Ollie's and Opal's faces were. It scared her. Kat looked like death warmed over. Morgan could not bear the sight. *No. No. No.* The tears were welling up in her eyes and she willed them back in. She would not let her children see her cry.

She bit the bottom of her lip until it almost bled and she sat up in her bed, stretched out her arms, 'Come to me my little darlings. I am fine. We will be fine. Everything is all right now and I'm so very sorry that you were scared. Please hug me. I love you both so very much.'

They held on to their mother tightly. Kat was standing behind them with her head down, wiping away teardrops. Morgan shook her head at her and Kat did her dead level best to straighten up.

Instantly, a big, fat arrangement of all sorts of red, purple, orange, deep blue, yellow, green, lavender, and lilac flowers – every colour in the rainbow – popped into the room and Antonio made a funny face as he marched in hiding behind the arrangement and then holding it high in the air.

'Look what I found! These flowers were in the shop downstairs in the lobby beckoning me to take them to Morgan. I heard: *Take me, take me, please. We want to be in Morgan's room!*'

Ollie and Opal were overwrought with joy and they ran over and hugged Antonio.

Kat took the vase from him, kissed him on his cheek, and sat the beautiful arrangement on a table by the window.

'Oh, Antonio, they're splendid!'

There wasn't a place on Morgan's body that wasn't hurting. It was her heart that hurt the most. Her first priority was not going to be the gun business when they returned to Memphis. She would ask her physician for a personal referral for a child psychologist. *What must Ollie and Opal be thinking?* She never wanted them to think that any type of life they had lived these last few weeks had been typical. Normal, loving, married adults do not act this way.

Kat stroked her daughter's hair and everyone made small talk. Morgan held her mother's hand, looked up at her and mouthed, 'Thank you.'

Kat bent down close to her daughter's ear and whispered, 'I love you.' She then shared, 'I'm going to take the children home. Dixie needs to be taken out. I didn't secure her in the kitchen as we normally do. Ollie and Opal, it is New Year's Eve so I'm going to prepare something especially lovely for dinner and we can watch the New Year arrive all around the world on Ash's big television screen. Would you like that?'

Ollie asked, 'Can mom come home with us?'

Antonio said, 'Not tonight, Ollie. You and Opal must be brave for your mother. Tell you what. I'm going to join you back home in a little while and you can help me with a surprise. Does that sound good?'

This piqued Ollie and Opal's interest. Their eyes widened and they kissed him goodbye.

Antonio pulled a chair up close to Morgan's bedside. 'How are you, really?'

Morgan looked down and Antonio shuddered when he saw her black and blue face up close.

'My entire body hurts like Hell, but not as much as my psyche. The police got him, right? I mean he is behind bars as we speak, right? This happened in broad daylight and you were due to arrive any minute. Antonio, that's the only reason I opened the door.'

'I arrived within minutes of the patrol car. Kat had immediately called for the police when she heard the kids' screams. When she returned outside, she only saw the monster's backside running down the driveway and scooting into the trees. He wasn't in a car, Morgan. He arrived in a car, someone must have driven him and parked in a predetermined spot; he high tailed it and so far, got away. He didn't manage this on his own.'

Morgan made a feeble attempt to sit up. 'What did you say? He attacks me in the middle of an afternoon on a private property with a restraining order attached to his head, my children see him with their own eyes, my mother witnesses the fact he was there and yet … he is free … again? He got away, Antonio?'

Antonio reached for Morgan's hand. 'It appears so. He may not have been caught this day, this time, but Morgan he'll be put away. Do not doubt it. He's really pissed off the local cops now and they're feeling quite foolish for not apprehending him. The Germantown and East Precinct police departments have received notifications to be on the lookout for him. The monster has not been living in his home for weeks. The cops told Ash's team that his mail is overflowing and they have someone driving by his house at different times during the day and night. For some reason, it took this incident in addition to Ash's accident for them to take the situation seriously. They want him as much as you do. The cops snapped photos of your face before the ambulance arrived, but they have asked the hospital staff to take further photos of any additional bruising or damage to your body. It's a wonder he didn't crack your head open or finish you off by strangling you. Your neck looks wretched if I may say so.'

Morgan muttered, 'Thanks.'

'Okay, so this is my groovy plan and you don't get a say in it. I'm popping back to Pickwick. I'm going to stop by the local super-market and see if they have any silly party hats for New Year's Eve for Ollie, Opal, and Kat and hang out with them for a bit. I'll get the kids an assortment of candy to have later and that will bring back their smiles. Then, I shall return with proper adult entertainment. The nurses are going to be taking you down for X-rays in minutes anyway. You're going to be tied up with tests and doctors for a while. I promise I'll be back before you know it.'

'Ash already knows what happened?' Morgan asked.

'One of the members of his team went directly to the hospital once the East Precinct contacted him. Ash became highly agitated, considerably upset. The doctor and nurses got angry with Ash's staff member and asked him to leave. Ash texted me on his new phone and told me to tell you he is thinking of you every moment. He is most distraught.'

Antonio looked quite cheeky. 'I'm glad Ash can't fully speak at the moment because I would have heard an earful.'

Morgan ignored that. 'Did you say new phone? What do you mean? Did his phone get destroyed or crushed in the wreckage?'

'Funny you should ask, Morgan. No, his phone wasn't damaged. Ash clearly remembers a black glove, an arm of a coat reaching down into the front windshield after it had been shattered and picking up his cell phone from the roof of the car. He was upside down, you know. He watched his phone slip away and then heard a car screech off.'

'The bastard. The scathing monster. Nothing surprises me. Nothing. It's all about control. He seriously thinks he's going to get dirt on me by having Ash's phone and he wanted to prove that he has power over Ash. He thinks he does have power in his sick, demented universe. Lee's right, Antonio. He brings out the worst in everyone.'

'Oh, and don't shoot me, please. I rang Lee and I put her in tears. I genuinely didn't mean to upset her. She loves you to pieces and I think it was a build-up of everything. This last attack sent her over the edge. She said she was hopping in her car without delay. I talked her out of it. I told her you would be leaving in a couple of days anyway. She did insist that I convince you to drive with the kids directly to her place after you dropped off Kat and move in with her. I advised her I would give it my best attempt.'

'I wish you hadn't Antonio. Lee doesn't need to know everything immediately. She's my sister from another mother and she's stressed out to the max. And, no, I'm not moving back in with Lee. I have faith the cops will catch up with him now.'

Antonio looked grim. 'Rightio, kiddo.'

A nurse entered the room with a wheelchair and Antonio gently kissed Morgan's head. 'I'll return in a while.'

With a wink and a wave, he was off.

CHAPTER THIRTY-THREE

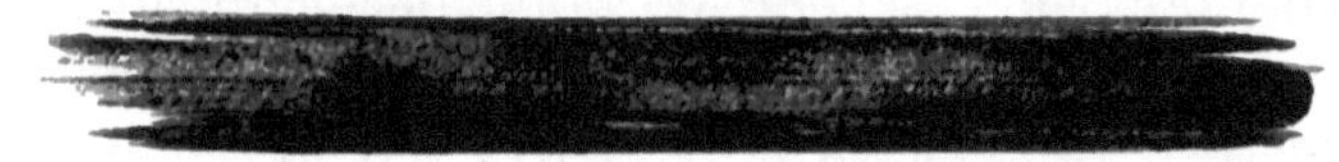

Dixie greeted Antonio with a happy bark and Opal had placed a new big, bold silver and gold ribbon around their furry friend's neck. Kat was busy baking oatmeal and raisin cookies, and she had produced a ham and potato casserole that looked delicious. She was chopping broccoli, cauliflower, and carrots to steam. He thought he could smell fresh bread baking in the oven. The kids were finishing Ash's get-well card and they had done an amazing job with it. Antonio complimented their efforts.

'Brilliant work, kids!'

They both thanked him as any serious artist would and Ollie decided to bow to Antonio!

Antonio pulled the brightly coloured assortment of striped party hats that had sparkly balls on top, metallic foil party horns, and other funny noise makers with extra silly bits and pieces he found, out of the grocery sacks to the children's utter amazement. He bought far too much candy for the kids. He picked up two new children's books in case Morgan was forced to stay a bit longer than she had anticipated. Their little hands clapped together while they jumped up and down.

Kat attempted to bring calm into the situation and announced in no uncertain terms, 'I am the candy manager, and I'll distribute some after you've had dinner.'

They begged her, 'Only one piece now, please?'

Antonio turned their thoughts to his task at hand.

'Remember when I said at the hospital that I wanted some help with a surprise?'

Ollie and Opal quipped 'Yeah!' with wonder and bemusement.

'Well, since your mom can't be here with you tonight, why don't you make her one special giant card and sign your names, and Kat's name, and Dixie's name?'

The children laughed hard at this notion and Opal said, 'Antonio, you're silly, Dixie doesn't know how to write!'

He just grinned. 'I would like to sign it, too. The front can say Happy New Year and you write whatever you like on the inside. Okay?'

Ollie and Opal were all over this wonderful idea. The scissors came out. Kat took the glue over to the kitchen table and their little hands went back to work cutting and designing.

Ollie suggested, 'Antonio, you can take her a hat and a horn, too, right? We can all blow our horns together at midnight.'

Kat was trying to smile.

Antonio checked out Ash's wine refrigerator and chose a quite divine, glorious bottle of chilled French Champagne. There it was staring him in the face – Louis Roederer Cristal 2009. All Antonio truly knew about it was it was known as the Tsar's wine and was made for the exquisite taste of Tsar Alexander II. He knew, too, that it was cellared for over six years. The most important fact he learned not long ago was that he enjoyed this drop immensely and had no doubt that Morgan would, too. It was screaming 'New Year's Eve' to him, and he grinned a little at the prospect. If Ash minded at all, which he sincerely doubted, he would replace the bottle the next time he came down. This day called for this particular drop and *not* because it was New Year's Eve. Antonio was Hell bent on instilling hope and appreciation for a future filled with new dreams in Morgan. His most precious colleague and mate needed it. He thought of his old friend, Ash, and said to himself that Ash would only want the best for Morgan, especially after the horrific intrusion forced upon her. He went into the pantry to get an insulated wine cooler bag and wondered how he was going to camouflage the champagne and two crystal flutes to sneak into Morgan's room. He found a bulky canvas carry bag in a dark rear corner of the pantry and he wrapped the flutes, placed ice in the cooler bag, and got a change of clothes to place on top to hide the contraband!

Kat watched in dismay. 'Antonio, are you being naughty?' Then she gave him a beautiful grin.

'Trying my hardest.'

They both laughed and Kat told him, 'Be careful, but what medication is Morgan taking?'

'The only thing I saw she was taking was some pain medication and I'll do my best to make certain that she is only consuming Champagne and not popping the hospital pills.'

'I don't think I want to know anymore. Please sit and eat dinner with the children and I'll make a small plate for my daughter. Hospital food probably hasn't improved greatly over the years.'

The kids held up their beautifully decorated card for all to see and Antonio reached into his inside pocket for a writing pen. The gang wrote a heartfelt message.

Opal chimed in, 'Don't close it. Dixie hasn't signed it.'

Ollie asked in a smarty pants' voice with his hands on his hips, 'And just how is she supposed to do that?'

Antonio smiled. 'Here. I'll show you.' He drew a perfect paw and inside of it a happy face.

The kids loved it and Ollie exclaimed, 'Oh, that's great!'

Kat got the kids' attention. 'Time to clear the table properly for dinner.'

Antonio called out to Dixie and picked up her lead. Dixie's tail went ballistic while they scooted out the back door together.

Kat was thinking what a dream of a man Antonio was and how it had been such a pleasure spending this much time with him. Then her thoughts turned to Morgan in the hospital, and she instantaneously felt sick to her stomach. She had no idea how to help except to tell her daughter how much she meant to her and to be there any time she was needed whether it was for Morgan, Ollie, or Opal. That's all Kat knew to do. She snapped herself back into reality.

'Children, please start setting the table.' Then she began to prepare the plates. Dixie appeared excited and proud looking, and her nose was seriously interested in the mealtime aromas.

Antonio poured the milk for the children and the remainder of a nice Spanish red for Kat and himself. They raised their glasses. 'To Morgan.'

Ollie said, 'To Mom.' Opal clinked her glass, 'To Mommy.'

CHAPTER THIRTY-FOUR

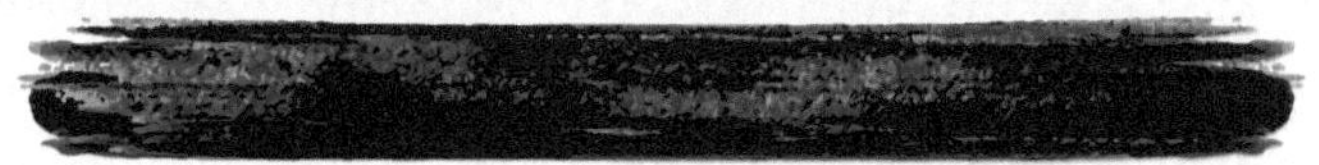

Morgan had been in X-ray for at least an hour, she felt, but nothing was happening. She was cold and her body was trembling uncontrollably from head to toe. A nurse apologised to her regarding the wait and got her two nicely heated blankets to place around her legs. In a matter of minutes, she was whisked away again. This nurse was a different one from the first who had wheeled her downstairs. She calmly and professionally told Morgan she needed to view her body for bruising or any other damage and take pictures for the police.

When she asked Morgan to turn around, Morgan heard the nurse gasp. 'My goodness, he did a number to your back, didn't he? It will be interesting to see what the X-rays reveal.' Snap. Snap. Snap. This went on for quite a while. Morgan's left thigh had a nasty bruise on it, too, that practically spread from the bottom of her hip to the top of her knee. She vaguely remembered being thrown sideways into the wall of the house before the monster started slamming her back into it. The nurse called for a technician and exited the room, but not before saying, 'I'm sorry this has happened to you.'

The efficient technician stood Morgan with her back against the X-ray machine. She took X-rays from assorted angles. Morgan wondered if the first nurse was supposed to comment regarding her injuries. Then she thought her back must look bloody awful for her to do so.

Yet still another attendant appeared before her and stated Morgan needed to meet with one more doctor in another section of the hospital. He said they wouldn't be travelling far in the wheelchair and the doctor was ready and waiting to meet with her now. *This must be the facial reconstruction guy.*

Morgan was wheeled into the examination room and moments later the door popped open to a very sophisticated and quite stunning looking doctor, but it was a 'she' and not a 'he.' That was fine. Morgan smiled to herself wondering why she had automatically imagined the doctor to be male. The woman had kind and interesting eyes. 'I've been informed you've had quite a day.'

Morgan tried to smile. 'Yes, but not the usual and not one I would choose to experience again.

The doctor was typing in her computer but stopped and moved Morgan under a better light. 'Let me have a good look at you.' After observing Morgan's face she commented, 'The emergency room doctor did an excellent job with the laceration. He used surgical glue. The benefits of using glue instead of stitches are lower rates of infection and much less scarring, plus stitches must be removed later and you won't have to worry about that now.' She continued, 'This should heal well. A mark may remain, but it should be minimal. I prefer doctors using glue instead of stitches, especially for wounds to the facial area, and, again, this is exceptionally good work.'

The physician warned Morgan it may hurt a bit, but she needed to check her entire cheekbone. The pain was sharp and Morgan winced. The specialist explained that if there had been more swelling, she would be more concerned and would order a CT scan of the eye socket area.

She took off her latex gloves and said, 'You took a big hit to the face. You're going to be in pain for quite a while. The face is fragile. As you know there is not a great deal of fat or tissue to protect it. I want you to carefully observe your face, especially your cheekbone. If you begin to experience any swelling, which I doubt very much at this point, or if a lump begins to develop or if a spot begins to appear sunken, please contact my office immediately. I am giving you worst case scenarios. I think your face will heal well in time. Be gentle in the shower. Don't linger with your face directly under hot water. Here is my card and I hope they get the bastard who did this to you.'

WOW! I really like this chick. 'Thank you very much,' was Morgan's only response to the doctor while she held onto her card.

Antonio, Kat, Ollie and Opal enjoyed a wonderful dinner together. Kat was busy cleaning the kitchen when she advised the children, 'Pack away your craft items as best you can, and I'll help you with your baths and pajamas.' She was talking up a storm about how much fun was ahead for the night and she promised to make them a hot bowl of popcorn, too.

She was encouraging both kids, 'Now, please get a move on.' Then it dawned on her that Morgan had absolutely no personal items with her in the hospital.

Antonio was taking Dixie out for a stroll again. These two seemed to adore one another. She knew Antonio was trying to help any way that he could. He could, she thought, walk a dog much better than he could clean a kitchen!

When Antonio stepped back inside, Kat quickly said, 'Morgan is stuck in the hospital with none of her personal belongings. I'm running upstairs, getting her purse, and her phone, and I'll put together basic toiletries, other items she may need, and a change of clothes, too. I have a nice bed jacket that I wear when I read and Morgan may like that. Hospitals can be so cold. You'll want to take her coat, too, Antonio.'

Kat could not believe she had not thought of these things sooner. Everything had happened lightning fast.

'Well spotted, you darling woman.'

Kat was heading back down the staircase with her arms loaded and Antonio went up to meet her. 'Let me take those. They will fit nicely into the canvas bag I've packed.'

'You mean they'll help you hide that nice bottle of wine and those two champagne flutes? Don't you forget to bring those glasses back to me young man and in fine shape, too. Understood?'

Antonio looked sheepish. 'Yes Ma'am.' He kissed his most favourite little people and told Kat, 'Morgan will be fine and we'll ring you at midnight or I will if Morgan falls asleep.'

He was loading his car and his cell phone was buzzing like mad. He wedged the heavy bag for the big New Year's Eve night at the hospital on the floorboard of the passenger side and answered his phone. 'Ash, you are not supposed to be talking. Why are you calling me?'

Ash huskily responded, 'Because I'm worried out of my head and no one is calling me. Why haven't I heard from you? How is she? Is she going to be okay?'

'Slow down, stop talking, and listen. I mean it, Ash, stop talking or I'll hang up. I only left the house seconds ago and helped Kat with the kids and now I'm heading back to the hospital. I promise I conveyed your words and concern with Morgan, and she is still more devastated about you. I assure you; that woman is a trouper, Ash. She is tough as nails and don't you forget it.'

Ash was about to say something and Antonio cut him off.

'Now, physically I know she has a laceration on her face, and they were sending her down to X-ray when I last saw her. I think the doctor was concerned about one of her shoulder blades and possibly the lower part of her neck. Ash, her neck looks like she had heavy ropes tied around it and as if she'd been dragged. It's a horrible deep purple and it looks alarming. You know what she said to me? She said her heart hurt the most. She looks like death warmed over. I'm happy there are no mirrors within her reach. And, she's angry. She's angry as Hell. No tears. I have not seen her cry one single tear, and this concerns me the most. She's certainly had enough. We all have. I cannot imagine what went through her head when she thought she was opening the door to me. It makes me sick, Ash. I want this bastard. I don't care how the cops get him. He's going to do something worse and he's planning it right now. Look, I'm pulling into the hospital. I'll have Morgan text you when we get settled. Oh and by the way, I took it upon myself to take your best bottle of Champagne for the best gal I know. Don't respond. Text me any time you need me. Text me when they think they are going to release you, too. Gotta run, buddy. Take care.'

Antonio found a parking spot close to the front door. It was well and truly New Year's Eve. He supposed the lot would be full once midnight hit and the party goers had too much to drink and made too many stupid decisions. He wondered just how full emergency rooms throughout the country would be on New Year's Eve. Hell, all over the world! He imagined they would reach over capacity levels.

Antonio made dramatic gestures singing, 'Hello and Happy New Year,' to the receptionist and headed towards the elevator to Morgan's floor. The bag was bulky and he was smiling to himself thinking of his surprise and hoping more than anything he would be bringing good cheer to Morgan.

He saw a floor nurse and she looked down at his bag and said, 'Will you be staying the night?'

He grinned flirtatiously at her. 'Yes Ma'am.'

The nurse told him she would have a cot, pillow and blankets brought up. He told her not to bother and that the sofa would be fine.

She grunted, 'I assure you it won't,' and went on her way.

Antonio didn't know if that meant someone would be coming or not. The least number of staff is what he preferred.

He stood at her door for a moment and breathed. He stood up straight, gently tapped on the door, and mustered a big, fat grin. Antonio couldn't wait to show her the adult entertainment – the adult beverages! He felt like a kid.

Her voice was soft. 'Come in.'

He opened the door with an enormous smile. 'Did you miss me?'

'You'd have to go away in order for that to ever happen.'

That response made him chuckle. 'Your mom is a star. She has not only prepared a fantastic New Year's Eve dinner for you, but she gathered your girly things she thought you may need.'

'What a relief! Mom is so astute - doesn't miss anything and yes, thank goodness, this is everything I needed. They're letting me know in the morning if I'm to be released, but it looks like that's what will happen.'

'First things first. Here is your phone. Text Ash, please. He was naughty and rang me to find out about you. He is still not supposed to be talking. I'll get your other things out for you and place them by your side. And I'll put your mother's dinner on your tray table, too.'

Morgan was texting back and forth with Ash and looking a bit distressed because she was concerned. 'Ash is most insistent about leaving the hospital as soon as possible. I told him he couldn't do that. Plus, he needs to stay as long as it takes to get him back to the original Ash I met.'

'Hmmm, well, he's very much like you...once he makes up his mind it normally does not change.'

Morgan saw her mother's light blue bed jacket with white, soft wool around the sleeves and the collar and she slowly slipped it on. It made her feel close to her mom and she was, still, quite chilly. Wearing the jacket made her happy and she felt cozy and comfortable. Then, she pulled her purse towards her and pulled out a mirror while Antonio was digging in the canvas bag. 'Oh, good God. I look like a creature from the deep lagoon. Antonio, why didn't you say something? I'll never look the same again,' she sighed in disgust and slammed the mirror shut. *That's okay. Another price to pay for bringing the monster into their lives.* Morgan truly didn't recognize her own face. The doctor was right. It was not swollen, but it was dark, black, and blue and her neck was even more frightful.

She caught the look of shock on Antonio's face.

This is exactly what Antonio didn't want to happen, but he wasn't paying attention. He walked over to Morgan and placed his hand out. 'May I have that, please?'

She stared at him. He took the mirror and placed it inside his jacket pocket. 'No mirrors allowed. Now, eat your dinner then we can get down to serious fun.'

Morgan wanted to cry but most certainly did not allow herself.

'Fun, in a hospital?'

'You bet.'

She wasn't the least bit hungry and it physically hurt her when she did attempt to eat. She didn't know if it was the position of her back in the bed or her shoulders when she moved her fork to her mouth, but something did not feel right, and she was in tremendous pain. 'Would you mind getting one of those pills from the bedside table? I'm not managing well.'

'I would, but what if I told you I had something better than hospital meds?'

'Like what? What do you mean?'

He pulled out the two crystal flutes that had been chilling inside the cooler bag along with the divine bottle in all its glory.

Morgan's eyes grew wider, 'No, no you didn't. You devil. I had no clue what you were talking about when you said adult entertainment earlier today. You had me perplexed. I should have known. You're the king of scrutiny and secret, covert activities! I'm overwhelmed by your kindness and generosity. Now, yes, damnit, please, pour us a glass.'

'It's more Ash's generosity and kindness because I raided his wine fridge.'

'Oh, Antonio, you didn't. We're never going to be allowed back in that house again!' They laughed together and Morgan held her ribcage.

They clinked the tips of their glasses.

'To you, Morgan, the bravest, the kindest, and the most beautiful woman I have ever had the privilege of knowing.'

Morgan couldn't speak and she had no control over her eye sockets. The tears burst through like a waterfall or a broken dam and she honestly couldn't stop the spillage. She placed her flute on the tray and put her hands up in the air.

'Oh, Antonio,' and he went straight to her and just held her.

'There, don't say anything. I've said it before. I shall say it again. You'll be fine.'

'It's not that,' Morgan said sniffling. 'I feel so close to you. You've been such a magnificent work colleague and we've hung out before, but never like this. Thank you for being in my life. I mean it. I treasure what we have and I want it to remain forever.'

He hugged her a little tighter.

They both collected themselves.

Morgan looked down at her dinner plate and said, 'Look how lovely Mom made this. Her trademark is written all over it and I don't have the strength or the appetite to eat it.'

Antonio covered it and removed it to the other side of the room. 'Kat prepared something for our champagne, too, I'll bring that out a bit later and you might feel like munching on a late-night snack.'

Morgan smiled sweetly at him. 'You two are quite the pair. How were Ollie and Opal when you returned home?'

'Well, that reminds me,' and brought out the brilliant New Year's Eve card. 'Morgan, they made this together. They put their hearts and heads into it without arguing or disagreeing and created this spectacular gem. They are the loveliest children. Truly.'

He held the card before her and Morgan examined every inch. Such peaches. The card was something she would cherish forever.

Antonio continued, 'They seem to be fine when they are working on projects together and I'm amazed at how very close to one another they are plus they love sharing the responsibility of

Dixie.' He went further, 'I do think having them see someone when you return to Memphis is an excellent idea.' He tried to explain, 'You never know if or when kids are faking being okay.'

'And why would they feel the need to fake it?' Morgan asked.

'My feeling is they want to appear strong for you, Morgan. They've been through seriously traumatising events lately. I know I feel as if I've been trekking through mud uphill; imagine what their little minds are thinking.'

FAKE. FAKERS. Dear God, please don't let my kids fake being happy. Please Lord, guide us towards a healthy, peaceful, and loving place.

Morgan closed her eyes. 'Mud,' she repeated. 'Mud is a most appropriate term for what we've been experiencing.'

Antonio poured more of the luscious bottle and a nurse's attendant walked in. She looked embarrassed and said, 'I'm just coming in to deliver extra blankets and a pillow, to pick up any empty trays, and to refill the water pitcher.'

She glanced at the patient. 'Do you need anything?'

Morgan tried to wink at her, but her face wouldn't work properly. 'No, thank you. I think I'm fine.'

The young girl said, 'Yes, Ma'am, I think you are, too,' and backed out of the room acting as if she saw nothing.

Antonio quipped, 'I think our secret is safe for the night.'

———

Back at Pickwick Lake, Kat texted Morgan: The kids are relaxing, but I would love to hear how you are feeling now. xxo Morgan sent a message back immediately: Thank you for being so observant regarding my personal items and the dinner you prepared was fantastic. I am feeling a bit better and I love you. xox She texted Kat again: I'm not sure if I'll last until midnight. Kat texted back: I'm certain you won't! xxo Morgan responded once more: I feel confident I'll be home around noon. xox

That is exactly the kind of information Kat was seeking.

———

Ash sent a joint text to Antonio and Morgan: I wish I could join you because your hospital room sounds tremendously more fun than mine. Morgan texted back: You're exactly where you need to be and we're raising a glass to you. Ash responded: Cheers and Happy New Year. I think I'm calling it a night. Morgan, this upcoming year will be YOUR year. Morgan sent one more quick text: Thank you for everything you've done and you're doing. Get better soon. She yearned to type 'xxo' but refrained. He was her attorney and would remain so for quite some time, no doubt.

Antonio joined the group text: Both of you – get well soon. My orders!

Antonio left the party hats and the festive trinkets in the bag. It wasn't that kind of night, no matter what he had tried to imagine for Morgan. It was a lovely, simple evening between two close friends. They sat for a long time without uttering a word.

Morgan reminded her friend, 'Please turn on the TV so you can watch the big ball drop in New York Times Square.' She felt as if she were beginning to nod off.

'I may do that, but I'm fine, right now, truly.' He went over to the cold, faux leather sofa and did his best to turn it into a comfy bed and kissed Morgan on her forehead. 'Happy New Year.' He turned back to look at her.

'See you next year.' She blew an air kiss.

Early, far too early the next morning, Morgan's doctor came in to see her. It was still dark outside and Antonio was snoring. The doctor flipped the overhead light on the headboard of her bed and said, 'I have good news for you. The X-rays appear clear. Nothing cracked or fractured at the base of your neck or your shoulders or your spine. You have the 'All clear' and I am releasing you this morning. A medical officer will be around mid-morning with insurance and other release papers, but you should be good to go by midday. I do wish you a happy and safe New Year and it's been a pleasure meeting you.'

Morgan smiled. 'I appreciate everything you've done for me, and I've enjoyed meeting you, too, but I would prefer if we didn't meet this same way in the future.'

Her words brought a big smile to the doctor's face. 'Agreed.'

Off he went with his white jacket flying behind him. He turned back once more at the door and gave her a wave. What a thoughtful, nice bedside manner the doctor had. She wondered why all doctors couldn't be that outstanding and turned her head sideways on the pillow and fell deeply into sleep once more.

This time it was Antonio gently nudging her. 'Morgan, Morgan, you need to wake up. Your signature is required.' She wiped the sleep from her eyes and had to think where she was. Antonio was raising blinds and turning on a few lights here and there.

An older woman with soft white hair, sparkling eyes, and a smile was standing before her with a clipboard. 'Good morning to you and Happy New Year, too. At least you'll be able to leave us and enjoy the first day of the New Year away from the hospital!'

Morgan replied, 'Happy New Year to you. I'm sorry you're working on this special day.'

The woman retorted, 'Oh, I've seen many New Year days in my lifetime and the money is far too good on this day for me to refuse work.' Morgan nodded and began signing her life away.

Antonio was busy collecting items from around the room and packing things back into the canvas bag. He had folded his blanket and, apparently, had a quick hot shower in the bathroom. Morgan thought to herself she wouldn't be showering here, but she'll be soaking a good, long while in a hot, steaming bath once they hit home. Morgan excused herself and made it slowly to the bathroom to at least brush her teeth and her hair. Once she sat up, she felt the pain travelling through her body. She wondered if this is how people felt when they had been in a car accident. She imagined Ash's body hurting everywhere. Poor sweet Ash.

Antonio tapped on the bathroom door. 'I'm going downstairs and pull the car around.'

'An employee from transport will be around in a matter of minutes and hospital procedures state you must leave in a wheel-chair,' the ward nurse advised.

Morgan managed to mutter, 'That's certainly fine with me.'

The woman wished her all the best and scooted out of the room.

She couldn't wait to see her beautiful children and Kat. She and her family were supposed to depart in the morning for home. Morgan mulled that thought over in her head and realized she would need to see how she felt in the morning. They might push the return trip back one more day and she knew Ash would not mind in the least. She would text Ash, too, once she was settled at his house.

Antonio was waiting for her, standing by the passenger side with the car door open. He placed a crisp $20.00 bill in the hands of the transporter and helped Morgan into his car. An ambulance was pulling into the lot and heading towards the emergency room doors and Morgan instantly felt fortunate to be leaving the hospital.

CHAPTER THIRTY-FIVE

On the way to the lake house, Morgan's cell was pinging. It was Ash. He had sent three different photos of the floral arrangement she had purchased. 'WOW' was the first caption. The second caption read: You truly made my morning. Thank you enormously. The third caption stated: I have been lying here contemplating, and I just realized I have never received flowers before in my lifetime. Not ever. What a wonderful surprise – such a treat. I'm in shock. Happy shock!

Morgan shared the texts with Antonio and he grinned from ear to ear.

'How fantastic, Morgan. You've obviously made him a happy man. This is great news.'

Morgan texted back: YOU are our delightful surprise. She deleted it, then texted: So happy you are happy. Enjoy. Get better soon.

They pulled up the familiar, winding driveway and Morgan's heart was racing. She was excited. The three lovelies opened the door and everyone was cheering, then, Opal burst into tears. 'Oh, Mommy, your face is still broken. You must be really sad and it must hurt a lot.'

Morgan had forgotten how she looked. She felt like the exact same mother on the inside, but now she was embarrassed and humiliated again and the fact she might have scared her own children didn't cross her mind when they left the hospital.

STUPID. EMBARRASSED. HUMILIATED. THOUGHTLESS.

Stop. Morgan winced inside.

Ollie was outstanding and he chimed in. 'Opal, it's okay. Remember, when you fell off your bike at the bottom of that steep hill? You were a mess. Your face and hands, elbows, and knees were all banged up and you looked terrible. You look fine now and mom will, too.'

There. It only took the words of a child. Out of the mouth of a babe and everyone was back on track. Dixie could not contain her excitement, and you would have reckoned Morgan had been absent for months. Morgan gently bent over, scooped Dixie into her arms with her poofy tail wagging wildly, and she covered her in doggie smooches and whispered sweet nothings into her white fluffy ears.

Kat tenderly hugged Morgan and took her things. Ollie and Opal stated they were taking Dixie for a walk, and Opal shouted behind her, 'No, we won't go too far.'

Antonio stood guard by the French doors watching them stroll with Dixie.

'How was New Year's Eve, Mom? Did everything go okay?'

Kat smiled and replied, 'The kids ate far too many sweets, but were darlings, and asleep by 9:45pm. I stayed up reading, had New York Times Square featured squarely on the television, but the sound was down. I surprised myself and stayed up past midnight.'

Morgan kissed her cheek. 'Mom, I need a long soak in a very hot tub.'

She needed to ring Lee, too.

Antonio vigilantly watched over Ollie, Opal, and Dixie before they returned inside.

The kids appeared in mere minutes and headed immediately to their corner puzzle table. Dixie let out a big sigh and curled up in a fluffy ball directly below them. Ollie and Opal could navigate the high bar stools easily by this time – clearly masters of their own destinies.

Before making his necessary phone calls Antonio told Kat, 'I'll meet you in the kitchen and we can whip up a fabulous New Year's Day celebratory lunch. Isn't it wonderful we've been able to be with each other for two special holidays this year?'

Kat agreed and slipped on her apron and turned on her fav music from an era long ago. She worked while listening to Ella Fitzgerald, Nina Simone, Dinah Washington, Frank Sinatra, Billie Holiday, Nat King Cole, Tony Bennett, plus Sarah Vaughn. She was planning on accomplishing a great deal this afternoon.

Morgan was undressing upstairs and refusing to look at her reflection in the mirror. *It doesn't matter. What can I do about it anyway?* She rang Lee who picked up instantly.

'Oh my God. I want to see you. Tell me how you really are, Morgan. Please.'

Morgan spoke in reassuring tones to Lee and was most relieved that Lee couldn't see the shape she was in. She spilled out the incident as quickly as she could, once again, tying up another episode, and tucking it away in a dark box hidden in a corner... somewhere. Her mental corner was now overloaded with boxes and she knew they would all come tumbling down soon.

Lee asked with sadness and urgency in her voice, 'When will I see you? When will you return home?'

'It was supposed to be in the morning, but I honestly think we should hang back a couple more days.'

'Well, I love you and can't wait to see you and the kids again. Hurry home. Give Kat a big hug, too.'

Morgan switched on the light in the gigantic bathroom and the best fragrance in the world drifted down upon her. She turned the heavy, opulent fixtures on full blast and hot, steamy water began to fill the tub. She added turquoise and dark blue bath crystals into the bath and stepped out of her clothes. Damn. The guest bathroom was lined with beveled mirrors from ceiling to floor. They were everywhere she turned. She caught the wretched sight of her damaged face, bruised back, her blackened neck, and her purple thigh in all their glory. It looked as if she had been pummeled. It was ghastly and she instantly felt nauseated. Shocking even for her eyes to take in, so, Morgan did what any sensible, hurt woman would do and flicked the light switch off and slowly slid into the magnificent, oversized tub. She must have been there for a while because her mom was tapping on the door and her fingers were incredibly wrinkled.

'My darling, are you okay?'

'Yes, Mom, I'll be out in a minute, but I'm feeling really drowsy.'

'Do you need help getting out of the tub?'

Oh God, no, Morgan didn't want her mother to gaze upon her battered body, but she did wonder if she had the strength to pull herself up from the bath.

Morgan called back, 'No, Mom, I'm perfectly fine, thank you. I think I'm going to have a bit of a lie down, if that's okay with you.'

'That's probably a good idea. I'll come and collect you when lunch is ready.'

Morgan toweled off her battered body and wrapped herself in a beautiful fuchsia and pale pink silk robe hanging from a brass dragonfly hook on the back of the bathroom door. It felt luxurious. She had no recollection of climbing into bed.

CHAPTER THIRTY-SIX

Ollie and Opal were gently prodding her and saying, 'Mom, it's time. Antonio and Nanna-Kat have made a pretty lunch for us. You must come and see. You must hurry.'

Ollie kissed her and said, 'I love you Mom and I'm glad you're home with us.'

Opal added, 'Me, too.'

That was the exact medicine Morgan needed to shift into gear. 'Go downstairs slowly and I'll be there in a jiffy.'

Morgan brushed her teeth, combed her hair, and got out her make-up bag. She did her damned best to hide as many bruises as possible, and she put on a nice burgundy lip gloss and lovely silver earrings. She decided on a green and blue flowing top and her best black pants. She added short, low-heeled, blue suede boots and thought what a difference foundation and powder can make on a damaged woman. She steered clear of the laceration. That was the best she could manage and it would have to suffice. Her smile, she thought, was what she really needed. Oh, and a short spray of Chanel Allure. The broken woman with her battle scars headed down to face the music.

Morgan's favourite people welcomed her exclaiming 'Happy New Year' in a theatrical gesture. Dixie just stood there wondering what all the fuss was about when food was sprawled about the kitchen and driving the furry being absolutely nuts. Morgan continued to be amazed. Antonio took off his apron and placed a towel over his arm, bending over, like a proper restaurant maître d' and pulling out the kitchen chair for her. Antonio must have slipped out and purchased a small bouquet of flowers because Kat had them sprinkled about the buffet in miniature, crystal vases and candles had been lit in between the decadent dishes. Kat had already peeled the fat, juicy shrimp and made her homemade cocktail sauce with plenty of horseradish cream and fresh lemons. There was pate with crusty bread. Kat, as always, making her own, fresh loaves. A medium ham topped with caramelised pineapple slices and cherries had been baked to perfection.

Antonio made the mashed potatoes and secretly shared with Morgan, 'I used Dijon mustard and real cream for these golden spuds!'

She couldn't wait to try them. There was the traditional pot of black-eyed peas and onions accompanied by a small oval pan of baked corn bread, too. Kat had grilled asparagus and steamed a pan of broccoli and zucchini for their daily portion of greens and baked small, round discs of sweet potatoes sprinkled with honey and sesame seeds on top.

'Oh,' Morgan grinned. 'Mom, you have no idea how much I appreciate seeing those mouthwatering devilled eggs! Look, Ollie and Opal, our favourite appetisers!'

She turned back to her mom. 'How could you two lovely human beings prepare this outstanding feast in such a short amount of time?' The cooks beamed!

Antonio said, 'You slept for almost three hours.'

The doorbell rang. Morgan froze. Her body stiffened and it took her right back to her last dark memory of the front entrance. Everybody stopped in their places – they looked stuck in time. You could have heard a pin drop. Dixie sensed something was wrong and she began to whimper. The kids looked as if they were about to burst into tears.

Antonio stood up. 'Rightio. Everyone stay where you are. I'll see who is there and I'll be right back. Do not move.'

Opal was already crying, ran to her mother, and Morgan held her close.

Antonio approached the door, looked out the side window and screamed, 'Good, God, man, what in the Hell are you doing here? It's so damned good to see you, but, again, who let you out of the hospital?'

The kids and Kat hurried towards the front door in sheer disbelief, downright delight, and unqualified relief. Morgan brought up the rear. When Ash initially saw Morgan, he missed a beat. He covered his face with his good hand, looked back down again and Morgan saw Ash cry for the first time. His face turned white. Morgan held him and Ash's shoulders were shaking.

Kat pulled the children back into the kitchen. Ash followed Morgan and they went directly to the bar. They held each other and stayed like that for a while.

He whispered, 'I'm so sorry he hurt you.'

'Shhh,' then she tried to joke. 'Sir, you have much to answer for. I think you may be an escapee and I'm going to have to call the authorities.'

Ash held on to her for ages.

When they entered the kitchen, Ash pulled a Boogie Board out of his briefcase and everyone stared, the kids especially. The little board was black with a thin, metal writing utensil which slid into a bar across the top of the board. His ex-wife, Alex, bought it for him and told him to use it every day until his vocal cords healed. Ash only had to write what he wanted to say on the blackboard with the strange pen and when he needed to erase it, he pushed a small silver button at the top and his words vanished! He could begin a new conversation with the touch of the button. So, while Kat prepared the luncheon plates, Ash wrote on his new Boogie Board that he truly did escape the hospital, but not for any one to worry as he hired a driver to deliver him to Pickwick. He could not stand being in the hospital. His personal doctor was a friend of his and he wanted everyone to know that if they ever wanted to escape from a hospital, New Year's Day was the perfect day to execute that plan.

Antonio, Kat, and the kids were laughing hard, but Morgan was not impressed. She scolded him and said, 'Ash, your body has a lot of healing to deal with and for an educated man you are not very smart, are you?'

Ash erased his last words and wrote on the board: Please be happy for me and kind and I promise if there is any sign of trouble, I will check myself back in.

The New Year's Day luncheon began with copious amounts of French Champagne, Australian Shiraz, New Zealand Sauvignon Blanc and ice, cold milk for two of the cutest and most loving kids on the planet. It was a perfect time for cheer and new joyful memories were becoming permanently etched in their brains.

Afterwards, no one could move because they had consumed such a vast amount of rich and delicious food. The Southern 'thang' to do, the tradition, at least in Morgan's family, was to leave exactly twelve black-eyed peas on your plate for New Year's Day. Those twelve peas would bring a person good luck for the following twelve months of the year.

Opal said, 'Ooops, Mommy, I forgot and I ate all my luck!'

Kat, Antonio, and Ash giggled and shook their heads and Opal turned red.

'Hold on, I'll get you another serve and you can begin again.'

Ollie chimed in, 'More peas, too, please.'

Everyone kept cracking up. It was hard on Ash because he probably wasn't supposed to be laughing either. Morgan noticed that he had a terribly difficult time eating. It must still hurt him to swallow, but she said nothing, of course.

One fat, luscious apple, brown sugar, and cinnamon pie had finished baking in the oven. Kat was going to offer it with vanilla ice cream on top and the table guests put their hands up in the air saying, 'No, no, please, we've had more than enough.'

Ollie and Opal looked at the adults like they were crazy! Ollie said, 'We want some, Nanna-Kat, but can we have it a little later, please?'

Slowly, but surely Antonio and Ash stood up from the table and began the motions of trying to assist with the clean-up. Kat kicked them out. Kat told Morgan to disappear, too. The kids took their plates to their nanna and told her, 'It was so yummy, Nanna.'

Ash wrote on his Boogie Board: Delicious. Thank you, Kat.

Antonio stood there with his hands up in the air. 'What about me?'

Morgan kissed Antonio on his cheek.

Ollie and Opal dashed back to the puzzle, but grabbed Ash's hand along the way, gently, with Opal pleading, 'Please come and have another look.'

He was every bit amazed as the last time and wrote on his board even he could not work a puzzle as quickly as they did.

Antonio made a fire and lit candles. Morgan turned on soft music.

Ash sat down looking completely flat, beyond tired, and in poor form.

Morgan asked, 'Can I do anything for you or get you anything?'

He wrote: Now that's funny coming from you.

'Seriously. You don't look so well.'

Ash continued writing: I think it best if I go to my study and stretch out for a bit.

Antonio offered to take Ash's briefcase for him, but Ash scribbled the words: Please, don't bother.

Morgan made up her mind. She had a long and deep restful sleep already and after one more nice night's siesta in Ash's home, she felt they needed to leave the next day. They would not hurry, however, it was definitely time to go home and return to reality. She felt it was important to make the move now – whatever helped them to get back to normal.

She announced her decision to Antonio.

He looked seriously doubtful. 'I was presuming you might stay another five days or so.'

Morgan smirked, 'In your dreams.'

'What's the hurry?'

Morgan looked at him like he'd gone mad, 'House, job, mortgage, responsibilities, bills, all the simple reasons everyone needs to go back home at some point.'

Antonio was standing with his back to the fire, his arms folded together behind him, and he was looking down at the bold coloured oriental rug. 'It's funny. It feels as if we've been a sort of bubble or time warp zone, even a dream. I can't find the proper words to describe it, but this last week does not seem real to me. What about you?'

Morgan agreed. 'Quite frankly, I don't like that feeling any more. I want a dose of reality. I want a routine to make me feel real. It puts me back in control. Does that make sense?

'Certainly.'

Kat entered the room and said, 'What's all this chat about?'

'Mom, I think we should return home in the morning. We won't leave particularly early, but you may want to pack a few items tonight. We need to get back to the real world.'

Kat gave a slight smile and didn't argue. Morgan thought her mom would want to check on her own home, too, and be back inside her domain.

Ash never returned to the sitting room, so Antonio went out to check on him. He reported that Ash was out like a light, under a cover, and had managed, at least, to take off his shoes and socks, but that was about it.

'Will you be taking Ash back when you leave?' asked Kat.

'Absolutely,' and he quipped, 'we'll probably argue on the way home if I should drop him into the hospital ER!'

Ollie and Opal had a small sliver of apple pie topped with vanilla ice cream and surprisingly, Antonio joined them.

Afterwards, the kids took Dixie outside and stayed for a good while and unbeknownst to them the adults stood behind as guards.

Ollie returned exclaiming, 'Dixie found something furry and she wouldn't listen to us to stop pulling on her lead.'

'The next time that happens, use your 'firm' voice.' Morgan opened a can of worms because describing what a firm sounding voice actually was and its uses turned into a fifteen-minute conversation.

Opal looked confused but added, 'Is a firm voice a mad voice?'

Then, Ollie began to practice. In his deepest voice, 'Dixie come with me, NOW.'

Opal got so tickled that she got the hiccups.

Kat advised the kids, 'Time for your baths.' She turned to Morgan, 'I'll handle everything tonight and pack for the children, too.'

Opal asked, 'Pack? Why are we packing?'

Morgan explained and the groans began and continued all the way up the spiral stairway. Only the words 'bubble bath' and 'new book' broke their attention span and got them back into happy mode.

Antonio and Morgan shared a bottle of red from the Bordeaux region. It was a Chateau Bonnet Bordeaux Rouge 2012, and this was the last remaining bottle of Morgan's stash. It was not expensive but a nice tasting Cabernet Sauvignon. She insisted that Antonio stay away from Ash's wine cellar and his wine fridge. Ash had been far too generous and maybe, not even willingly! She doubted that, but still, Morgan had purchased her wines for the specific reason to enjoy throughout the holidays.

They made another toast with the hope of a brilliant, safe, healthy, happy New Year for all, but Antonio commented, 'Morgan, your light...your essence has disappeared again, and I completely understand.'

It was a wonder she had not been hospitalised with a nervous breakdown. *Do people have those anymore or does everyone wear a mask and pretend?*

'Antonio was rubbing his forehead and sipping the gorgeous ruby drop of red. Ash and I may be at Pickwick a couple of more days because he needs to recuperate further. Either way, not much is happening at the office and Mike can handle it without me if he must.'

Kat returned downstairs. 'Ollie and Opal had been asking for you, but they fell asleep in my bed as I read them their new book.' She glanced Morgan's way adding, 'The children have been such a joy to be with and I, for one, shall never forget this Christmas, Morgan, for all the right reasons I will treasure being here with my family.' She kissed Morgan on top of her head.

Morgan grabbed Kat's hand and said, 'Thanks, Mom. There certainly have been special and interesting moments.'

Antonio was observing his favourite ladies and drinking in the precious moment. 'New Christmas memories for me, too, and I suddenly feel like I have another family.'

Kat snipped, 'Well you do and don't you forget it!'

Antonio poured Kat a glass and the three sat in front of the fire, each dreaming their own sweet dreams and revisiting newly created memories.

CHAPTER THIRTY-SEVEN

Morgan was the first to rise and she got the coffee started. Dixie appeared fatter and that made her giggle for some reason and Dixie didn't seem too keen to saunter out into the cold air either. Morgan fiddled with the security panel, grabbed a jacket from the mudroom, and attached the lead to Dixie's neck and off they went. Quiet, beautiful stillness and serenity. Yes, a new year was upon her, and she did have hope. Her pain had lessened, and she wanted to put everything behind her. They walked a good distance, as it gave her the time she needed to reflect on the kind people in her life. She counted her blessings that Kat, Lee, Antonio, and Ash were part of her circle. She had never imagined that she and Antonio would become kindred spirits, and she was most thankful Antonio had introduced such a fine human being as Ash into her life. The leaves crunched under her feet, Dixie stuck her nose into anything and everything, acted inquisitive, and for a moment looked as if she were a rabbit hopping about. The ground must have been much too cold on her tiny paws.

They stomped back up to the rear of the house and Ash was standing at the glass door with a hot, steaming mug in his one good hand. He raised it towards her and she beamed. What a wonderful face he had. She admired every inch of it. Dixie barked and they shuffled into the house together. She took Dixie over to the sink and washed her cold paws with warm water and dried them. Dixie scampered off to gobble down her breakfast.

Ash wrote on his Boogie Board: Good morning, Morgan. How are you? And drew a huge smiley face!

'Much better today, thank you. What about you?'

Ash made the words vanish and he scribbled quickly: I don't think I had one good night's sleep in that damned hospital bed, but last night did wonders for me.

Morgan grinned. 'Good. It shows.' She poured a cup of dark, steaming black coffee.

Ash scribbled again: Antonio told me you're leaving today.

Morgan felt strange, didn't know why, but nodded. 'Yes, as soon as I can feed the munchkins a bit and pack the car, we'll be on our way. And, Ash, there are no words that I can possibly think of to thank you enough. Your house has been a dream, a blessing for my family. I regret enormously that you were hurt and the word 'sorry' doesn't begin to describe how I feel about everything that's happened to you.'

Ash regarded her, paused, and slowly wrote the words on his electronic board: But it wasn't a safe house, was it, Morgan? My original intention was to keep you safe and I failed miserably.

Ash's face looked broken.

Morgan read Ash's written words and would not have a bar of it. 'No. Stop. Or the monster gets his way. We don't get ours. We must find a way around this Hell. I must find a way to keep going no matter what he has in store for me, and you know what, Ash? Quite frankly, that's what I've been doing. What I despise most is that the monster involves my closest friends and I have despicable thoughts about him now. I am making concrete plans to ensure my family's safety when I return to Memphis.'

Ash was writing furiously now: What plans? Have you called the security company I told you about?

Morgan stopped. Shit. She wasn't talking about electronic security systems, she was talking about learning how to handle a gun properly, but she didn't mean for her plans to slip out. She avoided the question. 'I've been researching different security companies,' because that much was true. 'Are you and Antonio going to stay a few more days?'

He jotted quickly on the Boogie Board: I feel as if I should. I don't feel much like going anywhere right now, but a couple of days should get me right as rain.

Morgan gingerly touched him on his forearm and excused herself. 'I'm going upstairs to make sure everyone is moving towards the departure goal and to finish packing.'

Ash surprised her and pulled her close to him and kissed her cheek, then he looked directly into her eyes and pressed his lips on hers and kissed her tenderly and lovingly as he held on to her tightly. He took her breath away. She didn't pull back. When he stopped, Morgan felt her own heart pounding right out of her chest.

'Oh, my!' and she kissed him again.

The momentum changed. Energy was in the air. The atmosphere was spinning, and she couldn't explain how she felt that all was right with the world. Morgan admired and respected this fine and gentle man. She knew he was much more than just her attorney. It felt like a part of him was always with her. *I cannot think about this now.* She had a plan, a direction in which to move, and steep hurdles ahead of her before any normalcy could appear in her life ever again.

In that moment, Ash's eyes filled with tenderness, generosity, and pure love.

Once upstairs, Morgan saw Kat fussing over the children, straightening their clothes, and helping Opal with her hair. It was such a happy picture that she wanted to relish it for a moment.

Kat smiled like a Cheshire cat. 'You look brighter. I promise, Morgan, there is a sparkle in your eyes. Last night's sleep did wonders for you, my darling one.'

'Yes, Mother, it must have.' She was bursting on the inside and stopped in her tracks, only for a second, to remind herself exactly *how* pure joy felt.

Antonio had just stepped out of the shower and had his jeans on. He was towel drying his hair and walking up and down the upstairs hallway singing loudly in an operatic manner just to entertain her kids. Morgan adored him. He passed Morgan and slapped her on her butt with his towel.

Antonio stopped in his tracks. 'Gheeez, woman, you look good. I swear, Morgan, you look completely different from yesterday. I'm not blowing smoke – you look gorgeous!'

Morgan chuckled. 'Well, thanks, I feel good.'

Antonio ceased his fantasy opera and walked back into his room to finish dressing.

Kat, Morgan, Ollie and Opal were quite chirpy, and Dixie was in between their feet and legs as they descended the now, extremely familiar staircase. Morgan would miss this fantasy house and she would dismiss any of the nasty memories. The house was full of goodness.

Ash looked content, happy, and relaxed. More importantly, he felt familiar. He appeared filled with appreciation and Morgan thought his eyes didn't look so sad after all.

Kat sliced apples and oranges, popped in the toast, and got the butter and jam from the fridge. She asked Ash if he wanted anything and he politely smiled and shook his head 'No.' He continued browsing the newspaper with a full mug of coffee. The children gathered at the kitchen bar and Kat added sliced bananas sprinkled with cinnamon on top of their fruit bowls. She poured the cold orange juice and buttered the toast. Within minutes every skerrick of food had disappeared from the breakfast plates. The little cherubs were hungry this morning.

Morgan reached for a piece of toast and gazed at Ash. His has been her favourite face for a while now.

'Hello gang, we must get a move on,' she announced.

Ollie said, 'Dixie needs to go out. We'll take her and we'll be right back.'

Antonio helped the kids attach Dixie's lead and they were gone in a flash. Kat kept her guardian stance at the kitchen window with a watchful eye. Antonio was sipping his coffee, but Morgan felt like he was watching her and glancing at Ash, too. *Am I being paranoid? Doesn't matter.* It didn't make a difference if Antonio had picked up on their happiness or not. He would be aware sooner or later. *Preferably, later.*

Ollie and Opal rushed back in complaining, 'It's too cold out there!'

'Gather your hats and gloves and be sure to get Dixie's food and water dish and please don't forget her dog coat either.' They were shuffling about gathering the items as best they could.

'Please place everything you've collected by the side of the car, and I'll pack it myself.'

Kat was already stationed in the garage doing that very thing.

When the kids returned from the car, Morgan advised them softly, 'Remember your manners.'

Both children perked up and ran over to Ash. Opal started. 'Thank you for your house and for our Christmas and for your pretty decorations.'

Then a wave of panic covered Ollie's face. He said, 'Mom, our puzzle. We worked so hard, and it's not finished. What are we going to do with it? We *can't* leave it.'

The men looked at each another. Morgan put on her thinking cap.

Then Ash pulled out his Boogie Board. He wrote: Dear Ollie and Opal, yes, of course, you can leave it right where it is and I will make certain my cleaning lady steers clear of it. This way you are guaranteed to come back to visit and finish the puzzle one weekend. Would that be okay with you?

'Mom, what does 'guarantee' mean?' Ollie asked. He couldn't say the word quite properly and he looked concerned.

Morgan explained, 'It's like an assurance or a promise.'

Ollie looked over at Ash and said, 'You could have just written the word promise.'

The gang enjoyed a giggle. Hugs all around with Dixie bouncing in the middle and Ash and Morgan held on to one another a little longer than they probably should have.

Morgan looked over at Ollie and tilted her head.

'Thank you for letting us have our Christmas in your big house. I hope we see you soon,' and Ollie truly meant it.

CHAPTER THIRTY-EIGHT

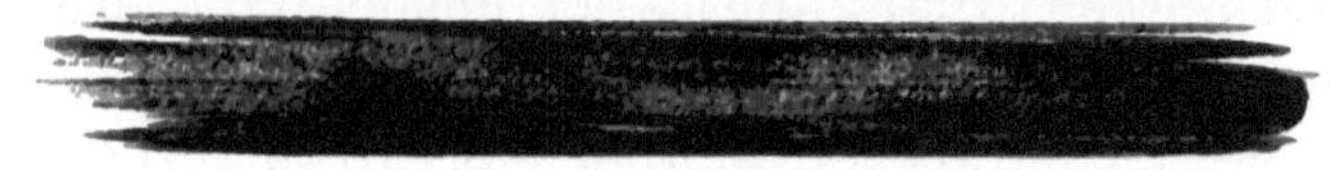

The happy passengers and the driver buckled up safely.

Kat mentioned to Morgan, 'I'm more than capable of driving and would be glad to do so.'

'I feel quite well, Mom, but I'll certainly keep your offer in mind.' The gang headed down the now familiar driveway.

'I loved being here, Opal commented, 'and I'm going to miss it.'

'I can't wait to finish the puzzle and I thought Ash's idea was good,' added Ollie.

Kat turned to the back seat. 'Me, too, kids.'

Dixie curled up looking like a white ball of fluff in the middle directly between the two children.

'US-72, here we come,' Morgan sang-out sweetly.

It was a noneventful journey. It seemed much shorter on the way back than it did driving towards Pickwick. Morgan assumed her mom and the kids were reliving the past days and thinking about the magic parts, not the nasty bits. That was her hope at least. She looked in the rearview mirror and two little heads were side by side with their eyes closed. Car rides still put her kids to sleep. She couldn't help but think of Ash in trouble and hurting upside down in his car! She wondered which part of the road the monster shoved him off, but quickly turned her mind to something more pleasant.

They were soon to be approaching Memphis when Morgan had an idea. They all looked presentable. Morgan's face was still a shocker, but she could pull her hat down. She glanced over at her mom. 'You did so much for us the entire time. You acted as our private chef, and I don't much feel like cooking tonight, and you won't either once you get your bags unpacked. Please let me take you and the children to dinner. We'll go to the Half Shell where the food will be hot and fabulous. C'mon, Mom, you deserve a treat.'

Kat replied with a huge grin, 'Do you really feel up to it?'

'Yes, yes I do.'

Morgan headed with renewed energy directly towards the Half Shell.

'I'll pull up, drop you off, and see if you can manage a table for four, preferably in their darkest corner.' Morgan tried to wink at her mom, but she should have known better by now. 'I'll find a parking spot and be right back with the kids.'

Kat reminded her, 'Don't forget to leave the windows cracked a bit for Dixie.'

By this time the children were awake and ready to get out of the car. Morgan attached the lead and walked Dixie up to the front door with the children and told them to wait for her in reception. Dixie did her business in the side bushes and Morgan kissed her black, button nose and reassured her they would be back soon.

When Morgan walked in, Ollie and Opal were already seated with their Nanna and, wonderful, it was indeed a table for four in a seriously pitch-dark corner. Kat had ordered water all around. She told Morgan she didn't feel like any wine. Morgan ordered iced tea, too. She secretly wanted a mean Bombay Sapphire martini because the Half Shell bartenders made the best in Memphis, but she was too tired and didn't want to indulge on a night she was driving. Martinis would have to wait. Hot, fresh, succulent Oysters Rockefeller would not have to wait. Morgan surprised herself and ordered an entire dozen.

Her mom just looked at her. 'What? I'm hungry – famished is more like it.'

The kids would share a basket of fries and they split a burger with ketchup only, but lots of pickles.

Opal asked, 'May I have a serving of broccoli, please?'

Morgan was a bit surprised at the request but pleased, too. 'You bet.'

Kat ordered the grilled, pan-blackened tilapia dinner with a baked potato and fresh vegetables.

In no time at all the table was covered with hot, yummy looking plates and baskets and Morgan had to make room for two burning hot stainless-steel platters of oysters. A bit of heaven was before her. The Half Shell never ceased to amaze Morgan. No matter what day of the week or time of the year the place was hopping. It looked only slightly tired, but that didn't matter because the servers were friendly, the bartenders welcoming, and the martinis the meanest! She had always loved the atmosphere at the Half Shell, located smack dab in the middle of 'her' beloved Memphis.

They finished in no time and Morgan wrapped up the uneaten portion of the burger so Dixie could have a bit of a treat when they arrived home. Home. Morgan didn't know what to think, so she did what she was used to doing and pushed any expectations out of her head. They each thanked their server, and Morgan left a most generous tip due to the season and the good service. Dixie was thrilled to see them again acting as if they had disappeared for a month. She snuggled up to the children instantly and away they went.

Morgan made the quick trip to Kat's house. The kids jumped out of the car and helped with the luggage, gifts, and the massive load of baking dishes, too, because that's how Morgan's mom rolled. Kat unlocked the door and tentatively peeked inside. Things appeared normal. The house needed airing out. Morgan brought the last load of items up the stairs.

'Mom, let's turn on all the lights and have a quick look around.'

'Sounds like a wise idea to me.'

The two women did exactly that. Everything seemed to be in perfect order. They had another group hug which included heaps of kisses. The kids held on tightly to their Nanna.

'Please, Morgan, don't forget to call and let me know you're safe and settled. And thank you, my love, for a splendid Christmas.'

'Promise, Mom. Sweet dreams.'

Off they went. Dixie perked up and her tail started wagging when Morgan rounded the corner to their house. *How do dogs know when they're close to home when they're riding in a car? It's dark. Dixie's eyesight couldn't be that good. It had to be intuitive.* Morgan pulled up to the garage and hit the opener. The light popped on and she slowly entered. She pushed back the memories of the last time she was in a garage. She did not need those bleak images muddling her mind.

'Ollie, Opal, please wait in the car for just a bit while I do a fast run through the house and turn on some lights.' Nothing. The house looked a bit unloved and lonely, but there was truly nothing out of the ordinary. *Fantastic. This is nice.*

'Kids,' she called out, 'Grab your things and I'm going to close the garage door, but don't forget to come back and get Dixie's bits and pieces, too. She'll need to go out one more time. Please, be neat. Don't just toss your stuff in your rooms. I'll have tons of laundry to do and I don't want the place to look like a bomb hit it.'

Opal giggled. 'Mommy, my room always looks good. It's Ollie's you need to watch out for!'

'Too right.'

There. They were snug as a bug in a rug. Lights on low. Washing machine humming. Dixie had been out and seemed perfectly happy to be right under Opal's feet. Morgan was feeling quite upbeat, and her shoulder was not as painful. It felt great to be back home. *What was everyone so concerned about?* Morgan left her cell on the countertop and she saw it wiggling back and forth. Lee.

'What's up, Morgan? I'm pleading with you and Ollie and Opal to be my house guests. The sheets have been freshly washed. I want you here with me...hmmm...when are you going to decide to change your mind, girlfriend?

Morgan tried to toy with her a bit. 'How do you know we're not heading your way right now?'

Lee got super excited. 'Are you, Morgan?'

Then, she felt instantly rotten for having suggested such a thing. 'Look, seriously, no, we're all settled at our house and everything's fine. I'm not putting you through any further trauma and, Lee, the cops are furious. They truly are fuming and want him now as much as we do. They'll get him. I have complete confidence. You do remember that we haven't had our Christmas yet and once things settle down you and I are going to celebrate the New Year somewhere incredibly fabulous together, like Folk's Folly.'

Lee murmured, 'Oh, Morgan, I haven't been there for a while. It's my favorite place and I'd like that very much. This gives me something wonderful to look forward to. Thanks for the reminder! Now, how are you feeling?'

'Much better today, but after the drive, unpacking, and starting the laundry, I'm pooped and I'm fading fast.'

'I understand. Love you. We'll catch up for coffee soon.'

Morgan put the news on. She couldn't remember the last time she settled in to watch world or current news events. Antonio was right. They had been existing in a bubble. Ollie and Opal were yawning and trying to stay awake.

'How about this? We aren't on any schedule tomorrow. Forget about baths tonight. Hop into your jammies and I'll come and read to you, but you must brush your teeth.'

They liked the sound of her idea, and their tiny bottoms went running down the hallway. 'Stop running!'

She read Ollie and Opal to sleep in her bed. She didn't mind. The three of them had been through enough and if they only needed a few extra cuddles and the feeling of being close, what on Earth could that hurt? She turned off the lamp on her chest of drawers and turned on the nightlight in the hallway directly outside of her bedroom door, then adjusted the heating. The house was quite cold even though she had left the heat on a low temperature while they were away. Dixie was acting a bit strangely; more anxious than anything else and Morgan thought that was curious. She double checked the deadbolt locks and made certain her new window locks were bolted, too. She turned on the big, bright, glaring, yellow backyard light she was quite certain her neighbours would not appreciate and decided to keep the front verandah light on until the morning.

'Ooops!' Morgan remembered to ring her mom.

Kat remarked, 'I was just about to pick up my phone.'

Morgan assured her, 'We're secure for the evening and I'm going to watch a bit of news and head to bed.'

They each said, 'Love you. Goodnight.'

CHAPTER THIRTY-NINE

She fell asleep in front of the television, but Dixie woke her growling. In a matter of seconds Morgan was fully awake and the hair on the back of her neck was standing on end. She didn't like what she was feeling. She felt frozen in place. Morgan took a quick survey of the room and everything seemed normal. It had to be sometime in the middle of the night; she wasn't certain. *Why is Dixie growling?* Morgan pulled Dixie next to her and rubbed her and tried to calm her. Dixie stiffened. *Okay. What the Hell is going on?*

Morgan forced herself to stand up in her sitting room lounge and she peered down the hallway, then she saw or heard - she's not sure - the garage door handle turn. The monster slowly walked in from her garage, calmly shut the door, and stood there...with his briefcase. He reached inside and pulled out a small, black caliber pistol and pointed it. Morgan recognized it. It was Stevie's gun. She became weak in her knees. Dixie went wild barking furiously! Morgan didn't want her waking Ollie and Opal. She was shushing her, loving her, and stroking her fluffy head all the while trying to get an angle on the monster's mood. She closed the French doors from the sitting room that led into the hallway hoping with all of her might the children would not leap out of her bed.

She noticed something different about the monster. He was not moving quickly. He was not lunging towards her, and he wasn't saying anything but her name, slowly, over and over. 'Morgan, Morgan, we need to talk. We need to sit down together properly and you need to listen to me.'

He didn't sound right. He seemed to have taken something because his words were difficult to understand. He appeared to have been crying. His face was red and puffy, and he wasn't pointing the gun at her. It was dangling down by his side now. But damnit, her instincts had been right. *He had been in her house and he found the gun after going through her personal items. He must have been into every closet, every drawer, everything she owned. Shit.*

'Morgan, Morgan, I want you to sit. Sit down now.' He was slurring his words. He pointed the gun directly towards her and she sat. 'You don't seem to understand. We're not getting divorced. We're in the middle of a crossroad. You are my wife. We were married before God. You and I took an oath and we cannot break…that. So, don't you see? We'll be together permanently. I am your husband. You are mine. That's how this works. It's so simple and you're making it extremely difficult for me. You have caused me serious problems. Are you aware of the pain and damage you've caused? You see I'm the only person who loves you because no man would stay and fight for you. I fight for you, Morgan. I do that because God says you're mine. You must remember that…always.'

His eyes were half-way closing and his words were sloppy. If Morgan could just get to her phone. By complete accident or mad luck, she felt it. Her fingers fumbled around between the sofa cushions and her phone was right below her hip. It must have fallen through when she fell asleep in front of the news. Morgan repositioned Dixie to the other side of her lap to cover up the crack and the possibility that the monster might see her phone. So far, no motion or sound from her bedroom. Morgan could hear her heart beating.

The monster said he was thirsty. He ordered her, 'Get me some water.'

She softly said, 'I'm afraid that if I move, Dixie's going to go ballistic and wake the kids and I only got her calm. The glasses are in the cabinet right next to the refrigerator.'

He stood up like a robot. He was not in his right mind, but she didn't have a clue what was happening. The moment he passed the sofa and entered the kitchen, Morgan pulled out her phone. Antonio was first on her contact list and she punched in '911'. He was the smartest man on the planet. He would get it.

The monster turned as she was putting the phone back under the cushion. He screamed, 'What are you doing?'

She couldn't think and she couldn't swallow, and her mouth couldn't form any words. This time he shouted even louder. 'I asked you what you were doing.'

Dixie shot off the couch and went straight for him, snarling and growling like she was madder than a hornet. He backhanded her like he was playing a game of handball. She landed hard against the wall and yelped and shook her head, panting. She stayed put. *Good girl.* Morgan looked at Dixie and felt her own heart break.

The monster threw his water glass and came straight towards her. She didn't see the gun. She didn't see anything except his hands going for her damn throat again. The pain was excruciating as she felt the skin tear from her neck. Morgan heard the pitter patter of feet running down the hallway. The monster released her, yelled like fury down towards her children while they screamed demanding, 'Get back into the bedroom and do not come out until I call your names.' He got down on their level and shouted like the monster he is. 'DO YOU UNDERSTAND ME?'

Morgan heard their little feet run like crazy back down the hallway and a door slam shut, and she thought she might puke. She was worried like Hell that Ollie would want to be clever and try to help her, so would Opal, but Ollie was the planner, the schemer. Morgan begged to herself. *Please, Ollie, don't try to be brave and don't make plans. This will be over soon.*

Morgan had not moved. She was still standing up against the wall. He grabbed the back of her hair and pulled her down onto the rug. They were right next to the brick fireplace and antique mantel piece. There was an assortment of fireplace tools, and she eyed them carefully. He didn't miss a trick. The monster turned around and saw what she was staring at, picked them up and threw them across the room. He kept the poker in one hand. She heard her children's screams when the tools hit the wall. Now he had 'the look.' Now he was in full form – total and complete rage had engulfed his body and his mind, and he was going to be a force to be reckoned with. Morgan's strength was completely depleted due to his previous attack. *At least he could not stay on track with his thoughts.* If so, he would have found her phone. He had forgotten that he asked her what she was doing and now he was only concentrating on frightening and hurting her. *Good God, please let Antonio see his phone.*

The monster was now bending down and climbing on top of her. He punched his knee into her thigh, and she screamed. His weight was too much. The pain was intense and she felt she would either pass out or vomit.

He snarled, 'This is the kind of pain you cause me. How does it feel, Morgan? It's going to take a long time for me to love you again, but we have all the time in the world.' He pushed his knee harder into her thigh and now his hands were back around her neck. He had blood on his hands now.

Morgan did not dare look for the gun. She did not dare search for her phone. She kept her eyes closed until he screamed at her to open them. 'You're going to look at me. You will know who is in charge. Who's in charge, Morgan? Who tells you what you can and cannot do, MORGAN? ANSWER ME.'

Ollie and Opal were screaming in the background and Morgan's body began shaking violently. The monster began to laugh a shrill, maniacal, evil laugh. His laugh. He continued that laugh for what seemed like a wretched eternity.

'I can't believe I scare you. We're just playing. We're playing husband and wife. Don't you get it Morgan? I can do whatever I want with you.'

He drove his knee harder once again into her thigh. Morgan was wincing in pain and wanted to cry out, but she stopped and listened. She heard a car. She swore to herself she heard another car door.

The monster looked at her. 'What is it, Morgan? Want some more?'

The monster heard something, too. He grabbed her by her hair and pulled her up. 'You're coming with me.'

This time he pushed something hard and cold into her waist. It had to be her gun. She didn't breathe. Dixie was all over them again, barking like crazy.

'Get her to stop or I'll kill her right here.'

Morgan was doing her best to calm Dixie.

The next thing she knew the garage door flew open and the front door simultaneously. Police officers were entering from the side, but there was Antonio's face. There was Ash's face. Was she dreaming? Lee's voice. Was that Lee she heard?

Something was trickling down her neck. And...the monster was gone.

She remembered being pushed and she saw Dixie race out the back side door to the yard. The yard was natural with no fencing and they lived on a corner lot. It was vast and huge and there were trees, but there were also two police cars and four officers if she had managed to take in the scene properly.

One of the officers yelled. 'His car. He's going for his car. It's white and it's hidden around on the other side of the cul de sac. He's on the opposite side of the cul de sac. I saw him entering his car and he's carrying something white. Get on it, guys. Let's go now.'

The radio announcement buzzed throughout Morgan's house.

Morgan screamed, 'He has Dixie. He must have grabbed Dixie. Oh, Good, God, Antonio, Ash, we must get her back.'

Morgan pushed through the men, Lee, and the cops remaining behind, and went straight to her babies. Lee followed. Ollie and Opal were huddled together in the corner of Morgan's room, shaking and sobbing. Morgan bent down, pulled them towards her and with every ounce of reserve and fortitude she had left in her, she said, 'I promise you that you will never endure another night like this in your life. I am so sorry you were scared. I am so sorry I could not come to you. I am so sorry you're hurting in any way. I love you both. You are my strong angels and none of this is your fault nor do you deserve any of it.'

'Mom, where's Dixie?' Ollie asked.

'Is Dixie gone?' Opal joined in. 'Mommy, is she?'

Morgan looked down. 'I'm afraid so, my darlings.' Shrieks. Tears and screams and the howling of Dixie's name through their sobs. It was awful. It was physically painful to hear her children. Morgan could not bear it a moment longer.

She swallowed hard. *That's the one thing I can do. I can get Dixie back.* Her mind was full speed ahead.

She looked at Lee. 'Kids, Lee has been pleading with us to stay with her and she has fresh sheets and beds ready and waiting for you. I want you to go with her now and I'll be back at Lee's before you know it. It's late at night still and you have lots of sleep to catch up on. Go. Go with her now and I'll see you in the morning. I love you both with every beat of my heart.'

With tears streaming, Lee gathered them together and wrapped blankets around their small, quivering bodies.

Morgan marched up to Antonio and Ash with her pale, distorted face, body shaking, and demanded, 'Wherever he is we are finding him...you are driving me to him and I'm getting Dixie back. Now.'

CHAPTER FORTY

The police radios were bursting with chatter and instructions. An officer responded to another one standing in front of Morgan and repeated on the radio that the assailant was driving a white four door Volvo and heading at a high rate of speed towards downtown Memphis. A garbled voice shouted, 'He's on the interstate now.'

Antonio, Ash, and Morgan piled into Antonio's car.

A police officer came out and advised them that the home was a crime scene and someone needed to stay behind.

As respectfully as she could muster, Morgan said, 'This is my home and I'll be right back.' She lied. A big fat lie. *LIAR*.

The officer immediately got on his radio and reported, 'The victim is leaving the scene of the crime, and it appears she and some others are going to pursue the suspect.'

Antonio said, 'Morgan you're bleeding,' and he reached towards the glove compartment for napkins or anything which looked useful.

She appeared unmoved. 'It doesn't matter.'

Antonio gave her a serious look of concern. 'I have a police scanner 5-0 radio that is connected to my Bluetooth and we could hear live police action as it's occurring, as crimes are being called in.'

'By God, man get it happening now,' Ash said in a hoarse voice.

Antonio tuned in and at first, they heard a bit of crackling and popping and sounds of rushing air, then police conversations came through loudly and clearly.

'Suspect, white male, approximately 40 years of age, speeding towards downtown Memphis in a four-door white Volvo. Approach with caution. The defendant has a gun. Divorce pending. Held wife against her will at gunpoint. Proceed with caution.'

The police radio was buzzing, and it continued. 'Assailant taking right two lanes to go I-55/US-61 exit at a high rate of speed heading towards St. Louis/Little Rock. Be on high alert.'

Still another announcement, 'Person of interest is using cell phone. Speed increasing.' Helicopter pilot reported white Volvo in sight, nearing Ornamental Metal Museum Road.

An officer on ground reported, 'Assailant is turning towards Exit 12C, continuing on Metal Museum Drive and nearing W Illinois Drive.' Another patrol car piped in there was a restrictive usage road not far from assailant.

The officers' voices were sounding hypervigilant, but reports became terribly scratchy and difficult to hear. Another officer announced, 'Assailant heading into restrictive usage road.'

The helicopter pilot reported a dark older model vehicle was parked ahead on the bridge. A separate announcement stated the assailant was continuing to use his cell phone.

'Please, Antonio, we'll be fine, go faster,' Morgan pleaded! 'The cops are everywhere. He's surrounded. I need to get Dixie for my babies – I must! He only took her to hurt me. Please get me to her.'

Then she calmly asked... 'How is it you were able to appear at my house?'

Antonio responded sheepishly, 'We both felt you were unsafe, and we simultaneously decided to make the drive back early and left not long after you departed. I'm so sorry, I should have texted you.'

Ash turned around to look at Morgan. His voice was more than hoarse. It sounded like it hurt him to speak. 'Please try and calm down. Breathe and listen. I know you're on high alert and adrenalin has taken over, but Morgan, rest assured the officers are not going to let you or me or anyone near him. Imagine the scene right now in your head. When they stop him, we'll be advised to withdraw. I'll do everything in my power to get as close as I can. Please, Morgan, please let me do the talking.'

First helicopter voice reported lights had gone out on the bridge and an officer on ground believed shots had been fired. A second voice returned, 'Copy that. Additional lighting out in middle of bridge. Report: shots have been fired.'

First helicopter pilot's voice reentered the radio waves. 'A white sedan has pulled over to the side in the middle of the

Memphis-Arkansas Bridge. An additional vehicle has pulled to the front of the white sedan and appears to be a black or dark grey utility van. A double rear door is opening.'

The pilot added, 'Visibility is good. I can see clearly with search lights. No assailant in sight. Repeat: No assailant in sight.'

A second helicopter pilot confirmed through thermal imaging at least one or two items had gone over the side of the bridge. The pilot stated he turned his nightsun search lights on because the forward-looking infrared radar could not assist once items became submerged in water. The nightsun beams would enable those individuals above, and on the ground, to see precisely. The officers on foot were approaching the point on the bridge where the pilot claimed an object or objects had gone over.

Antonio reached the entrance to the Memphis-Arkansas Bridge. It looked gigantic, far more expansive than Morgan ever remembered. They could see a substantial number of police cars ahead of them in the distance with their lights spinning around the top like an electrical storm. There was a beehive of activity. Sirens had been turned off, but the cars had formed a protective barrier.

Ash instructed Antonio, 'Ease forward and see how close we can get.'

Morgan felt like it was taking hours to move inches. They had not moved far when an officer with a flashlight and a walkie-talkie came towards them with his hand up in the proper stop mode. Antonio opened his driver's window.

Ash spoke from the passenger's seat and said, 'Hello, I'm Ash Downing and I'm representing the victim of tonight's crime.' He continued, 'Would you mind if I get out of the car to speak with you?'

The officer asked for identification and Ash handed it over to Antonio. The police officer ushered Ash out of the car.

Morgan ignored Ash's previous instructions and pleaded with the officer through tears. 'He has our dog. He has our Dixie. Please, officer, get our dog back.'

The officer pulled Ash to the side and they both began to walk towards the commotion.

Ash explained, 'I've lost much of my voice through an accident which, in all likelihood, was caused by the assailant, but I want – I need desperately to retrieve the family dog. I'm the victim's acting attorney. Please, can you share any details regarding the current situation?'

The officer stood in front of him and just stared. He took off his police cap and said, 'We don't have an assailant. He's gone. His phone is not in his car. His keys are in the ignition. There was a scribbled note left on the floorboard. The search lights provided us with enough light covering a specific area where at least three different officers saw a white object and a black object drifting across the top of the water. The helicopter pilot confirmed through thermal imaging and a zoom lens camera that the white object appeared to be a small to medium sized animal and the darker object appeared to be a brief case or a piece of luggage. We're going to have to send the divers into the river in the morning.'

Ash's heart sank. He did not have the proper words to share this horrific news with Morgan. He and the officer stood together in silence.

Ash appealed to the officer. 'Look. She's lost her dog – her children's best friend. This dog was like another child to her, and the entire family has been brutally traumatised for weeks now. Can you get me the note...at least?'

The officer scoffed, 'Not a chance. Evidence.'

Ash lashed back, 'Damnit man, can you work with me? I need something. I must return to that car with enough information that can confirm this nightmare is over.'

The officer put his cap back on his head and sighed heavily. 'Hold on.' He disappeared into the cluster of cops and was gone for a while.

Antonio flashed his lights a couple of times.

The officer reappeared in front of Ash. 'I told you we would never divorce.'

The cop went on to say, 'That's it. Those words were the only thing scribbled in blue ink on a scrap piece of paper. Look, the idiot knew he was cornered. There was no place for him to go and he decided to take himself out. I thought for sure, we all did, it was going to be suicide by cop, but there's no trace of him. The mighty Mississippi River has him now. That's all I have for you. I need to get back to the team. Please tell your client I'm sorry for her loss.'

Ash put his one good hand in his pocket and made his way slowly back to Antonio's car. Morgan had already jumped out from the back seat, and was running towards him crying, screaming, pleading, 'Where's Dixie? Where's my Dixie, Ash? Can't you get her for me? Please. We need her.' Morgan collapsed and was bawling. 'Oh, Ash, we love her. Ollie needs her. Opal needs her. Oh, God, I need her. Please get her for us. PLEASE!'

Antonio and Ash tenderly picked Morgan up and placed her gently on the back seat of the car.

They sat there in silence as Morgan tried to pull herself together.

Morgan began picturing her beautiful mother's face in her mind. She cringed at the thought of telling her what had transpired. Tears swelled in her eyes and she felt grateful, fortunate to have a mom as wonderful and loving as Kat...but this thought made her tears worse. Then she pictured Lee and how distraught she was, and she recalled her treasured children and the shape they were in. Morgan knew she was surrounded by the best human beings on the planet – angels indeed – and not one deserved the horror story they had each just lived through. This was all beyond real comprehension. Dixie most certainly didn't deserve anything except an abundance of love for her entire life. Tiny precious Dixie never hurt a soul. Morgan wanted to be held by her mother, and she wanted to hold on tightly to her kids – that's all that mattered to her now. She must keep the people most important to her...safe...for as long as she lived.

After what felt like an eternity had passed, she found her voice. 'I trust you, Ash. Please don't hide anything from me. Exactly what did that officer say to you?'

Antonio leaned forward as if he were wondering the same thing.

Ash took a deep breath. 'The first officer on the scene found a note on the floorboard of the car.'

'What did it say?'

'Well, Morgan, normally that information is not given out because it's held as evidence, but I pleaded and told him we needed something to know this nightmare was over. The officer pulled the necessary strings and came back and told me the note said: I told you we would never divorce.

'The cop went on to say that he was cornered, no way out, every cop on the scene had the same feeling it would end as suicide by cop, but he chose to do it *his* way and end it when he wanted to do so. He's gone, Morgan. In his mind, he remained in control until the very end. Like the cop told me, the mighty Mississippi has him now.'

Everyone became silent.

Morgan put her head down, allowed the pain to radiate through her body, the tears to stream, and softly muttered, 'No, Ash, you're wrong. The monster loves himself far too much.'

The End.